THE ZULU CURSE

An Archaeological Mystery Thriller

By Bradford G. Wheler

BookCollaborative.com
Cazenovia, NY 13035

Doug, 7/29/19
Great to see you. Enjoy Brad

BookCollaborative.com
PO Box 403
Cazenovia, NY 13035
BookCollaborative.com@gmail.com

ISBN 978-1-7332026-0-2

Mystery, Thriller, Archaeology

PRINTED IN THE UNITED STATES OF AMERICA

Cover image by Tproud

Interior design by Lorie DeWorken, Mind*the*Margins

Also by Bradford G. Wheler

MONGOLIA AND THE GOLDEN EAGLE:
An Archaeological Mystery Thriller

INCA'S DEATH CAVE
An Archaeological Mystery

LOVE SAYINGS
wit & wisdom of romance, courtship, and marriage

GOLF SAYINGS
wit & wisdom of a good walk spoiled

CAT SAYINGS: wit & wisdom from the whiskered ones

HORSE SAYINGS
wit & wisdom straight from the horse's mouth

DOG SAYINGS
wit & wisdom from man's best friend

EIGHTEEN 6/10/71
The Poetry of John G. Hunter III

SNAPPY SAYINGS
wit & wisdom from the world's greatest minds

THE ZULU CURSE

**An Archaeological
Mystery Thriller**

Chapter 1

The underbrush parted into the edge of a clearing, I'd never seen anything like it. They were all dead, more than a dozen of them, around two long cold campfires. Strangely there were also dead buzzards around the now decaying human corpses.

I'm not a big fan of snakes and there were lots of snakes. Why weren't the snakes, like the buzzards, dead?

Chapter
1

Chapter 2

[Several days earlier at Cornell University, Ithaca, NY]

I was reading *The Archaeological Journal,* published by the Royal Archaeological Institute, with my feet on my desk when I sensed more than heard someone's presence. I looked up and saw the Dean staring down at me. I'd begun wearing cowboy boots as my preferred footwear. I took my feet off the desk. They left a small clump of what looked like horse manure on the desk. I hoped the Dean wouldn't notice.

I said, "Good morning, Dean. There are a few interesting articles in the latest *Archaeological Journal.*"

"I'm sure there are but that's not why I'm here. The President would like to see you in her office at 11:30 this morning."

He seemed miffed that he hadn't been invited.

He knew I didn't have any classes then. I said, "No problem, Dean. Please tell the President I'll be there and I'm always willing to stop by if she needs my help or advice."

The Dean wasn't a bad guy really. A nosy busybody, and a bit of a prig, however these seemed to be the traits the University looked for in their academic Deans. Because he was such a stuffed shirt and I was a tenured full professor, I enjoyed pulling his chain.

He bent forward and took a tissue out of the box at the corner of my desk. He then picked up the piece of horseshit and put it in the trash. After one more disapproving look he turned and left.

I left my office in McGraw Hall and walked across the quad to the administration building in Day Hall. As I walked I knocked any remaining horseshit off my boots. It probably wasn't a good idea to visit the President's office with droppings on your footwear.

I went into the President's outer office where her assistant greeted me and buzzed the inner office.

She came out and said, "Professor Johnson, Rob, how nice to see you."

Now I had met the President several times at various functions, but I don't think she ever remembered my name.

She continued, "Please join us in my office."

As I went in I saw Walter Falone, Ned Harris, Chad Dillon, Laura O'Hara, and a woman who looked vaguely familiar. Working for Walter I'd been shot twice. I had a bad feeling about this.

Chad raised a hand and then gave me the thumbs-up. Was he reading my mind? One quick shot by him had saved my life in Mongolia. A CIA field agent and a bit too cocky, he probably went to Harvard.

There was also another man seated somewhat apart

from the others. He didn't smile and he didn't move.

President Garrison said, "Professor, your leave of absence has been approved effective today."

A bit dumbfounded I said, "The Dean won't like that." I'm not sure I liked it.

"I'll handle the Dean. Now you folks feel free to use my office as long as you need to."

As she started to walk out I said, "Paid? My leave, is it paid?"

She looked at me. "No it is not, Professor Johnson." She went out closing the door. From her tone I guessed she didn't subscribe to "There is no such thing as a dumb question."

Walter stood, shook my hand, and said, "You know everyone except perhaps Professor Mia Wang. Ms. Wang teaches here at Cornell in our Department of Molecular Biology and Genetics and is a leading scientist in the CRISPR-Cas9 genome engineering revolution."

I wasn't sure what that was so I said, "Very pleased to meet you." Then a thought flashed into my head. "Didn't you testify before a congressional hearing on making designer babies last June?" She was good looking, that's probably why I remembered.

She said yes and it was nice to meet me, quite matter-of-factly.

Walter made no attempt to introduce the man who sat motionless in the corner. I wasn't sure what was going on but that dark feeling stuck with me. I said hello to the others but skipped any small talk.

Walter said, "Rob, sit here next to me, we have a potential situation I'd like your help with. There are some strange, troubling, and perhaps quite dangerous things going on. They have an archaeological component I believe you can help with."

Since President Garrison just put me on leave from the University, I didn't seem to have much choice. Best to keep my mouth shut so I just nodded.

I looked around again at the group. Walter Falone was a tech billionaire, founder and CEO of Falone Advanced Technologies, and a lover of archaeology. His firm did remote sensing, mapping, researching, and more, primarily for the mining and oil industry. I read that his company had just acquired a cybersecurity firm. Walter sponsored my archaeological work in Peru and Mongolia. He did his undergraduate studies at Cornell.

Ned Harris worked for Walter's firm in the security department. Ned viewed himself as a cyber warrior. He was on my team in both Peru and Mongolia. Ned didn't fit neatly into any mold.

Chad Dillon, the last I knew of him he was in Mongolia attached to the US embassy in Ulaanbaatar pretending to be something other than the CIA agent he actually was.

Laura O'Hara, I didn't see how she fit in with this group. She was a Cornell research librarian, a friend, and a wonderful help if you were trying to research an obscure topic.

Walter smiled and said, "There are numerous troubling events that have our government concerned. Since several aspects seem to involve, at least tangentially, Cornell and our work, they suggested we might be helpful and I agreed. Falone Advanced Technologies works with the US government in several areas. Most recently the company has been involved with cybersecurity work for NSA.

"It seems that a graduate student of Professor Wang's has gone missing. He is especially talented in the field of gene editing and genetic engineering. It has since come to light that this young man was researching genetic engineering methods for creating what could be considered biological weapons."

I was having a hard time understanding what any of this had to do with me.

Walter seemed to sense my mood and said, "I'm sure you are curious about why we are involving you. So let's jump to that part and come back to the other later. I believe you remember that the National Library of Mongolia was robbed last fall."

I did remember Abbey telling me about it. I said, "If I remember correctly it was a sophisticated break-in in which dozens of rare volumes were stolen, all of them relating to ancient medical practices. I assumed they were stolen for some collector. I understand the black market for rare books is quite strong."

He said, "That was everyone's assumption. But now it seems there could be more to it. Laura, tell Rob what you have been hearing."

"As you know, my area of expertise is rare and ancient books. Research librarians in this field are a small and somewhat tight-knit group.

"Over the last six to nine months there have been several robberies similar to the one at the National Library in Ulaanbaatar. Similar in that what was taken was ancient manuscripts having to do with medicine, diseases, plagues, etc. All the robberies were well planned and professionally executed.

"Several libraries in India, one in Rome, St. Petersburg in Russia, Istanbul, and Peru. There are probably others that I don't know about. It seems a bit much for one collector to be doing."

Ned spoke up. "Now there is something else interesting that is in your field, Professor. There's been a rash of ancient grave and tomb robberies during this same time period."

I looked at him. Graves are looted all the time but I hadn't heard of any big increases outside of the war zones of Syria and Iraq.

Ned went on. "You know how I like to know things, well since working with you in Peru I've kept up a bit on archaeology. I set up a bot to search the web for any new archaeological news. I use an AI program, you know, artificial intelligence, to organize it and feed me the really interesting stuff. When I saw the big increase in grave robberies I decided to look more closely.

"What did I find? Many but not all of these gravesites were in a location of and dating to a period of plague. Graves dating from 541-2 in Constantinople were robbed. That is during the period of the Plague of Justinian. Then grave robberies from the time and places of the worst of the Black Death in the fourteenth century, and the Great Plague of London around 1665. Plus the list goes on. Scary, right?"

I looked around the room. No one spoke up. Finally I said, "So what's the theory? Someone is robbing graves and stealing ancient books on disease so Professor Wang's missing grad student can genetically engineer biological weapons?"

Given who was in the room I knew it couldn't be a joke.

"There is more to it," Walter said.

I didn't have breakfast, now it was way past lunchtime. My stomach was grumbling. I was just put on unpaid leave again, didn't these people know I actually enjoyed teaching?

I stood up. "You should put all the data into Elizabeth's super spy software, the one that supposedly could have predicted the Pearl Harbor bombing and the 9/11 attacks, and see what it spits out.

"I'm hungry and I need to go home and put my horses out."

The mention of Elizabeth's software got the first reaction out of the man sitting in the corner. His eyes narrowed and his jaw clenched slightly as he looked towards Walter.

Walter calmly said, "We might do that, Rob. Now let's you and I go get lunch and let your horses out. I haven't seen your new place and I want to say hello to Beast. We can talk more about this later."

He put his hand gently on my back and guided me to the door. Walter, just my billionaire buddy with nothing better to do than take me to lunch and say hi to my dog. I'd said something to throw a spanner in the works but I wasn't sure what.

Chapter 3

As we headed out of Day Hall, I said, "How did I screw up back there?"

I thought his response might be "let me count the ways."

He said, "There seems to be a difference of opinion among the security agencies as to how this situation should be handled. There is some skepticism if any of these events are related and if so how. The different agencies have very different opinions on who should be told what or even included at all. Each seems to have a different security concern plus assets and turf to protect."

I said, "I thought putting all the agencies together under Homeland Security was supposed to fix all the interagency squabbling."

Walter looked at me. I said, "Right, even I'm not naive enough to believe that."

We went to a table in the back corner of the barroom at the Statler Hotel. Once the waiter left menus Walter said, "Not many people know just how powerful Elizabeth's mega-data software is. I'm negotiating an exclusive license to the NSA for a very large sum. Having you so casually but accurately describe it in front of several people with no security clearances hit a raw nerve."

I said, "The guy in the corner, he was the only one who reacted. Ned knows about the software but Chad Dillon didn't seem to and no one else had a clue what I was talking about."

"You're right, Rob, Dillon isn't high enough up to know anything other than NSA has good software. The other gentleman is a different story He is high up the chain of command and a skeptic of the NSA's and CIA's approach to this potential threat."

"What kind of threat are we talking about? It can't be as far-fetched as what I said back in the President's office. And how did you get involved?"

Walter waited until the waiter took our order, when he left he said, "Some of it sounds even stranger than what you said.

"How I or our company got involved was when we were doing demonstration runs of the software for NSA. I had Ned dream up some threat scenarios and NSA staffers made up others. People were very impressed, however one of Ned's test runs came up with very strange connections. NSA dismissed it as just what you get when you throw a lot of jumbled info into a test run. Garbage in garbage out, they said.

"But Ned wouldn't let it go. He ran more runs using the company's computers. The more connection he found, the stranger it got. Ned convinced his boss, Major Ian

Campbell SAS retired, that I needed to see his results.

"As crazy as it seemed, that is what the data was telling us. I've built this company by generating good data then trusting it."

His phone vibrated and he went out on the patio to take the call.

I remembered how Walter had started. After dropping out of grad school, he developed a system to combine available site data with search engine capabilities that scoured all available databases and added a layer of artificial intelligence. He used it to make his first fortune in the gold fields of Canada and then in the petroleum industry and then more. He saw things in data others missed and built a multibillion-dollar company.

I also remembered when I first met him at his ranch in Houston. I had visions of being summoned to his football field-sized office by a butler. Instead he came to the guesthouse where I was staying, knocked gently, and apologized for interrupting me.

His wife had recently died of cancer. He said his love of archaeology was the only thing that could fill the lonely nights. It helped restore his balance after the loss of his wife, and perhaps even saved his sanity.

I had developed great respect for him.

When he came back I said, "I have a family now, it's not so easy for me to just leave for months at a time."

My family members were all furry and had four legs, but with family come responsibilities.

"I know you do and I have Mrs. Lopez working on that."

Regina Lopez was the assistant who handled the items

on the more personal side of Walter's affairs. She was in her mid-sixties, very organized, and had a friendly way of making sure everything got done.

"I don't understand what is going on and I don't see how I can be of much help. What is it you want me to do?"

"I want you and Abbey to follow up on several of the events related to the ancient grave and tomb robberies. I want you two to try to understand in more depth what is in those ancient manuscripts that were stolen. I want you to discover how these events relate to a series of other strange events that our software runs indicated are all related."

I just looked at Walter. I wanted to say "you must be joking." But it was Walter and I knew he wasn't. All I could think to say was "Abbey is in Mongolia."

He replied, "Actually she is on a company jet headed for Ithaca. Let's go see your new ranch. I'll drive you to your car and follow you there."

We went out the front door of the Statler Hotel and Walter's limo was waiting. Walter opened the door for me and we both got in. I told the driver where my truck was parked.

As I drove the six miles to my small farm I thought of Walter calling it my ranch. His ranch in Texas was 3,200 acres and his ranch in Peru was much larger. I had a couple dozen acres, two rescue horses, two cats from the pound, and my dog Beast, a Mongolian Bankhar who was almost as big as a pony. That was my family.

When I pulled in, Beast was waiting in front of the barn as always. I'm not sure how far away he could hear my truck but he knew who it was. Other vehicles could go by and he didn't bat an eye.

Next Beast bounded over to greet Walter. Walter played with him as Beast got slobber and dog hair all over Walter's finely tailored suit. He didn't seem to care.

He had me walk him through the barn, around the property a bit, and then into the house. He had nice things to say about everything, I think he meant them.

Then he said, "I want your help on this. I know I'm taking you away from a place you love and I might be putting you in danger."

I didn't like that. When I worked for him before he never mentioned danger and we ended up with plenty of it.

He went on. "Mrs. Lopez has her niece and her niece's husband lined up to watch your ranch. They have a nine-year-old daughter who loves horses. I'm having them fly up so you can meet them."

"Walter, I walked into the President's office at 11:30 this morning. It is now 2:45 in the afternoon and I've been put on leave from the University and my life is being turned upside down. I'd like time to think. I'd like to know more. I'd like a choice."

"Of course. I know this must feel like a bum's rush. Abbey will be here tomorrow. You two meet with Ned, Chad Dillon, and Professor Wang. They will go over what they know. That will probably make everything seem even stranger.

"Then meet with Mrs. Lopez's niece and her husband. Talk it over with Abbey. Then call in by tomorrow evening. But Rob, it is important and I need your help."

All I could say was "Why me?"

"Because I trust you. I trust you, Rob. Now I need to go."

"Wait, what happens if we say yes?"

"Then in three days you fly to Houston, we meet, and you fly on to Peru. Peru will be your base of operations. I'm sorry to have so little time. I look forward to your call."

He took a second to pet Beast, and as he headed for his limo he took out his cellphone. He was on to the next issue he had to deal with.

I said to Beast, "Let's saddle the horses and go for a ride."

Riding one horse and leading the other along the trails I thought about Abbey arriving tomorrow. I first met Abbey when she was a fifteen-year-old freshman. I was her adviser and it quickly became clear that she was gifted. She stood out even among the many brilliant Cornell students. I was thrilled when she decided to pursue her PhD in archaeology at Cornell. Then there was our time in Peru, the first time working for Walter, she completed her PhD, and became a faculty member at Cornell. Next was our adventure again working for Walter in Mongolia. Abbey decided to stay in Mongolia and continue the archaeological work at the site we discovered while I returned to Ithaca.

Tall with red hair and green eyes, she was bright, attractive, and had an easygoing sense of humor, but I worried that all the people she killed had to have affected her.

Chapter 4

The next morning I headed to campus. After stopping at my office and spending a couple hours emailing my class notes to the professors who were taking over my classes, I walked to the Biotechnology Building. It is said to be the largest single research building on the Cornell campus and a far cry from McGraw Hall where I had my office. McGraw Hall looked like it was from the Flintstones and the Biotechnology Building looked like it was from the Jetsons.

I made my way to a conference room. Ned and Professor Wang were there deep in conversation.

Ned looked up, no greeting, just, "Professor Wang is doing some way cool stuff. This gene editing is almost like writing computer code but for life forms. Is that cool or what?"

I said, "Good morning." Professor Wang looked surprised by Ned's outburst. "That seems like a ringing endorsement of your work, Professor."

She said, "Let's not call each other professor, I suspect

it will be awkward enough working together without using formal titles."

She didn't seem too happy about being involved in whatever this was we were doing. "Mia, were you put on leave as well?"

"No. I mostly do research but they reassigned the one grad course I was teaching and told me to take whatever time was needed to help you out." She then softened a bit. "I am worried about Justin. He is a very bright young man but I fear a bit troubled. He wasn't a problem for others to work with, just somehow distant and self-isolating."

I assumed she was talking about her missing grad student. I was about to ask more about him when Abbey and Chad Dillon walked in.

Chad had apparently picked Abbey up at the airport. She looked like she had been up a while.

I introduced her to Mia Wang. At a university as large as Cornell it wasn't unusual for faculty in different colleges not to know each other.

Abbey was polite to everyone and then gave me a "what now?" look.

We all looked at each other for a moment. Then I said, "Where do we start?"

Chad Dillon said, "My boss told me I was at Mr. Falone's disposal, to facilitate your investigation, and report in regularly." He smiled. It somehow reminded me of the Cheshire cat. It struck me that he thought this whole thing was a big waste of time.

Mia Wang said, "Don't look at me. I was told to help when asked."

"Just like the old days, you're in charge, Professor," Ned piped in.

Abbey had a bewildered look on her face.

Great. Walter put me in charge but didn't tell me I was in charge or what it was I was supposed to be in charge of.

I looked at Ned. He was enjoying this. He knew I didn't know what was going on.

I pulled out the chair at the head of the table, sat, and said, "Ned, report in on what you have found out to date." I said it as if this was a daily briefing and I had been in charge for months.

Ned said, "Some folks at NSA think our software isn't that great and it gets more things wrong than right. Walter wants to prove them wrong and save the world at the same time."

Well that explains part of it, I thought. With Walter there is always a business angle. He wants a bundle for his software from NSA and they aren't convinced it is worth it. I remember when Elizabeth developed it in Peru, Walter made sure none of the work was done in the US. Plus Falone Advanced Technologies is technically a Canadian company, so Walter wouldn't be restricted from selling it to another country. But no one else could afford to pay as much as the US and the fact the US didn't want it would greatly diminish its worth.

I said, "OK, let's focus on saving the world and the other part will take care of itself.

"Ned, give us the Cliffs Notes version of what you found in your software run."

He thought for a moment. "Well lots of strange stuff

is happening and the software shows a common link back to one website. When I start from the other end with the website as the main data point I find more weird stuff that ties back, including the stolen manuscripts and old graves being robbed."

He stopped. I saw Abbey stir. She knew all too well how Ned made you pry the information out by asking him lots of questions. It was some kind of game for him.

I waited and then said, "I see why NSA wasn't very impressed."

He looked a little miffed. He opened his laptop and wirelessly connected to the flat-screen on the wall. I saw the first page of the PowerPoint document was labeled 1 of 87. This wasn't going to be the Cliffs Notes version.

When Ned finally finished I didn't know what to think. There was so much it didn't seem believable. Much of it on the surface sounded innocent even, other parts very scary. I hoped Walter was going to give us a better idea of what we were to do.

Abbey said, "I've just flown halfway around the world. I need to shower and change."

I said, "OK, Ned, give me a copy of your presentation. Walter wants us in Houston tomorrow. Find out the flight arrangements and let us know."

"Houston. I'm not going to Houston," Professor Wang said.

"That's up to your boss and Walter. From what little I was told we will be working from Peru and probably headed there straight from Houston."

She seemed to like that even less. My phone vibrated.

A text from Mrs. Lopez: "My niece is arriving at Ithaca airport shortly. I've arranged for a car service to take them to your ranch. They should be there in about an hour."

I held my phone out to Abbey. The pace at which things happened in Walter's company was so different than the glacial pace of most things at the University.

I said, "We need to go. Ned, let us know tomorrow's schedule."

I picked up one of Abbey's bags and she grabbed the other.

As we walked I said to Abbey, "What did Walter tell you?"

"I got a message from him saying it was important to meet with you and him in Ithaca ASAP. I was told to meet a plane at the Ulaanbaatar airport the next day. I'm an employee of his company while I'm on leave from the University. He's the big boss. I was hoping it would be a bit of a vacation in Ithaca.

"It all seems so crazy. But Ned is really good at this cyber spy stuff. The last I saw of him Major Campbell was having him sent from Mongolia to Canada under armed guard thinking the CIA might try to kidnap him because of everything he knew."

"It appears Walter has worked that issue out," I said.

I thought about the file I was given on Ned when he was first going to work with us in Peru. Ned attended Gateway Community College in New Haven, Connecticut. He was in an associate's degree program in Diagnostic Medical Sonography but kept sneaking into the Yale University engineering library. After he was thrown out several times one of the library's management staff gave him an application for a part-time job. As an employee he could spend as much of his free time in the library as he wanted. Somehow he taught himself advanced computer coding and computer analytics. I started to smile thinking back on it. You can't make this stuff up. Ned gets hired by Booz Allen Hamilton, which is probably the largest technology-consulting firm in the country, with 99% percent of the company's revenue coming from the federal government. He is assigned to the NSA account. The same Booz Allen Hamilton that hired Edward Snowden to work for the NSA, who leaked all the classified documents on the NSA's mass surveillance and data collection program PRISM. After two years there Ned joined Falone Advanced Technologies.

Ned's mother had always wanted him to finish college. After our time in Peru I helped him apply to receive a joint Bachelor's and Master's degree in computer engineering from Cornell. He was with us again in Mongolia. That was the last time I'd seen him before yesterday.

When we got to my farm Abbey went for a shower after saying hello to Beast. I went to feed the horses.

Beast barked, so I came out of the barn. A car service vehicle was just pulling in. I told Beast to sit.

A slender woman in her thirties with dark hair and dark eyes got out of the car. As I walked over to the car she walked towards me and put out her hand. "I'm Regina Lopez's niece Sofia Nunez. It is a pleasure to meet you, Professor Johnson."

She turned back to the car where the other two passengers had gotten out. She said, "This is my husband, Carlos, and my daughter Gabriela."

We shook hands and I told them to call me Rob. The whole thing felt awkward. I imagined they probably had as little notice and choice in having their lives turned upside down as I did.

Gabriela was holding on to her mother's hand, trying to look brave. I said, "I understand you like horses. Would you like to see my two horses?"

She nodded yes but held tight to her mother's hand. "Is that your dog?" she said still not letting go of her mother's hand.

"Yes, his name is Beast."

"He is big. May I pet him?"

"Sure." I looked at Beast. He was dying to run over and join us. "Beast, come here, say hello to Gabriela."

Beast bounded over then approached slowly and very gently. He had always been good with children. Gabriela finally let go of her mother's hand.

We walked into the barn. I introduced them to the two horses and the cats. Carlos ran his hand over each horse's neck and then their rumps. I could see him looking at each hoof. I wondered if he was going to check their teeth. He obviously knew horses.

Sofia said, "My husband is one of Mr. Falone's ranch managers in Houston."

I said, "This isn't much of a ranch compared to Mr. Falone's."

Carlos spoke for the first time since we were introduced. "You have a most fine ranch here. I will take excellent care of it. Mr. Falone sent me because he trusts me to do a good job and I will not disappoint him."

Abbey came into the barn. Her hair was wet and pulled back in one loose braid. She had on jeans, a sweatshirt, and boots.

I made the introductions.

Abbey said, "Gabriela, I understand you like to ride."

She looked up at Abbey with big brown eyes and nodded yes.

"OK. Let's you and I go for a ride while your mom and dad talk to Professor Johnson."

I brushed the horses while Abbey and Carlos got the tack. I watched Carlos expertly put the saddle and bridle on the horse for his daughter. Abbey, who had become a strong horsewoman from her time in Mongolia, saddled the other horse. Horses were our main method of transport to the archaeological site in the Altai Tavan Bogd National Park in western Mongolia.

Gabriela sat comfortably in the saddle. Her mother was totally at ease, that told me Gabriela was a good rider. After seeing children as young as three or four riding in Mongolia, it didn't surprise me that Gabriela could ride well.

As Abbey and Gabriela rode off at a slow trot, Beast looked at me and whined. I said, "Go with them" and pointed to the horses.

Beast ran after them with his whole rear end wagging.

I went through where everything was in the barn and then we went to the house. I made a list of everything I thought they needed, feed store, vet's number, etc.

I said, "I'll set up accounts at the stores for you in the morning."

Sofia put up her hand. I thought, just because I'm a professor you don't have to raise your hand to speak. I smiled at her.

"Professor, my Aunt Regina set up checking and credit accounts for us and told me not to let you pay for any of the expenses while we are here. She said it was part of your employment package with the company."

One more thing Walter hadn't bothered to tell me. But knowing I was going to be paid was nice.

She went on, "Aunt Regina also registered Gabriela in the local school and our cars will arrive shortly. We can stay at a hotel until you leave so we won't bother you."

Yes, things do move at a much faster pace at Walter's company.

I said, "No, please stay here. It's a big old farmhouse and we will be gone soon."

She thanked me and I showed them to one of the spare rooms.

They started unpacking so I went to pack. As I packed I kept thinking what the hell is going on, what am I getting into, and why me.

Once the horses were fed after their ride, I took Abbey aside in the barn and said, "Ned sent a text saying to be at the airport at noon. A plane will be waiting to take us to Houston. From there we go to Peru. He also sent a video to my secure laptop. Only you and I are to watch it."

"Prof, this is crazy. What I saw of that website Ned claims is important reads like it could have been done by a few fifteen-year-old do-gooder hackers."

I said, "Walter thinks there is something to it. So it isn't just Ned's imagination running away with him."

Abbey said, "OK. Let me wash up a little and I'll join you in your den. I hope you have some wine."

"I always have wine for you." It was odd to see Abbey out of sorts. She was normally upbeat. It could just be flying halfway around the world. Even on Walter's private jets it's hard to sleep and keep your bio-clock on track.

I cleaned up and went to the kitchen. Sofia was going through my fridge and cupboards deciding what to make for dinner. I was well stocked with beer, dog and cat food, and snacks but probably not up to her standards.

Gabriela was at the kitchen counter doing homework. I said, "Can I help you find anything?"

"No, Professor, I need to figure out where everything is. Will you and Abbey be joining us for dinner?"

"That would be great if you can find anything to cook."

I opened a bottle of white wine and grabbed a bag of chips. Sofia handed me a bowl. Not wanting to admit I wasn't going to use one, I carefully poured the chips in and took the wine, two glasses, and bowl to my den.

Cybersecurity was a big deal at Falone Advanced Technologies. Companies, countries, and others were constantly trying to hack into the company's system and steal the valuable customer data the company produced. It had become such an issue that Walter had acquired a cybersecurity company and added its work to the company's service offerings.

I had a company-issued laptop and phone with all sorts of security protection I didn't understand. I booted it up and loaded the video from Ned.

When Abbey came in I gave her a glass of wine and asked, "Do you want to relax for a while and enjoy your wine or jump right into the video?"

She held up her glass to me and said, "Gabriela seems like a nice young girl and she rides well. I hope this works for them."

She looked into her wine and didn't speak for a long moment. Then she took a sip and said, "Let's see what Ned thinks is so important."

I started the video. It showed the length as eight minutes. Good, whatever it was at least it wouldn't take all night.

It opened with an aerial scene of Africa. There was an undulating hilly terrain with a small river. This gave way to a grassy plain with wetlands in the distance. The voiceover spoke of the beauty of the eMakhosini Ophathe Heritage Park in South Africa's KwaZulu-Natal province, known as "the garden province" and the region of the traditional Zulu Nation.

Next the camera zoomed in to show two black rhinos lying in a pool of blood. It looked like they had been machine-gunned. The horns were cut off and the bodies left to rot. The voiceover spoke of how few of the endangered black rhinos were left. How poachers killed them for their horns that were worth more per pound on the black market in Asia than gold.

The scene switched again. Now there were five black women in ceremonial dress. They were dancing and drums were beating in the background. The voiceover said these were Zulu sangomas or shamans. The killing of black rhinos had upset the harmony between the living and the dead. The ancestors must be shown respect through animal sacrifice. The strongest of curses is being invoked on anyone who kills the black rhino. The commentator stopped, the drums beat louder, and the women danced at a frenzied pace. The lead woman fell to her knees and from out of the camera's view someone poured blood over her head.

The camera panned away. Next it was a scene going through the brush. The underbrush parted into the edge of a clearing, I'd never seen anything like it. They were all dead, more than a dozen of them, around two long cold campfires. Strangely there were also dead buzzards around the now decaying human corpses.

I'm not a big fan of snakes and there were lots of snakes. Why weren't the snakes, like the buzzards, dead?

Abbey let out a small gasp. The voiceover said these were rhino poachers and their gruesome death was from the Zulu sangoma's curse. It then went on about how this would be the fate of all poachers in Zululand.

I shut my laptop. "Well there's a nice scene before dinner."

Abbey asked, "What did Ned say?"

"Not much. That only we were to watch it and he asked Chad to send it to CIA's analysts to see what they could make of it, also that we could discuss it tomorrow on the plane in route to Houston.

"Let's not worry about it until tomorrow when we will know more." I poured Abbey more wine.

She was quiet for a while and then said, "I shot another poacher in Mongolia. Ranger Batbayar and I were riding back to the ranger station at the end of Lake Khoton. We spotted two men. They had tied their horses and were behind a small rock outcropping that overlooks a path the ibex use to come down from the mountain for water.

"Ranger Batbayar wanted to capture them and not just scare them off. So we dismounted and went on foot. As we approached we saw two ibex coming down the trail. We were about 400 yards from the poachers. Ranger Batbayar handed me his rifle. He looked at me and said, 'We both know I can't make that shot. Don't let them kill the ibex, take the shot, Abbey. I'll try to scare them off.'

"He fired his pistol in the air. The ibex froze and the poachers looked back at us. When they saw how far away we were, one raised his rifle and took aim at the now still ibex.

"I aimed for the leg above the knee and dropped him. The other poacher dropped his rifle and went to help the wounded man. Ranger Batbayar radioed for help and we mounted our horses and rode to them. We both had our guns ready but there was no more trouble.

"It turned out to be two brothers. The younger one, who wasn't shot, kept saying we didn't know you were rangers. We thought you wanted our ibex. As if that made it all right. The older brother bled to death before help came. We put a tourniquet on his leg, but I must have hit an artery.

"The rangers treated me as a hero."

I wasn't sure what to say. We sat quietly and then she said, "Perhaps there are some skills it is better not to have."

I put my hand lightly on her shoulder. "You saved my life more than once and you have saved other people's and

your own." Then I let it go and we sat quietly again.
Shortly Sofia called to say dinner was ready.
Perhaps tomorrow we would get some answers.

Chapter 5

After a busy morning Carlos drove us to the general aviation section of the Ithaca Tompkins County Regional Airport. We each had two medium size bags. Our secure laptops and a few clothes were pretty much all we packed since we had no idea what we might need.

Carlos said in his accented English, "Don't worry, I take good care of your ranch."

We thanked him as a young man in a pilot's uniform met us. He introduced himself and took two of the bags.

Abbey said, "Look, it's the same Cessna 525B Citation Jet 3 we rode on when we went to meet Walter for the first time."

I looked at the pilot and said, "It is 1,200 nautical miles to Houston. I hope this plane has long-range tanks."

"Yes sir, it does," he said very sincerely.

Abbey poked me in the ribs. It was an inside joke from our first trip.

He loaded our bags and we went onboard. Chad Dillon

and Professor Wang were already onboard. She didn't look happy.

I said, "Good morning. Where is Ned?"

Chad said, "He's in the office with the other pilot."

A minute later Ned came bouncing up the stairs. He was all smiles and full of energy. He was the only one who was enjoying this.

The second pilot came onboard and closed the door. He asked us to fasten our seatbelts and then told us the flight time once airborne would be a little over three hours. He went to the cockpit. No closing and locking the cockpit door as there is on an airliner.

Mia Wang looked worried. I said, "Do you enjoy flying?"

She responded with an edge to her voice. "I don't mind flying. I mind being here."

That was a bit of a conversation stopper. Abbey spoke up. "I know how you feel. Seventy-two hours ago I was in the Altai Mountains of western Mongolia. Now I'm not even sure what day it is. What were you told?"

"My Dean told me to be of whatever assistance I could be. He said President Garrison was firm on her request for my assistance. It seemed more of an order than a request. If I wasn't so concerned about Justin I would have refused. I'm a tenured full professor. They can't just order me around."

Abbey said, "Tell me about Justin."

She thought for a moment. "Well his name is Justin Barry. I am his faculty adviser. He received a Bachelor's degree in Biochemistry and a Master's degree in Molecular Biology both from Stanford. He is or was at Cornell

38

for a PhD in our Department of Molecular Biology and Genetics.

"He was interested in research topics such as DNA replication, DNA repair, membrane trafficking, the cytoskeleton, signal transduction, metabolic regulation, enzyme structure and mechanism, organelle function, biophysics of protein-protein and protein-lipid interactions, and virology. Really quite a broad range of topics and I told him if he ever wanted to finish a thesis he needed to decide on a narrow topic of research.

"He said he needed to know more about all these things before he could find something truly important for his thesis. We've all seen gifted PhD candidates who do years and years of research before getting around to finishing their thesis. Some never finish."

She stopped and Abbey asked, "What was he like personally?"

"He was a polite young man. No one had trouble working with him. He kept to himself, no girlfriend that I knew of. When he went missing we asked the other students and no one knew anything. While none of the other people had anything negative to say about him they also didn't consider him a friend or socialize with him.

"There was no response to the contact phone numbers and email addresses he gave the University. He had a furnished apartment in College Town that the Ithaca and Cornell Police say is now empty of any of his belongings. He just left over one weekend.

"Then one day the Cornell Police came to my office with Ned and a gentleman from Homeland Security asking questions. None of it makes any sense.

"Now I'm to do God knows what for Walter Falone and the CIA." She pointed to Chad. "I'm not even sure where I'm going."

Ned, who can't seem to keep quiet for long, jumped in. "You're going to Houston and then Peru. Walter has a very cool ranch there. It is going to be great. Think of it as an adventure. Cyberspace is like the old Wild West. You could become a cyber warrior yourself, Professor. A Molecular Biology and Genetics Cyber Warrior Queen. How cool would that be?"

Everyone was staring at him. He said more softly, "I bought a dozen bagels at College Town Bagels. Who wants one?"

I had to smile. Ned wasn't yet twenty-five and he was charging forward to save the world. He truly thought of himself as a cyber warrior. It then crossed my mind that Walter may have involved me to babysit Ned.

I had a bagel then asked Ned and Chad what the story was with the video they sent me.

Chad nodded to Ned. Ned said, "The software says it ties to the 'Save the World' website and that it ties to other strange deaths that connect somehow back to Justin Barry. Chad had his CIA people look at the video. He can probably tell us more."

Ned booted up the video on his laptop.

Chad said, "According to our analysts the video is a compilation designed to scare poachers. They found versions online with the voiceover in several languages, everything from local African dialects to Afrikaner to Chinese.

The Zulu Curse

"The first part of the video is from a travel video on the iSimangaliso Wetland Park. The part with the two black rhinos lying in a pool of blood is from a BBC documentary on poaching in Africa. The five black women in ceremonial dress dancing to drums have nothing to do with a curse on rhino poachers. It is from a YouTube video of a Zulu sangoma initiation ceremony. The blood on the woman is goat's blood that is always part of that ceremony.

"The final scene is the most interesting. This was not chopped out of some online video. Those are poachers and quite notorious ones according to what we could find out. They died in a very gruesome and unusual way. It was reposted to the park authorities that then investigated the scene. They were afraid they might be dealing with some contagious disease so they buried the bodies where they found them.

"They have agreed to let us send in a team of experts to take samples of the remains for testing. But our analysts noted some disturbing things from the video. Ned, focus in on that one body. Notice the nose, the lips, and the fingers are black. It is ecchymosis, that is the escape of blood into the tissues from ruptured blood vessels. Ecchymosis that looks like this is most commonly associated with the bubonic plague."

I looked. It was much worse looking now that Ned had enlarged the image.

Chad went on. "It gets stranger. Bubonic plague usually manifests itself in three to ten days with flu-like symptoms. If untreated there is a 30 to 90 percent chance of death in approximately ten days.

"That isn't what the video shows. It appears that all these people died together at the same time. There doesn't appear to be a struggle. They are all around the two campfires as if they just fell asleep at the same time and then died.

"Our analysts' best guess is that it was something they ate or drank that caused them to peacefully pass out and then die of internal bleeding. They didn't want to speculate on what the agent of death might be until they get samples from the graves."

I said, "The buzzards were also dead but not the snakes. Why?"

"I don't know. But perhaps the buzzards ate or drank whatever killed the men and the snakes didn't," Chad said.

Abbey said, "So this is tied to the website, I can see how that might be. The website has about every do-gooder cause you can think of, from save the whales, to find a cure for cancer, to stop trafficking of children. The list goes on and on. There are even pro and opposed groups on the site for things like genetically modifying crops and using antibiotics when raising livestock. It is no surprise that someone on the site is opposed to rhino poaching.

"But being opposed to rhino poaching on a website is a far cry from killing poachers like this or even knowing how to kill poachers. What's the connection?"

We looked back and forth between Ned and Chad.

Ned looked at Chad. "OK. I assume Professor Wang will pass her security background check. The rest of you have clearances that cover what little I know.

"The FBI and a few other law enforcement agencies

have been monitoring this site for quite some time. They have had some limited success in stopping situations based on information from the website.

"The FBI found out about an animal rights group that was planning a surprise protest in NYC. The group was going to throw paint on women wearing fur coats on Fifth and Madison Avenues. They also planned to ransack some stores that sold furs. The NYC Police were told the details of the planning and were able to break it up before there was any real trouble.

"They also discovered a Greenpeace group's plan to occupy an oil platform. There were a few more incidences of this sort either discovered or corroborated with information obtained from this website.

"There is a minority opinion at the FBI that this site is a front or recruiting site for something much more sinister. People are identified that may fit into the group's more radical plans. Contact is then made outside this website and potential recruits are further screened and some are recruited for various tasks.

"A little while back NSA told the FBI that the Falone Advanced Technologies super software they are trying to sell NSA points to this website as a major problem. Because some of the issues are outside the US the CIA got involved. The agencies can't agree if this is a big problem or not and if so what to do about it. Plus, as is quite common, even within an agency there is no agreement. But since it is Falone Advanced Technologies and not some unknown software house, it's agreed that something needs to be done.

"Because I had the pleasure of meeting you three in Mongolia, some boss at the CIA decided I'm the guy to work with Walter's investigation."

"Not your first choice of assignment?" I asked.

He smiled his shit-eating smile and said, "I don't get to pick my assignments."

Abbey said, "But what's the specific connection of this video to the site and to Justin Barry?"

Ned broke in. "Barry was a frequent visitor to the site. One of the areas of the site he often visited was saving endangered species. He clicked yes to questions regarding taking direct action to stop poaching."

Abbey cut him off. "I'm for saving endangered species. I hate the killing of elephants, lions, ibex, and the rest."

Ned jumped in again, now a bit worked up. "You, better than most, know how this software works. It looks at billions of bits of data, more than a thousand people could analyze in a lifetime, and finds patterns and connections people could never see. They say Facebook's data analytics can tell your religion, politics, income level, and probably the color of your underwear from just five to seven of your posts.

"If our software says there is a connection, there is a connection."

Abbey said, "OK. I've used the software, it is great. I'm just saying correlation doesn't necessarily mean causation."

I thought about how the software worked. There had to be more that they weren't telling us.

I looked at Chad. "What else?"

"When we get to Houston there will be people who can

44

give us more details. We will be landing shortly," he said.

We landed at Ellington Airport, a joint public and military airport about 17 miles southeast of Houston. Falone Advanced Technologies had a facility at the edge of the airport. Our jet taxied to the company hangar. We were met by a van that took us a short distance to an office building. Our bags stayed in the van and we were directed through the security at the entrance to a conference room.

We sat, a woman came in and asked if we wanted coffee, juice, or soft drinks. No one seemed in the mood for small talk. Ned was typing away on his computer.

I heard the door open and looked at my watch, we had been waiting fifteen minutes. It seemed much longer.

Walter walked in talking to a man in a dark gray suit. He stopped and looked around the room at us. He seemed to sense our sour mood. He frowned briefly, then came the rest of the way in.

He introduced the man in the suit as the director of the FBI's Houston office. The director smiled broadly and shook everyone's hand. Behind him were three men and one woman all in dark suits. He told us these were government agents. He gave no names of the people or the agencies they might work for. They displayed no ID badges. One of the men was the same man who didn't smile or talk when we were in President Garrison's office. He wasn't smiling today.

Behind them Elizabeth Walters more bounced in than walked. She had a big smile on her face.

"Abbey, Professor Johnson, how wonderful to see you two. You'll have to tell me all about your time in Mongolia, it had to be so exciting." She then introduced herself to Professor Wang and Chad Dillon. Finally she gave Ned a big smile and greeted him.

Elizabeth had big blue eyes, blond hair and a bouncy, cheery air to her. When I first met her in Peru I pegged her for head cheerleader, valedictorian, captain of the field hockey or tennis team. If they still had bake sales she would have been one of the main organizers. I was basically correct. But she was more a brilliant computer programmer and the inventor of the software at issue here.

After our time in Peru she became Falone Advanced Technologies' Chief Technology Officer. I'd also found out her bouncy, cheery manner wasn't an act. She was a truly nice person.

Walter said, "Our time is short and we have a lot to cover so I'd like to get started. The director has been kind enough to bring several people who can brief us on some troubling events that may be related and have bearing on what our company software has revealed."

The woman stood first and said, "I believe Mr. Ned Harris has briefed you on the theft of ancient manuscripts having to do with diseases and their treatments. Also on ancient tombs and burial sites being robbed. I won't repeat those.

"We have reason to believe that there have been additional thefts of this type. Tu Youyou, the Chinese pharmaceutical chemist, educator, and Nobel Laureate in medicine in 2015, recently had her laboratory broken into.

"She is best known for investigating the historical Chinese medical classics and for visiting practitioners of traditional Chinese medicine all over the country. She received the Nobel Prize for her discovery of a treatment for malaria. Tu says the preparation was described in a 1,600-year-old text, in a recipe titled, 'Emergency Prescriptions Kept Up One's Sleeve.' She then perfected a low-temperature extraction process to isolate the effective antimalarial substance from the sweet wormwood plant used in the ancient treatment. With her team she has evaluated over 2,000 traditional Chinese recipes.

"There are just too many of these types of incidences to believe it is a coincidence or a rare book collector. Some person or group believes there is information in these ancient manuscripts that they are willing to devote substantial resources to obtain. If a legitimate organization wanted them for a valid scientific purpose, they wouldn't steal them."

She stopped and the Houston director pointed to one of the three men. He rose and like the woman didn't introduce himself. He handed Ned a memory stick and asked him to display it on the flat-screen on the wall.

The first image was a map of South America with Bolivia shown in green. The next slide showed the nine administrative departments of Bolivia. The third slide showed the Bolivian department of Pando with its provinces. The provinces of Manuripi and Madre de Dios were shown in red.

He then used a laser pointer to indicate a river. He said, "The Madre de Dios River has its headwaters in Peru and forms the border between the Provinces of Manuripi and Madre de Dios in Bolivia. It is one of the principal waterways in the provinces. Manuripi and Madre de Dios are two of the five provinces of Pando Department in Bolivia and are situated in the Amazon lowlands of Bolivia. It has a 60-mile border with Peru on the west and extends about 130 miles from northeast to southwest. It is remote and poor. There are few roads. What little commerce there is mostly along the river. About 90 percent of the people in this area have no electricity and 60 percent have no sanitary facilities.

"Last week we received a report from the World Health Organization on a strange disease outbreak on the Manuripi side of the river. It was at a ferry crossing about 70 miles east of the Peruvian border. It was reported that some 80 percent of the residents in the village on the north side of the river came down with what appeared to be a common cold.

"However no one in the village on the other side of the river reported having a cold. The ferry connects the two villages and people travel back and forth all the time. The only people who got the cold were on the north or Manuripi side of the village. People with the cold traveled to the south side of the river but didn't infect anyone.

"The WHO had a survey team in the region and decided to investigate. No one died and after a week to ten days everyone recovered just as you would expect with a cold. However the survey team was puzzled why a cold strain that was so contagious that it affected 80 percent of the village didn't spread beyond the confines of one small village. They sampled the people who were sick and those who weren't sick from the affected village on the north side of the river. They also took samples from people on the south side of the river where no sickness was reported.

"Now here it gets interesting. When they sent the samples to the Centers for Disease Control in Atlanta for analysis it was a rhinovirus. Rhinoviruses are the most common viral infectious agents in humans and are the predominant cause of the common cold. However it wasn't any of the ninety-nine recognized types of human rhinoviruses.

"Further study suggested it was a genetically modified virus. It is a very contagious virus and yet apparently unable to spread beyond a small local area. The CDC is conducting further tests."

Walter spoke up. "The company software shows a high probability of a link between this incident, the website, and Professor Wang's student Justin Barry. But again we don't know why."

I looked at Professor Wang. She looked worried but said nothing.

The Houston FBI director pointed to one of the other unnamed men.

He stood and said, "We have unconfirmed reports of robberies of ancient graves and tombs in the Madre de Dios region of Peru and farther south towards Lake Titicaca. This can be a bit confusing because there is the Madre de Dios River, the Madre de Dios Province in Bolivia, and the Madre de Dios Region in Peru. Madre de Dios literally means Mother of God in Spanish and is an often-used name.

"There are also two reports of poachers dying a gruesome death along the Madre de Dios River. The reports told of black fingers and eyes. While these are second-hand reports the descriptions are similar to what we saw in South Africa.

The director said, "The various agencies in the Homeland Security Department receive strange reports all the time. Now NSA is telling us that the software your company is trying to sell them sees a connection between a mishmash of reports from all over the globe that are related and somehow tie to a website that acts as a chat room for about every do-gooder, save-the-something group there is.

"People in the FBI and other agencies are skeptical, Walter."

I noticed he didn't say he was skeptical but it was clear from his tone he was. I looked at the others. The three that had presented information looked like they didn't care one way or another. The fourth man who didn't speak had no expression on his face. Just as when he was in President Garrison's office.

The director said, "Perhaps if we knew how this software worked we would be able to be more helpful."

He glanced at the man who hadn't said anything and received a slight nod.

Walter was watching the two men closely. Then it struck me. NSA wasn't sharing any information on how the software worked.

Walter looked at the Houston FBI director and said, "I assume you have completed Professor Wang's security clearance. So I'll ask Elizabeth to give you a detailed explanation of how it works."

He nodded yes.

She began, "I started with the existing company software that uses site data and then uses search engine technology to scour all available databases but also adds a layer of artificial intelligence…"

Then she got really technical. It was clear to me that no one but Ned and Walter had a clue what she was talking about. Perhaps one of the unnamed analysts was getting it. This probably was what Walter had intended. However the director didn't look amused.

Perhaps I should have kept my mouth shut, but I broke in. "Elizabeth. How about the train example you gave me?"

She looked at Walter and Walter smiled. "That's a good idea, Professor."

I almost thought she was going to say, "If you can understand it then they can." But Elizabeth is far too nice for that, she probably didn't even think it.

She said, "I used trains for my analogy for Professor Johnson. He claimed he likes trains because they are old-fashioned and slow.

"Imagine lots of parallel train tracks. Those are our search runs. These trains are all electric trains and they are powered by one substation. Now this won't be a perfect example but I hope you will see what I'm doing. We start the trains down the tracks and as they go faster, they need more electricity. In our searches we need more server capacity because the searches keep expanding like a fractal or like an evergreen tree that keeps branching out. To keep from a combinatorial explosion or an overload of options I've done several things. First I've turned off the part of the company software that automatically shuts down unlikely branches. This is how the company software keeps from bogging down by going down too many pathways. Most search software does this.

"The artificial intelligence (AI) used to do this is very effective for what the company does. In our petroleum and mining areas we are usually looking for one or two specific things so it is relatively easy to identify and shut down unlikely search branches. NSA's needs are different. They often don't really know exactly what clues will be helpful. They need to look at everything from every direction.

"Now that the AI that trims the branches back is turned off, we need another way to not crash the program when we run out of server capacity. So one thing I did was to program a code that would move anybody else's train off the tracks. That puts other people's computer work at the back of the queue. Once our searches needed more capacity or in our example our trains needed more electricity than our substation had, we would tap into another train system's substation. First we would use any spare electricity they had and then we would start parking those trains to get more of their electricity. When we were using all their electricity we could go to the next train system's substation and use that and so on.

"Now we can't just keep having billions and billions of more branches of our parallel searches. So this is the fun part. I wrote a program, and I'll go back to my train analogy, that looks back and forth across our train tracks and sees the big picture across all the tracks. We can program a sensitivity level in this with multiple parameters for what we want to be searching for. This program tells each train how fast to go or in search terms which paths not to go down. But it does it globally, not each train individually, or as most search software does within that one search. As new information emerges my new software remembers the pathways that were shut down and can restart them if they now look useful given new information.

"In a classic search you pretty much know what you want. For example if you want to buy a digital camera, just plug the term into the Google search engine. You get a million hits ranked in order of how likely they are to be what you want. Now you can compare prices, look at the different features, read reviews, and so on.

"For much of NSA's work a simple search is only marginally helpful. You could plug in terms that you think might be relevant all day and not get anything useful.

"This software setup allows you to search a large number of documents at once with a large number of search terms. Then look across all searches as they are running, identifying potential useful patterns, and shutting down paths that hold little likelihood of being helpful. This not only greatly speeds up the process but it increases the chances of finding the patterns that will be useful.

"There are other situations where the amount of data is much greater and time is critical or the search has to be ongoing. Let me give you some examples from the past. The Boston Marathon bombing, the 9/11 attacks, or the Japanese attack on Pearl Harbor. After the event people looked back and found clues that together would have warned of the situation. Congressional committees and reporters love to point fingers and blame people for not seeing patterns that in hindsight seem obvious. The reality is those six, ten, or even twenty clues were mixed in with millions, if not billions of other pieces of information, and it is almost impossible to see any meaningful pattern."

I saw the Agency people stir a bit. They knew, all too well, about getting blamed by politicians after the fact.

She continued. "We now have computing power that is literally a million or more times as powerful as it was a decade ago. With my system of programs and the vast computing power that now exists, it is possible to look at billions of pieces of information in real time and pick out those clues. Some false patterns will emerge but the number will be small enough that they can be checked out manually. The NSA could set up a real-time search for terrorist plots using numerous likely search terms and run the program continuously with a given amount of server capacity. If there is a credible threat then they could start letting the program put low-priority computer work at the back of the queue, adding more and more government servers as needed. Now you don't want to start a panic so the system turns off the alarm systems as it goes from server to server. To eliminate the problem of people seeing their work sidelined, the appropriate government officials could say that they are performing maintenance on the system or some story like that."

I think the idea was beginning to sink in with the director. He said, "Can the NSA jump to any government computer and sidetrack their work?"

Elizabeth answered, "It all depends on how the system

is configured. Our company recommends that a priority hierarchy system be set up between government agencies. So once NSA's capacity is used up, it could be agreed to go to the FBI's computers for domestic issues next. If it were international it might go next to CIA's computers. For a defense issue it could be DOD computers. For each scenario you would decide which computer system to go to second then third and so on."

The man who hadn't spoken looked at the director and gave him another small nod.

The director said, "We have one more item for you."

The unnamed woman handed Ned a memory stick and asked him to play it.

The scene was Africa with elephants walking through dry bush land. There was no sound. Next there was a lone bull elephant with large tusks. The camera pulled back and there were three black men. One was sighting down the barrel of a hunting rifle. To the left the elephant walked along slowly. It was clear the man was preparing to shoot. Then his head exploded into a spray of blood and gore.

Professor Wang screamed and the rest of us jumped. The camera pulled back away until the barrel of a rifle with a scope was in the foreground and the elephant was running away in the distance. A hand reached up and using the rifle's bolt, ejected the spent cartridge and loaded a new one. The video stopped.

Abbey said, "Ned, play back the last part of the video and freeze the frame with the cartridge being ejected."

She watched closely. "Not everyone can make that shot. It looks like 500 yards."

The unnamed woman said, "Our estimate is closer to 600 yards."

Abbey went on. "It's an M40-A3 sniper rifle used by the USMC since about 2000 and sold all over the world. They have probably made over a million of the various M40 rifles. It's harder to find someone who can shoot like that than to get hold of one of those rifles."

The unnamed woman stared at Abbey. She didn't expect a female archaeology professor to have that depth of knowledge with firearms. The man who never spoke didn't seem surprised.

The Houston director stood and said, "You should run that through your software. Mr. Dillon will coordinate with the CIA and FBI. We will send you the results of the additional CDC tests and forward other information we believe might be useful to you.

"Please keep us informed on anything you discover. Thank you for your time, Mr. Falone."

He shook Walter's hand then his people all got up and walked out behind him.

I said, "Well that was interesting. The director seems to be in the group that doesn't think much of your software. Some of the folks at NSA aren't sure your software is worth the money. Lots of folks in the other agencies don't like the idea of NSA having powerful software that can grab their server capacity and put their work on hold even if it is in the national interest. Others at NSA are worried that if your software really is that good and they do nothing, some other government is going to end up with it. So they are willing to help you try and prove there is some big sinister plot going on involving this do-gooder website.

"You are pushing this because you want your company to make a couple hundred million bucks on the sale to NSA. But why us?"

Walter said, "Your summary is a bit blunt but it does cover most of the issues in play. As to your question why I need your help, there is an archaeological aspect to this with the grave robberies and stolen ancient manuscripts that you are qualified to investigate. The grave robberies and manuscripts all seem to have a disease or even biowarfare component that may be tied to Professor Wang's student. The analysis of the runs Ned has performed indicates the intensity of activity is going to increase."

I wasn't convinced but said, "OK what now?"

"The five of you go to Peru. You set up headquarters at my ranch. From there you investigate the grave robberies, stolen manuscripts, poacher deaths, and that strange illness. Start with these occurrences in Peru and Bolivia then we will decide what to do next."

I said, "Is Elizabeth part of the team?"

"No. She stays in Houston but feel free to call her. She can consult with you to the extent her schedule allows."

That didn't sound promising. I looked around the room. Chad had a smug look on his face, Ned was back typing on his computer, and Professor Wang looked in shock. I looked at Abbey, she shrugged her shoulders.

"Who else is available to help?"

Walter said, "I'm working on it. This is unfolding rather quickly. Your permits from the Peruvian National Institute for Culture will be waiting for you in Peru. They authorize you to investigate recent thefts and vandalisms at archaeological and burial sites. They also authorize you to evaluate the impact of the stolen manuscripts to the collections of the various institutes that were robbed.

"Letters of introduction have been prepared from Peru's National Institute for Culture, Ministry of Interior, and National Police. I'm still working on the permits in Bolivia.

"Mr. Dillon will be credentialed as part of the company's security department. Major Campbell will provide logistics and additional security as needed."

I said, "What is my budget and how do I report to you?"

"Rob, go to the ranch and get set up at the R&D center there. Start reviewing what we have. I'll be down in a few days and we can work out those details. Once again I must apologize for being short on time."

Walter had close ties to the Minister of the Interior and many important businesspeople in Peru. Abbey and I had worked well with members of the National Institute for Culture before in Peru. I was curious to see which archaeological sites were looted. The software's reliability and the more sinister matters, well we would see.

Chapter 6

I looked out the window as we started our descent into Lima's Jorge Chavez International Airport. It was just getting dark. Lima is a big, sprawling city with a population of almost 9 million and a land area of over 1,000 square miles. It is the capital and the largest city of Peru. It is located in the valleys of the Chillon, Rimac, and Lurin Rivers, in the central coastal part of the country, overlooking the Pacific Ocean. During the day you would see hang-gliders sailing off the cliff overlooking the Pacific Ocean.

Spanish conquistador Francisco Pizarro founded Lima on January 18, 1535, as Ciudad de los Reyes. It was the capital and most important city in the Spanish Viceroyalty of Peru. I hadn't spent much time in Lima when I was last in Peru. I hoped to have more time to explore the city this trip.

We taxied to the general aviation section of the airport. The flight attendant collected our passports and gave them to one of the pilots. As we came down the ramp a customs official handed us our passports and told us to enjoy our stay in Peru. There were definite advantages to flying on Walter's private jets.

A van was waiting for us. Our bags were loaded and we drove off. Walter's ranch was about 100 miles north of Lima. We headed north on the Pan-American Highway, also known as Peru Highway 1, towards the city of Huacho. It is in Huaura Province, one of the nine provinces of the Lima Region. Huacho was known for two things: being near the Lomas de Lachay National Park and holding the city's annual Guinea Pig Festival where guinea pigs are dressed up in fedoras and frilly dresses to participate in a fashion show. Must not be a lot else to do in Huacho.

We turned east off the highway. It was dark but I knew from previous trips that we were entering an area of peculiar geography called the Yungas. It is a stretch of forest along the eastern slope of the Andes Mountains and features a unique mist-fed ecosystem of wild plant and animal species. The ranch bordered Lomas de Lachay National Park. We turned onto a gravel road and through the open gate of the guardhouse. The ranch was over 10,000 acres.

The van took us straight to the guesthouse complex. Mrs. Lopez was there to meet us.

I said, "Hello. I like your niece and her family. I hope watching my place in Ithaca has not disrupted their lives too much."

"No, Professor, it will be a good experience for them. I'll have them give you updates each week."

I introduced Professor Wang and Chad Dillon. Ned said goodbye and headed off. He had accommodations in the employee area.

The guest complex consisted of two guesthouses on each side of a swimming pool. On one of the other sides was a pool house/gym building. The fourth side was a partly covered party patio with a cookout area. Each guesthouse had four apartments around a common area with a kitchen/bar and a large living room work area.

The driver brought our bags in and Mrs. Lopez showed us each to an apartment.

She said, "I'll have a light dinner sent over. The refrigerator is stocked for breakfast or you can eat at the canteen whenever you like. Major Campbell will meet you here at 10:00AM to take care of security matters."

Mia Wang looked lost. Chad Dillon seemed to like his new home. What was not to like? It was a luxurious place in a beautiful setting.

Mrs. Lopez left and Abbey went straight to the refrigerator. She pulled out a bottle of white wine and tossed it to me. "Open this, Prof, I need a drink." Then remembering her manners she said, "Mia, Chad, what would you like?"

Mia wanted wine, so I poured three wines and Chad grabbed a beer. Abbey looked at Mia and said, "It's an interesting place. It is more of a company R&D center than a ranch. The countryside is spectacular so not a bad place to work even if we don't know what we are doing."

She replied, "I don't see how being here will help find Justin." She took a small sip of wine. "I don't see why I need to be here."

I looked at Chad. He was drinking his beer and looking around the guesthouse. He seemed not to have a care in the world. I guess he was used to waiting.

Dinner was a subdued affair. Abbey talked to Mia about her work. Chad asked me about the facilities at the ranch. Then he excused himself and said he needed to check in with the office. Mia retired to her suite.

I looked at Abbey. "Delightful dinner."

She shook her head and said, "Remember how excited and energetic our team was when we were here before? They worked day and night and loved it."

"We have Ned, our cyber warrior. He's got enthusiasm," I said. "Walter must be planning to get others to help us."

"Help us do what?" But she was smiling. Abbey's smile was infectious. "Let's take a walk."

The next morning I was up early. I took a swim and then went to the research facility we used before. It was well equipped but no one was there. I walked around the ranch until a little before 10:00AM.

Mia Wang was on her laptop by the pool. Chad was on his sat-phone at the far end of the pool. When Major Campbell arrived I introduced him to Professor Wang. That got her attention. It was the first big smile I'd seen on her face. Was she batting her eyes at Major Campbell? He did cut quite a figure at six foot five inches of thin, hard muscle.

Abbey joined us and we started walking over to the security office. Mia was at Major Campbell's side asking questions about the ranch and hanging on his every word. Chad was following behind still on his phone. I looked at Abbey, she just shook her head slightly.

In the security office Major Campbell handed Abbey and me ID badges. He said, "You two are all set unless you want to be chipped."

We both shook our heads no.

He went on. "Let's start with you, Professor Wang."

She said, "Please call me Mia."

Was there more batting of the eyes or was I imagining it?

Major Campbell seemed not to notice. "Here is a cellphone and secure laptop. Please use it for all your work here. Transfer any data you need from your laptop with this memory stick."

The Major introduced her to David Fine. "David will take your photo, retinal scan, and fingerprints. He will also give you the computer access codes. The codes will be sent directly to your cellphone and changed every 48 hours. Secure area door locks have either fingerprint scanners or retinal scanners. You will be in the system for all areas you are cleared to enter. You can set the locks on your apartment.

"David will also explain the injectable RFID chip. But that is optional."

David led her away to start the process. I wanted to see the look on her face when he explained the injectable RFID chip. It is a tracking device about the size of a grain of rice that is injected under your skin and can be tracked twenty-four hours a day.

Major Campbell went over to where Chad was looking at the wall diagram of the ranch.

"I doubt your employer would want us to do a retinal scan and fingerprint you. We'll just do a photo ID and credentials showing you as part of the company's security department. I'll override the scanner codes for the places you need to go.

"However I'd like you to use a company sidearm. They are permitted with the Peruvian National Police. We have about anything you want. You can test them at the range."

Abbey said, "I'd like to join you."

Major Campbell hesitated for a moment and then said, "Let's meet at the range at 4:00PM. You folks are all set. I'll have David bring Professor Wang back to the guesthouse when she is done."

Abbey was going to check out the airstrip and see what was going on. I took Chad downstairs to the workroom I assumed we would be using again and then through the tunnel back to the guest complex.

We came out of the tunnel next to the pool house. Chad touched my arm and said, "Just the way you like your coffee."

I look at him puzzled then in the direction he was looking. She was black and she was very hot. In a pink one-piece swimsuit she was sitting back in a lounge chair sunning herself.

We walked in her direction. She stood up and was over six feet tall.

After looking at the two of us she said, "You must be Professor Johnson."

She extended a beautifully manicured hand. "I'm Dr. Carol Lord and don't say it."

"Say what?" I asked.

"Did I play basketball?"

How did she know that was what I was thinking? I said, "Volleyball?"

She broke into a big smile. She had very white teeth.

Her smile consumed her whole face.

"Yes, I played volleyball and I was good."

I introduced Chad Dillon. After a brief hello he walked to the far side of the pool and was back on his sat-phone.

After an awkward silence she said, "No one told you I was coming?"

"No." I didn't add that it was pretty much the way things had been. "Please sit. Tell me what you were told."

She sat and looked around. "Nice place here. They flew me in by private jet and had a car waiting for me. A Mrs. Lopez met me and showed me my apartment. Much better than the Motel 6 I'm usually in when on a field assignment."

She looked back at me. "You're the boss and you don't know what I'm doing here?"

I stifled a laugh. "I'm the boss but I'm just not sure of what or who."

"I guess that's how the government works. They told me to pack my bag for an extended trip to Peru and report to Professor Johnson when I arrived. What type of professor are you? They didn't even bother to tell me."

"I'm an archaeology professor. My area of interest is pre-Columbian archaeology."

Now she looked surprised. I said, "What type of doctor are you?"

She was shaking her head, not smiling, and then said, "Let's start again. Hello, Professor Johnson. I'm Dr. Carol Lord. I'm an infectious disease specialist with the Centers for Disease Control in Atlanta. I've been told that you are in charge of investigating disease outbreaks in South

America and elsewhere that could be of grave concern. My employer asked me to be of whatever assistance I can be to your investigation."

I said, "That helps. Things are moving a bit fast. Until a few days ago I was teaching my normal archaeology courses at Cornell University. Now I'm on leave from Cornell and employed by Walter Falone's company Falone Advanced Technologies. In working with the NSA Walter's company uncovered some potentially troubling things that may or may not be related. We will be investigating them."

I wasn't sure what her security clearance was. It was confusing enough without withholding information from our own team members.

She said, "Terrorism, bioweapons?"

"We aren't sure. But something like that."

David Fine arrived with Mia Wang.

I introduced the two women. Both were in professional mode. Very formal greetings were exchanged.

I was frustrated. "David, please arrange for these ladies to have a tour of the facilities here at the ranch. See if Chad wants to go also. Enjoy the afternoon. Dinner is on your own in the canteen tonight. We will meet at 9:00AM tomorrow in the workroom.

"I need to talk to Mrs. Lopez and Major Campbell. Perhaps they can tell me when Walter will be here. Where the hell is Ned anyway?"

David said, "Not my day to watch him."

I let it drop and headed to the main house to see Mrs. Lopez.

When I walked out of the main house after finding out

from Mrs. Lopez that she didn't know when Walter would arrive, Ned was waiting for me.

"You looking for me, Professor?"

I said, "Organize all the info we have so we can review it at 9:00AM tomorrow in the workroom. Get Chad to find out any new information or test results the CIA, FBI, and whoever has for us. Tell him to have the proper security clearances for Dr. Lord by the time we meet.

"I want a map showing the locations and dates of all the grave and manuscript robberies. Organize the other information in a way we can make sense of it. And no bullshit."

He said, "Don't get sore at me. I just work here."

I smiled. "You're a cyber warrior, you can take it."

"Dr. Lord, a pretty hot number. Did you know she was a star volleyball player for UCLA? She could have gone pro if she hadn't wanted to go to med school and maybe even have been in the Olympics. How cool is that?"

Since Mrs. Lopez had told me Major Campbell also had no idea when Walter would arrive, I decided to take a walk. As I approached the stables I thought maybe riding would improve my mood. Walter kept several horses because his daughters like to ride.

I found one of the stable hands and told him I'd like to go riding. He was a bit surprised because I'd never ridden when I was here before. He excused himself and said he had to make a call.

When he returned he said he would love to go riding with me. As we started out I looked around. The ranch was on a high open meadow that ran north-south. The buildings also ran north-south along the meadow. To the east you could see the start of the rain forest and the Andes Mountains beyond. To the west the terrain fell away towards the coastal desert plain. This was not so much a ranch as an eco-reserve.

This region is considered to have the most biodiversity in Peru. It is mainly composed of lucuma, cherimoya, and casuarin trees. Casuarin are evergreens growing to over 110 feet tall. The foliage consists of slender, much-branched green to gray-green twigs.

We rode for over two hours on well-groomed trails. We didn't speak but I noticed my companion studying the way I rode. I guess his instructions were to not let me get hurt. He relaxed a bit when he realized I could ride. In Mongolia we spent days in the saddle. It was the only way to get to our remote archaeological sites.

He was again surprised when after our ride I insisted on cooling and washing my horse. I brushed him and cleaned each of his hooves. By the time I went to the tack room someone had cleaned my bridle and saddle.

Much to my amazement my black mood was gone. It was almost cocktail hour. I went to see if Major Campbell was available for a drink and dinner.

Chapter
7

I was up early. I swam, ate, and then took my coffee over to the research facility. It was underground below the security offices. All the buildings were Spanish hacienda style. Nothing had a commercial or office look.

Abbey arrived about 8:15AM. I said, "Which office do you want?" Last time we were here Abbey was a grad student, not a professor, and she had a small office just outside my much larger office.

"Let's do it the same as before. Our last time here ended up well," she said.

I replied, "You weren't the one who got shot. Did you have a chance to meet Dr. Lord?"

"Yes. She seems to have a better attitude then Professor Wang. If whatever we are doing involves diseases and bioweapons, our archaeological expertise doesn't help much. When is Walter coming?"

"Mrs. Lopez didn't know. She said she would check."

Ned walked in. "You two ready to rock and roll? I was

up most of the night trying to figure out how to display what we have. I see why people are skeptical. Kind of a mish-mash."

I heard voices in the other room. "Showtime, Ned. Let's see what you did while the rest of us slept."

We walked into the workroom. I was surprised to see Major Campbell was also there.

I went into professor mode. "Good morning. Ned has organized the information the software algorithm indicated was all related to our do-gooder website. I've asked him to focus on two areas.

"The first is the robbery of graves and ancient manuscripts. We have permits coming from the National Institute for Culture that allow us to investigate these thefts in Peru. Ned will report on all the worldwide sites robbed. Then we will decide on the order in which we will investigate the Peruvian sites.

"The second area is the strange deaths of poachers in South Africa and Bolivia. Plus the common cold outbreak in Bolivia that appears to be caused by a genetically modified rhinovirus. Hopefully the CDC will be able to give us additional information.

"I have no idea how confidential or classified the information we have and will have is. I'm going on the assumption that we all have the proper clearances but no information should be shared outside the official reporting channels. If you have questions on security issues talk to Major Campbell and/or Chad Dillon."

Dr. Lord raised her hand.

"Yes."

She pointed to Chad. "Is he really a spook?"

I think I'm going to like Dr. Lord. "Yes and quite a good one. But to be politically correct he is a CIA field agent. However for anyone we talk to outside this room he is a member of Falone Advanced Technologies' security department."

She said, "OK. Ned here, he is a cyber warrior, and you and Professor Summers are archaeologists who dig up old bones and stuff in caves."

"Yes."

"This group's job is to save the world from some mysterious evildoers?" She was smiling.

I said, "As far as I've been told that is more or less the plan. However things are looking up now that we have you to help."

She let out a most unladylike guffaw and said, "I just like to get the big picture before we jump into the details." She really seemed to be enjoying this.

Ned's presentation was made up of the same material we had heard before. However he had done an admirable job of organizing it. All the grave and manuscript robberies were plotted on maps and dated.

There wasn't much more on the poacher killings or the rhinovirus outbreak. But now everyone was at least up to speed on what little we knew.

When this part of the presentation was done, I said, "Professor Wang and Dr. Lord, your thoughts."

Professor Wang was looking down at her folded hands. Dr. Lord was shaking her head no.

"OK. Let me ask a different question. Can you extract

from the centuries-old remains of people who died of the Black Death or some other disease something that could be used to make a bioweapon or recreate the virus?"

Dr. Lord said, "The Black Death is caused by bacteria not virus. In theory bacteria and even more so viruses can remain dormant for a long time but I've seen nothing in the research to suggest that live virus has been extracted from human remains that are hundreds of years old."

Professor Wang looked up and spoke to Dr. Lord. "There is another possibility. You could analyze the DNA structure of the long-dead bacteria or virus and then use gene editing to modify an existing bacteria or virus."

I said, "Have scientists done that?"

She said, "I haven't heard of anyone using bacteria or viruses from ancient human remains. But using the DNA code of one bacteria or virus to modify another is done in the lab all the time."

I said, "Wouldn't it be easier just to use some bad existing virus or bacteria? There is still a lot of nasty stuff like Ebola around."

Everyone was quiet for a moment. Then Dr. Lord said, "The advantage as a bioweapon is that if a virus or bacteria hasn't been around for a thousand years there won't be much residual resistance to it in the human population. Also no one has studied it or is working on vaccines or treatment methods. It could be a very virulent and nasty disease."

"OK. Here is what I'd like everyone to do. Abbey, you review the grave and tomb robberies in Peru and plan which sites we want to visit and when. Dr. Lord, please contact the CDC and get any additional information on the new rhinovirus strain. Also see if they have any other related information that may be helpful. Chad, see if your Agency was able to get samples from either of the dead poacher sites. Ned, keep poking around that website. Major Campbell, please try to expedite our permits from the National Institute for Culture.

"I'll look into the manuscript robberies in Peru. Let's meet back here at 9:00AM tomorrow and report on what progress we have. Any questions?"

Professor Wang said, "What should I do?"

I thought a moment and said, "Review with Dr. Lord the things that Justin was researching. Perhaps the two of you will see a connection.

"Ned, one more thing. Run a search and see if any other molecular or genetic scientists have gone missing.

"I'll be in my office or around. If you need me just send me a text. Thank you."

I got up and asked Abbey to have a word with me in my office. The two of us walked out. The others just sat there.

I sat and put my feet on the desk. Abbey sat looking at me. Finally I said, "Well at least now everyone has something to work on. It's better than having everyone mope around."

She said, "That takes care of today."

"We'll see what tomorrow brings. If I can't think of anything productive for them to do, you and I can go examine the robbed gravesites and they can work on their tans here.

"You figure out the most fun sites to visit and we'll start our investigation there."

73

"Brilliant plan," she said as she got up and walked out.

I pulled up my laptop and looked at the list of robberies of ancient manuscripts in Peru. There were only three: the National Museum of Peru, the Cathedral Basilica of the Assumption of the Virgin in Cusco, and the Larco Museum in Lima. I sent off an email to the contacts I'd been given for each institution. I also sent an email to the Monastery of Saint Catherine in Arequipa. I knew from our previous work in Peru that they had a large collection of rare manuscripts. That took all of twenty minutes.

Not feeling like I had earned my day's pay I started poking around the website we now called the do-gooder site. I'm not really up on this stuff so I just started clicking around the site. It was made up mostly of Internet forums or message boards on different topics.

I went to the forum on rhino poaching. Not surprisingly no one was supporting the poachers. There were comments on the number of rhinos left in each area of the globe. I learned that both African species and Sumatran rhinos have two horns, while the Indian and Java rhinos have a single horn. Vietnam is the largest market for rhino horn and it costs more per pound than gold. But the horns are just made of keratin, the same type of protein that makes up fingernails.

There were fundraising appeals to help protect the rhino, increase their habitat, and promote breeding programs. There were tirades against corrupt government officials and some graphic comments on what to do to poachers. In short just what you would expect.

I went to the forums for elephants, whales, polar bears,

and a few others, again pretty much what you would expect.

I looked at forums on genetics and bioengineering but it was way too technical for me. I shut down my computer and headed to the stables to go riding.

The next morning we met at 9:00AM as planned. I started with Ned. "Anything new to add about the website?"

Ned said, "I spent most of yesterday turning the rest of my work over to others. Major Campbell had me working on about a dozen things. Now I'm to be full time on this project. I ran the video of the elephant poacher getting his head blown off through our software. It showed a high probability of a connection to the do-gooder website.

"I looked for missing genetic engineers and molecular biologists but there were no mysterious disappearances I could find. Lots of job changing and some are making good bucks. I did find that a young scientist from the George Eliava Institute of Bacteriophage, Microbiology and Virology in Tbilisi, Georgia, has gone missing. He specialized in something called phage therapy. I'll keep digging."

I had another thought but I didn't interrupt him.

He continued. "So not much more but here's another item the software says may be relevant. It doesn't seem to fit. There are several schools in Philadelphia and Chicago that are reporting greatly reduced rates of teen pregnancy."

Everyone was staring at Ned. He said, "I'm just telling you that the software flagged it as a high probability of being connected."

I said, "Do we know who set up the website and runs it, or who the forum moderators are?"

"It says it was established and runs as a not-for-profit in the Netherlands. The not-for-profit is called 'Concerned Scientists to Save the Earth.' They go by CSSE. I haven't checked them out.

"Until a couple of days ago they had me doing other things."

I smiled at him. "Me too, Ned. Check out CSSE and poke around the website forums and chat rooms see what you can find out.

"Dr. Lord, anything from the CDC?"

"They said they hope to be able to get back to me in a day or two with more info. Professor Wang and I reviewed what Justin was working on. It is all interesting stuff and maybe we'll see a connection when we learn more."

Professor Wang just nodded yes.

"Let me ask you two, if Abbey and I are allowed to take samples of the same or similar remains to those that were stolen, what helpful analysis could be run on them?"

They thought for a bit then Professor Wang said, "There are all sorts of tests we could do. The question is which ones if any would be useful."

I said, "How about you two make a list of any you think might be helpful and what they might show. Develop some theories and think them through."

She was shaking her head and said, "We don't have a clue what we are doing."

She was right of course. I pasted on a big smile and said, "We're scientists, we solve mysteries. It's an adventure."

She wasn't buying it. So I moved on.

"Chad, any progress?"

"Some. They are sending people to investigate the buried remains of the poachers in Zululand. But they didn't say when. Unless it is related to jihadi terrorism it's hard to get them to allocate assets these days.

"We have the Bolivian government's permission to investigate the remains of the dead poachers there, assuming we can find them. That's about it."

Abbey reviewed the grave robberies in Peru and I filled them in on the little I'd accomplished with the manuscript thefts.

"Major Campbell, what is the status of our permits?"

"They are in process. The Peruvian government doesn't work at the same speed as Walter's company. I'll work with Chad on arrangements in Bolivia. The company has good relations in Bolivia.

"Walter arranged a videoconference with a bioterror expert at the US Agriculture Department for 11:00AM the day after tomorrow. Walter believes it may give us useful background information."

I thought Walter is trying to keep us busy so we don't all quit. I said, "OK. Follow up on any items you can and enjoy the ranch. Work on your tans. Once things start rolling there may not be much down time. Let's meet at 9:00AM the day after tomorrow to review before the videoconference."

I went back to my office and Abbey followed me. She didn't stop in her office but came into mine.

I sat and said, "Progress."

"You're kidding, right?"

I said, "No, I'm being optimistic. You always tell me

I'm too pessimistic.

"You make a list of all the tests you would like to run on the remains from the robbed graves assuming we can find any and they let us take samples. Don't limit yourself to what you think might help in this context. Everything you would like to test if money was no object.

"Also spend some time with Professor Wang and Dr. Lord. See what tests they are interested in and why. Compare notes."

"What are you going to do, Prof?"

"I'm going riding. Do you want to come?"

"No, I'm going to the range. Some of Major Campbell's men are doing long-range target practice."

Just then Ned walked in. Abbey said, "We're shooting the Remington Model 700 on the range, do you want to join us?"

Ned went pale. "No way." He began rubbing his shoulder as if he could still feel the bruises from the one time he had fired the rifle.

She punched him gently on the shoulder and left.

I said, "What's up?"

"I want to set up a few sock puppets…"

"Stop, what is a sock puppet?"

He gave me a look that I took to mean "how could anybody be that dumb?"

"Sock puppets are multiple pseudonyms used by the same person on a message board or forum. I'll use multiple IP addresses from different parts of the world. Sock puppets are usually found when an IP address check is done on the accounts in forums. Maybe I can stir something up."

I said, "OK. We don't know much, whatever you can find out could help."

"Check, I'm on it." He walked out.

I had a sneaking feeling I'd authorized more than I knew. Well cyber was Ned's world. I started checking my email. The nun responsible for the library at the Monastery of Saint Catherine said they had no robberies or missing manuscripts. The National Museum of Peru and Larco Museum were both in Lima so I set up appointments for Wednesday.

Then I sent an email to my favorite research librarian Laura O'Hara. I asked if she could contact her counterparts at the libraries and museums that had ancient manuscripts stolen and get as much detailed information as possible on the topics and time periods of the manuscripts. My thought from earlier was who could read these old manuscripts? They were in different languages from different centuries. Scholars often spent years trying to decipher just one manuscript. Plus we need to understand the science to know if any of the info was effective or useful. So I asked her to also check into that.

Not knowing what else useful to do, I went to lunch and then decided to walk up to the airfield. The airfield was short, about 1,200 feet. I'd learned last time I was here that the planes that flew in were all modified for short field takeoffs and landings. Plus they weren't that big. The biggest one was the Britten-Norman Defender. It could hold up to about ten people. The company flew a variety of drones here mostly to test new remote sensing equipment.

I heard voices in the hangar and wandered in. I saw Chad Dillon next to a workbench, talking to Peter Frank.

Peter called himself the fix-it man. He assembled and tested much of the company's newest and most advanced equipment. He referred to his wife, Dr. Dona Frank, as the brains of the team.

"Peter, a pleasure, I didn't know you were here."

"I wasn't until this morning. They flew me in from Lima to test some new miniaturized equipment. I heard you and Abbey are back on the payroll here. But nobody knows quite what you're doing."

I said, "I'll tell you as soon as I find out. Do you know when Walter is arriving by any chance?"

"No. Ask Mrs. Lopez. She'll know if anybody does."

Chad said, "Peter has some nifty toy here."

He held up what looked like a cross between a dragonfly and a child's toy helicopter. It was about four inches by one inch.

Peter said, "A Black Hornet nano-helicopter unmanned aerial vehicle."

I thought "I'm pretty sure it is unmanned" but kept my smartass comment to myself.

He went on. "It is probably too small to be practical for what we do. It was developed to provide troops on the ground with vital situational awareness.

"It is equipped with a tiny camera that gives troops reliable full-motion video and still images. Soldiers use it to peer around corners or over walls and other obstacles to identify any hidden dangers, and the images are displayed on a handheld terminal.

"We are testing a range of miniature UAVs from micro air vehicles like Chad is holding to portable UAVs that can be carried and launched by one or two people. Walter believes that they could be very effective for mine surveys where it is too dangerous or cumbersome for people. For smaller spaces we need a vehicle that can hover and back up. Plus radio control and most other remote control systems don't work that well deep underground."

I said, "What about Major Campbell's Aeryon Scout quadcopter, would that work in a mine?"

"It's the company's quadcopter and Ned is out playing with it now. But what I really want is something that will fly like a quadcopter and will travel over rough terrain on the ground."

He picked off the bench what looked like a giant yellow plastic six-legged bug. It was about eight inches long and stood about six inches high.

"Watch this. It's a hexapod robot or hexbot."

He pushed a button on the small remote control and dumped the plastic bug on the workbench. It tipped over but then righted itself and walked along on its six legs. It went over tools and parts on the bench. When it tipped over, it righted itself and went on.

He turned it off and said, "What I need is a UMV that flies like a quadcopter and climbs rough terrain like a cockroach."

I picked up the yellow plastic hexbot and said, "What you need to do is to take this hexbot and attach the quadcopter arms with the rotors on the middle of each side of it."

I pointed to the spots I meant.

"Did anyone ever tell you you're a genius?"

I shook my head. "No one, not even my mother."

He took the plastic bug robot from me and began turning it around in his hands.

Chad said, "I'm going to join the others at the range."

I said, "I'll walk with you." We let Peter get back to work. Abbey, Major Campbell, and four other men from the security department were there. Ned had the Aeryon Scout quadcopter set up on the ground ready to take off. I waved and kept walking to the stables. I had no interest in shooting.

We reassembled as a group Tuesday at 9:00AM in the workroom. It was an uninspired looking group. I asked Ned to start.

He said he was making progress on the background and funding for the not-for-profit called Concerned Scientists to Save the Earth. The directors all seemed to be legitimate concerned citizens. Their annual report had a list of donors but didn't show amounts. It was more a recognition and thank-you list than a financial disclosure.

He was working on several areas but it might take a while. Then he said, "I could use some help from Professor Wang. I'm fishing around several chat rooms and forums relating to genetically modified organisms. But I don't know all the GMO terms and slang or even much of the science. I need to sound authentic and knowledgeable to get anywhere."

I looked at Mia Wang. She said, "Sure, I'll help you. I don't have much worthwhile to do here and they won't let me go home."

Ned said, "Cool, I can really use your help, I've got way too many balls in the air."

She didn't seem very enthusiastic about it. Well Ned had enough enthusiasm for both of them. Now he could try to turn her into a Molecular Biology and Genetics Cyber Warrior Queen. It would probably be good for her.

Abbey, Carol Lord, and Mia Wang reviewed their long list of tests they wanted to run on the remains from grave and tomb robberies. The tests covered sequencing the genome, looking for all sorts of potential diseases, and several other areas.

Dr. Lord asked, "How much can we spend on testing? Many of these tests are expensive and I'm not sure what the CDC is willing to pay for."

I said, "Walter hasn't given me a budget yet. He doesn't waste money, however I assume we have a reasonable amount to work with since the sale of the software to NSA is worth a boatload to the company. Put some budget numbers together and prioritize the tests."

Abbey said to Ned, "Do you have any more on those schools in Philadelphia and Chicago that are reporting greatly reduced rates of teen pregnancy?"

Ned shook his head no.

Abbey turned to Dr. Lord. "Those reports make no sense to me. There are nine high schools reporting that the teen pregnancy rate has dropped to almost zero in the last few months. The school officials are claiming it is the result of the sex education programs they have implemented.

"I checked and those programs have been in place for years. The other schools in Chicago and Philadelphia haven't seen any real drop and they have basically the same programs. Now these nine schools had the highest rates of teen pregnancy in those cities.

"The Overbrook High School in the west region of Philadelphia is typical of all nine school. It is over 95 percent black and the students are largely from very low-income families. This is typically the hardest type of situation in which to have a successful sex education program. Plus these types of programs when they work usually show gradual improvement over time, not dropping to almost zero in a few months.

"It makes no sense."

Dr. Lord looked puzzled and said, "Send me all the info you were reviewing. I'd like to read it and then I'll talk to our people in those cities.

"My boss at the CDC told me they came up with some strange additional findings on the rhinovirus samples taken in Bolivia. He said he wanted an additional expert to check the results before he sent them on to me. That is about all I have."

I looked at my watch. "Let's take a fifteen-minute break before the videoconference with the gentleman from the Department of Agriculture."

Ned had the video link set up on the wall-mounted large screen hi-def TV. At exactly 11:00AM the link went live. A gentleman was facing the camera much like you see in a TV news interview. The background appeared to be a laboratory.

He gave his first name and said he was a bioterror expert at the US Agriculture Department.

"Mr. Falone has arranged for me to give you a restricted briefing on several areas of concern related to potential bioterror attacks on the US agriculture industry and/or food supply. I've been told all of you have the proper clearances. If your work uncovers anything that indicates there is likely planning of anything that resembles the examples I outline, please contact us immediately.

"I'll be using a PowerPoint presentation. It is part of a presentation I gave recently to the United States Senate Subcommittee on Internal Security."

OK, I was impressed. He put up the first slide.

The insects fell into the Romans' eyes and the exposed parts of their bodies...digging in before they were noticed, they bit and stung the soldiers, causing severe injuries. — Herodian, a historian of ancient Antioch (c. 170 – c. 240)

"Biological warfare has been around in one form or another for a long time. Early evidence of insects being held in military esteem is seen in Egyptian hieroglyphics dating to the First Dynasty, more than 5,000 years ago.

"By 2600 BCE, the Mayans had weaponized bees or wasps. The sacred text Popul Vuh tells of the people building dummy warriors topped with headdresses to conceal both the inanimate condition and the real purpose of the manikins. The heads were hollow gourds filled with stinging insects. When attackers smashed the gourds, the insects retaliated, precipitating a chaotic retreat that allowed the Mayans to defeat the attackers.

"History books are full of examples of bioweapons used in warfare. Most with only limited success. That all changed during World War II with the Japanese in China, under the direction of a brilliant and possibly demented medical doctor who became the general in charge of what was called Unit 731. General Ishii Shiro, the mastermind of Japan's Unit 731, was responsible for developing biological weapons during the war. His program made extensive use of human experimentation. He set up facilities in Manchuria where he could use Chinese prisoners for his experiments.

"After outgrowing two facilities in 1939 he had a facility constructed that was a bizarre cross between a biomedical death camp and a resort spa. Within its two square miles, the compound comprised more than 150 structures: headquarters building with a moat, administrative offices, laboratories, barns, greenhouses, a power station, a school, a brothel, recreational facilities including a swimming pool, housing for 3,000 scientists, dormitories for technicians and soldiers, and a prison for the inmates, along with the requisite crematorium.

"The facility researched all sorts of diseases and massed produced plague-infected fleas. At its peak the Japanese could produce more than half a billion plague-infected fleas per year. They experimented with several ways of delivering the plague-infested fleas. In the end they primarily were using two methods. In the first they packed the fleas in small porcelain bulbs set within a ceramic bomb casing. A small, timed charge exploded the ten-quart payload and thereby released fleas from an altitude of about 500 feet. The second method used later directly sprayed the fleas from airplanes.

"It is estimated the Japanese killed a total of 580,000 Chinese with biological weapons during World War II.

"Well you folks don't need any more gruesome examples from history to know this is a real worry. The area my group is concerned with is a terrorist attack on the agricultural sector. Others in government are worrying about the water supply, diseases, the power grid, etc.

"There are hundreds of possibilities but there are three at the top of our list. If you uncover any information suggesting potential threats in these areas please contact us immediately.

"One scenario is a terrorist posing as a tourist travels to the Napa and Sonoma Valley wine country. Along with the usual tourist items he has a small jar with some common label that actually holds thousands of a foreign strain, Phylloxera vitifoliae, commonly known as grape lice. These tiny aphid-like insects kill vines by infesting and destroying the roots. Moving through California's wine country the terrorist spreads the tiny insects. By the time the vineyards begin to show signs of stress it is too late to stop the invasion, and the insects spread to thousands of acres by the time the problem is identified. It is estimated that such an attack could kill two-thirds of the infested plants and cost the industry billions of dollars.

"Another scenario involves the New World screwworm. It is a loathsome creature. Its species name hominivorax is derived from hominis meaning 'man' and vorax meaning 'voracious' so its literal name is man-eater and for good reason. The insect was responsible for hundreds of gruesome deaths on the Devil's Island penal colony. A French physician, Charles Coquerel, who was investigating the deaths, named the insect. A female fly laying a mass of eggs around a wound starts the infestation. In just 12 hours the eggs hatch and the larvae begin eating the injured flesh with their mouth hooks. The gore of this feeding frenzy attracts more females as the maggots expand the open sore by the hour. Death almost inevitably results unless the wound is treated. After five days of feeding, the larvae drop to the ground, burrow into the soil, and form pupae. A week later, bluish-green metallic adults emerge, mate, and the cycle starts again.

"The New World screwworm was eliminated in the US in 1966 and in Mexico by 1991. The large-scale breeding of sterile male flies that outcompeted the fertile males did this and the majority of female flies began to lay sterile eggs. Irradiating the males was used for sterilization.

"A large-scale reintroduction into the US could be devastating to the livestock industry. An outbreak in North Africa in 1989 spread rapidly killing about 2.7 million sheep over a 10,000 square mile area in just three years. The US would eradicate the screwworm again but not before hundreds of millions of dollars of damage had been done.

"The final example of concerns we are on the lookout for is a terrorist attack on the honeybee population. As funny as that may sound, bees play a vital role in the agriculture industry. Virtually every plant relies on bees or other insects to spread pollen for their breeding process. Farmers hire beekeepers to bring hives to the fields to assure their plants are pollinated.

"It has been widely reported in the news so most of you have probably heard of colony collapse disorder or CCD.

The Zulu Curse

Beekeepers in the US have been reporting slow declines of stocks for many years. However in 2007 an unprecedented decline occurred with die-off rates of 30 to 70 percent of the bees in the hives. It is unclear whether this is simply an accelerated phase of the general decline or a new issue.

"Evidence is leaning towards CCD being caused by a combination of various factors rather than a single pathogen or poison. With our country's bees already stressed and in serious decline, they become more susceptible to a deliberate terrorist attack. One of our biggest concerns is the Varroa destructor mite. It can only reproduce in a honeybee colony. The Varroa destructor mite first appeared in the US in 1987. It attaches to the body of the bee and weakens it by sucking the bee's blood. In this process it transfers viruses such as deformed wing virus and others that kill the bees.

"If terrorists found a way to effectively spread Varroa destructor mites between bee colonies the entire US honeybee population might be in danger with billions of dollars of losses to our agriculture industry.

"I know this may sound a bit far-fetched but consider that from 1906 to 1991, an estimated 553 nonnative organisms successfully settled in the United States, and two-thirds were insects. For the forty-three insect species for which careful loss assessment has been conducted, it is estimated that the losses total $93 billion. This occurred often with as little as one ship's cargo carrying the insect eggs or larvae.

"Again if your work uncovers any evidence of a threat to our agriculture industry, contact us. Thank you for your time."

The screen went blank and we all sat quietly. Finally Ned said, "Very spooky stuff but I haven't seen anything like that in our work. We have weird shit going on but not like that.

"Are we done here? As I've got a boatload of work to do."

On that cheery note I said, "OK, everybody keep digging, let me know if anything big comes up and I'll schedule another meeting in a few days."

I walked to my office and plopped into my chair. I was in a black mood. I had my head down reading a text on my phone when I heard footsteps. I looked up.

Abbey said, "That was inspirational, Prof. You really know how to keep the group's spirits up and everyone motivated."

I held up my phone so Abbey could read the text from Mrs. Lopez. It read: "Walter is in Asia for at least another week."

"Abbey, let's go to Bolivia. You haven't ever been to Bolivia. I'm sick of sitting around here not really knowing what we need to do. Let's get out of here and go find the dead poachers.

"We'll take Chad and Dr. Lord, plus whoever Major Campbell wants to send with us. I'll go talk to Major Campbell and Chad about arrangements. You talk to Dr. Lord. Plan on leaving first thing in the morning. That's an order."

I smiled. I was starting to feel better already.

Chapter 8

We met at the airfield at 8:30AM. Major Campbell had the Cessna Skymaster parked in front of the hangar.

I saw Dr. Lord looking at the plane. I said, "It's funny-looking, isn't it? It is a push-pull engine configuration, one engine mounted in the nose and the other in the rear of its pod-style fuselage."

I patted the engine cowling and went on. "It is a Cessna T337B Turbo Super Skymaster. It has two Continental turbocharged fuel-injected 210 horsepower engines, a service ceiling to 33,000 feet, a cruise speed to 233 mph, and a range to 1,640 miles. It is pressurized and has Robertson STOL modifications."

Abbey poked me in the ribs. "An aviation expert now?"

I blushed a little and said, "That's what Major Campbell told me. He loves flying." Then I was quiet. Was I just showing off for Dr. Lord? I left the two women and went into the hangar to find Major Campbell.

I had given him the list of archaeological sites I wanted

to fly over. Mostly I wanted Dr. Lord to see Machu Picchu from the air. There were four other sites we would pass close to. Two were Inca and two were Wari. I'd marked them on a map and asked Major Campbell to fly over them.

Major Campbell came out of the office at the back of the hangar just as I was getting to the office door.

"Good morning, Rob, the weather looks good. Is everyone set to go?"

I said, "The ladies are here but I haven't seen Chad yet."

We walked out. Chad had arrived.

Major Campbell said, "With our detours to overfly the archaeological sites it is about 800 miles to La Paz, Bolivia. In La Paz we will clear customs and pick up one of Chad's associates. From there we will fly about 350 miles to Blanca Flor and meet up with Bolivian officials who will take us down the Madre de Dios River to the village that had the rhinovirus outbreak and to where the poachers died.

"The first leg to La Paz will take a little over four hours including our sightseeing and the second leg to Blanca Flor will be about an hour and a half."

I said, "Abbey, how would you like to be tour guide for the sites we fly over? Dr. Lord, you take the copilot seat, Chad, you and Abbey sit in the next row, and I'll crawl in back. I've seen these sites from the air before."

We put our bags in the cargo area and got in. Major Campbell finished his pre-flight check and got in. We taxied out to the runway and did a run-up with Ian revving each engine and checking all the gages. He set the altimeter and taxied to the very end of the runway. Then he stepped on the brakes and pushed both throttles to full. We rolled down the short runway and lifted off smoothly. On my first flight with him the plane seemed to jump forward like a jackrabbit and leap into the air. He wanted to show me how the STOL special modifications worked. This time it was smooth as silk.

Our flight path would take us south through five of the twenty-five regions that make up Peru. We would fly south and east through the Lima, Junin, Cusco and Puno regions and then on into Bolivia. As we climbed we could see the coastal plain to the west. We shortly reached the western edge of the Andean mountain range. The border area between Lima and Junin has snowy and ice-covered peaks. Farther to the east, there are high glacier valleys that end up in high plateaus.

Continuing east there is an abundance of narrow and deep canyons with highly inclined hillsides covered by woods. The Waytapallanna mountain range is located in the south central area of the region. This range holds a great fault, the source of the area's earthquakes.

My attention was next drawn to Lake Junin, the largest lake entirely within Peruvian territory. Lake Titicaca is much larger but its eastern half is located in Bolivian. Lake Junin covers over 200 square miles. The southeastern end is in Cusco region.

The Cusco region is where all five of the archaeological sites we would fly over are. This region was the heart of the Inca and before that the Wari cultures.

First we passed over Winay Wayna. Abbey was explaining that this meant "forever young" in Quechua, the language of the Incas. She went on to say it is built into a steep hillside overlooking the Urubamba River. The site consists of upper and lower house complexes connected by a staircase and fountain structures. Agricultural terraces are above and below the houses. All of which was clearly visible from the air.

Major Campbell circled the site twice and Abbey answered Dr. Lord's questions.

Next we flew south and east along the Urubamba River towards Machu Picchu, perhaps the most famous archaeological site in South America. It is situated on a mountain ridge above the Sacred Valley at an elevation of almost 8,000 feet. Most archaeologists believe that Machu Picchu was built as an estate for the Inca emperor Pachacuti who lived from 1438 to 1472. It is commonly known as the Lost City of the Incas. The Incas built the estate around 1450, but they abandoned it during the Spanish Conquest about a hundred years later. It was unknown to the outside world until 1911 when Hiram Bingham, an American historian, rediscovered it. Machu Picchu is situated above a loop of the Urubamba River that surrounds the site on three sides. The cliffs drop vertically for 1,480 feet to the river below. The location of the city was a military secret. Its deep precipices and steep mountains provided excellent natural defenses. The city sits in a saddle between the two mountains Machu Picchu and Huayna Picchu. It has a commanding view down two valleys and a nearly impassable mountain at its back. The water supply is from springs that cannot be blocked easily. The hillsides leading to it have been terraced, providing farmland to grow crops and steep slopes that invaders would have to ascend. There were two routes from Machu Picchu going across the mountains back to Cusco. The first was the Sun Gate, and the second was across the Inca Bridge. This Inca Bridge, also called the Trunk Bridge, was a part of a mountain trail, which was a stone path cut into a cliff face. A 20-foot gap was left in this section of the carved cliff edge over a 1,900-foot drop. This was bridged with two tree trunks. Removing them would leave the trail impassable to enemies. Major Campbell flew low over the site. We could clearly see the three primary structures: the Hitching Post of the Sun, the Temple of the Sun, and the Room of the Three Windows. They are located in what is known as the Sacred District of Machu Picchu. He circled twice as Abbey explained all this and then headed southeast.

Next we came to the first of the two Wari sites we would fly over. Wari culture flourished from about 500 to 1100AD in an area that covers much of today's west coast of Peru, a part of western Bolivia and the northern part of Chile. The first site, Patallaqta, is situated southeast of Machu Picchu at the confluence of the Kusichaka and Willkanuta Rivers and on a mountain called Patallaqta.

Abbey explained that the site had housed a large number of occupants, including travelers and soldiers who manned the nearby hill fort of Willkaraqay, and a shrine with rounded walls known as Pulpituyuq that had ceremonial functions. During his retreat from the Spanish in Cuzco, Manco Inca Yupanqui destroyed Patallaqta in 1536 along with several other settlements. This may be the reason the Spanish never discovered Machu Picchu.

Pikillaqta was the final site on our aerial tour. This Wari site is located in low ridges in the eastern Valley of Cuzco. The area is hilly with no rivers, but small lakes are located near the city. It may have been a large feasting site. There was a large patio in the middle of the architectural structure that probably was the center of the administrative rituals and religious practices.

Because there were no rivers close by and little rain, the city depended on a system of reservoirs and aqueducts to water the terraced fields. Canals were built of stone and were connected to the Lucre River and Chelke stream. There are over 30 miles of canals in the system. The site appears to have never been finished and was abandoned about 1100AD.

We then flew straight southeast to La Paz. I'd asked Major Campbell to fly over Lake Titicaca. It is the highest navigable lake in the world, with a surface elevation of 12,507 feet, and is the largest lake in South America by volume. The west side is in Peru and the east side is in Bolivia. Its surface area is 3,232 square miles. The views from the air are spectacular.

Shortly after we crossed the lake we could see the city of La Paz. The city sits in a bowl surrounded by the high mountains of the altiplano or Bolivian Plateau. It is a sprawling city of just under a million people that climbs up the sides of the surrounding mountains to an elevation of 13,500 feet.

We landed at El Alto International Airport and taxied to the general aviation section. Major Campbell followed the instructions given by the air controller and parked.

Two men walked up to the plane, one was a customs official and the other introduced himself as an economic and trade specialist with the US Embassy. This was our CIA contact. He introduced himself as Harry Jones. He and Chad showed no sign of knowing each other or having any connection to each other.

The customs agent asked us to follow him. We entered the small terminal building used by general aviation passengers. He told us to use the restroom if we liked while he reviewed our passports. It took all of ten minutes and as we walked out to the plane the gas truck was just finishing refueling the plane.

Abbey got in the third row with me and Harry Jones took the seat next to Chad. We took off and headed north. Not much of a visit to La Paz and we were off on our 350-mile flight to Blanca Flor.

As we flew north and a little east we could see the high Andean plains of western Peru. In front of us was the Bolivian Yungas, a tropical and subtropical moist broadleaf forest eco-region. This northeast region is situated in the Amazon lowlands of Bolivia. It is hottest and wettest region of Bolivia.

The Blanca Flor Airport wasn't much, just a grass airstrip, a few one-story buildings and dirt roads heading in three different directions. There was no control tower so Major Campbell circled once looking at the windsock then descended and lined up on final approach.

Two members of the National Police Force met us. The uniformed police are referred to as Carabiniers. They introduced themselves. Mariscal was the senior officer and Simon his subordinate. They explained that they were with the POFOMA, which is the forestry and environmental protection police.

I helped Major Campbell tie the plane down and we all got in two Toyota Land Cruisers. I sat in back with Dr. Lord. As we bounced along dirt roads she explained to me that Bolivia had the worst health ranking in the Western Hemisphere except for Haiti. After about forty-five minutes we reached the village on the south side of the Madre de Dios River that hadn't experienced any of the flu cases.

Dr. Lord, Harry Jones, and one police officer would question people on both sides of the river about the flu outbreak. Abbey and I would work with the other officer and Major Campbell to find out what we could about poaching. Chad Dillon wandered off to a shack that had a sign stating it was a bar. It was already 4:00PM so we agreed to meet back at the vehicles in two hours.

After our two hours of investigating we went to a small inn. It seemed we had the whole place. The first floor consisted of a one-room dining, bar, and sitting area. There were four rooms upstairs. I was bunking in with Major Campbell.

As we gathered in the sitting area a young girl took our drink orders and her father made the drinks at the small bar.

"Dr. Lord, what did you find out?" I asked.

"It's all very strange," she said. "After about six weeks the virus seems to have burned itself out. No new cases after that but about 80 percent of the villagers seem to have contracted the disease during the six weeks and it never spread outside the village.

"When we get back I'll do some research and see if there are other similar cases."

Abbey said, "The CDC report indicated the rhinovirus wasn't any of the ninety-some known strains and was possibly genetically engineered."

Dr. Lord nodded her head.

Abbey went on. "A highly contagious airborne virus with an infection rate of over 80 percent that is confined to a specific geographic area for a limited time period. That seems like the perfect bioweapon to me.

"Historically the major drawback to bioweapons was the risk of infecting your own troops or starting something you couldn't stop."

Chad Dillon and the other CIA agent were fully focused now.

Dr. Lord said, "Yes, but it just caused a mild cold."

I said what others were thinking. "They're testing the time and geographic aspects of the engineered virus. Once they have that down they can weaponize it with a really nasty virus. But why here?"

Abbey said, "It is an out of the way place. If the World Health Organization hadn't had people near here we might never have heard about the outbreak.

"There are some species that live only in very small specialized environments. But the village on one side of the river seems much the same as the other side and CDC believes it is a genetically modified virus. Can the CDC test for something like this?"

Dr. Lord thought for a moment then said, "It isn't necessarily that easy. The blood samples probably have no living virus. We are just beginning to understand what genes cause what to happen. Plus most of the time it isn't as simple as one gene causing one trait. Often many genes are involved. Other times genes are there but aren't expressed. I need to talk to my office and to Dr. Wang."

On that cheery note Dr. Lord said, "Tell us what you found out."

I nodded to Abbey. She said, "Not that much. The great river otter is an endangered species and protected under Bolivian law. However poaching is a problem along the river here as well as throughout the greater Peruvian Amazonian basin. It is estimated that there could be as few as 5,000 left in the wild. As the number shrinks, the price of their velvety pelts keeps going up on the black market.

"We talked to several villagers who heard about the strange death of some poachers. All of them seem to have heard it second-hand, no one said they saw the bodies and some villagers believe it is a rumor spread by the government to try to discourage poaching. Most villagers don't seem to care much about the fate of the river otters.

"Tomorrow we can go downriver to the areas where the otters live and poaching is known to occur."

Abbey stopped and shrugged her shoulders.

I looked at Chad Dillon. "How did your afternoon go?" The sarcasm was clear in my tone.

He smiled his Cheshire cat shit-eating grin. "Not much of a drink selection in that bar, but an interesting group of regulars in there between 4:00 and 6:00PM and quite talkative after a few free drinks.

"It seems two white men were here a week or two before the colds broke out across the river. They had a local with them from downriver. The men spoke Spanish but not like Bolivians and they spoke English but not like Americans. After one day here they went back downriver again.

"One of my new friends said his cousin was with the group that found the dead poachers. His description of the bodies matches what the FBI told us in Houston. After some hemming and hawing and several more drinks he admitted that his cousin's group dumped the bodies and took their pelts and gear. I'll poke around some more when you go downriver tomorrow."

Dinner was family style and not much small talk. I excused myself early and went to bed. The officers wanted to start downriver at first light.

The Madre de Dios River was peaceful in the early morning light. We had coffee and rolls from the inn as we cruised downriver. The police boat was sturdy looking with two outboard engines. I watched the mist rise from the tree-lined shores.

After about an hour Officer Mariscal slowed the engines to an idle. He handed me binoculars and pointed ahead to the north shore of the river. At first I didn't see anything. Then they came into view as I focused the binoculars. Even from here they looked big.

I handed the binoculars to Abbey. The engines were off and we were quietly drifting downriver. Abbey had a big smile on her face as she handed the binoculars to Dr. Lord.

She refocused the binoculars and said, "So cute and big like a seal. Are they playing?"

Officer Mariscal said, "Yes, otters are very social, they sleep, play, travel, and feed together and typically live in family groups of six to eight. They can grow to over five and a half feet with the males weighing up to seventy pounds."

"So cute," Dr. Lord said again. "Who would want to kill them?"

We drifted past the playing otters to a point where there was a path worn in the shoreline vegetation. The officers nosed the boat in and tied it.

We walked into a clearing that looked like a camping area. As the officers were examining the area, a shot rang out. Officer Simon fell backwards to the ground.

Major Campbell screamed "down" and fired four quick shots from his automatic in the direction of the shot. A second shot came at us. Dr. Lord was standing there with her hands over her mouth. I jumped up and tackled her. As we went down, another shot rang out and my feet snapped around.

Officer Mariscal and Major Campbell lay on the ground slowly firing into the brush where the shot had come from. Abbey had Officer Simon's handgun. She was scanning the brush but not firing.

Dr. Lord rolled me off her and crawled to where Officer Simon was down. Blood had pooled on the ground next to him. She pushed him onto his stomach and tore open the back of his pants.

A fourth shot was fired towards us. Abbey fired a quick volley of shots and there was a scream from the brush.

Dr. Lord said, "I need the first-aid kit from the boat."

I started to get to my feet but Abbey pushed me down hard and sprinted to the boat. She did a diving roll into the boat and was sprinting back to Dr. Lord in a matter of seconds.

Dr. Lord opened the box and dumped out the contents. She cut away the blood-soaked rear of his trousers and poured in a powder. Officer Simon groaned. She then cleaned the area and bandaged it.

Major Campbell and Officer Mariscal moved cautiously to the edge of the clearing. Abbey sat next to me. "Prof, are you OK?"

My ears were ringing from the gunfire. I've never really gotten used to the loud noise of guns. "I think so."

She had my foot in her hands and was removing my boot. Now that hurt. I tried not to scream but did let out a grunt. The boot came off and the sole was flapping.

Abbey examined my foot. "You're not bleeding but you probably will have a big bruise. Shot in the boot." She held it up and the sole hung down.

I rubbed my foot.

She grabbed a roll of surgical tape and began taping my boot. She said to Dr. Lord, "How is he?"

"He has severe trauma to his gluteus maximus or more simply, he was shot in the ass. He should make a full recovery but he'll have trouble sitting on this side of his butt for a while."

Major Campbell and Officer Mariscal came back. After checking on Simon, Mariscal said, "There were two or three of them. Abbey wounded at least one. There is a tributary stream in that direction. They probably have a boat. I'm not going after them with a wounded officer and four civilians with me. Can we move Simon to the boat?"

Dr. Lord said yes and they carried Simon to the boat as I put on my boot. He was propped on his good side with life vests. Dr. Lord gave him some pain pills and fussed over him a bit more.

I went and sat in the back of the boat. Abbey stood alone in the front of the boat looking out over the river. Again I worried about her.

Dr. Lord came and sat next to me. She said, "You saved my life. That bullet would have hit me if you hadn't tackled me. Maybe you are a little like Indiana Jones. Not as cute as Harrison Ford but he's getting a bit old."

She smiled, shivered, and slid closer to me. She said in a lower voice, "How did Abbey know to do that?"

"Do what?" I said dumbly.

"You saw her. She took Officer Simon's gun and took up a firing position like you see in the movies. She knew Major Campbell and Officer Mariscal were trying to draw their fire and then Abbey would know exactly where to shoot.

"I read her résumé on the Cornell website. She graduated early from high school and went straight to Cornell. She has been affiliated with the University ever since. No military or police training. She acted as if being under fire was second nature to her."

I looked at Abbey standing in the bow of the boat, her long red hair streaming behind her in the breeze, still in her mid-twenties. I said, "Abbey is an exceptional young woman."

Officer Simon groaned and tried to sit up. I said, "I'll tell you about it some other time."

She smiled and squeezed my arm. "I'll hold you to that, Professor." She went to Officer Simon. She had a beautiful smile.

Officer Mariscal had radioed ahead. A medical van and several policemen met us. Dr. Lord and the medics took Simon by stretcher to the van.

I went to Abbey and just said, "Thank you."

She smiled and said, "You're the hero. You saved Dr. Lord's life, the damsel in distress. Just like Prince Charming and you know how that story ended."

She poked my arm and walked over to where Major Campbell was talking to the police. She still had Officer Simon's gun in her belt.

I looked at my watch, it wasn't yet noon. It seemed like ages ago when we started downriver.

Chad Dillon came over. "Sorry I missed the action. Officer Mariscal said you surprised some otter poachers."

I said, "Did you find anything else out about the two men who arrived before the virus outbreak?"

"From the descriptions they appear Caucasian. As I said last night they spoke English well but not with an American accent and Spanish but not like a local. I would guess European. We have a reasonable description of them and we will work with the authorities to see if we can find out any likely matches entering the country at that time. It is a long shot."

The medical van left and Officer Mariscal went with several officers back down the river to look for the poachers. We decided to fly back to La Paz tonight and then on in the morning.

We really hadn't accomplished much. Chad would stay in La Paz to see if they could get anything on the mystery men. Dr. Lord was keyed up and wanted to talk to her colleagues at the CDC. Abbey was quiet and I could feel that black mood overtaking me. Winston Churchill called it his black dog and it dogged him his entire life.

We landed back at the ranch in the early afternoon. I dropped my bags in my suite, changed, and went to the barns. I asked for a horse. The cheerful stable hand from my other ride appeared in a minute with two horses. It didn't take him long to sense my mood. He quietly saddled one horse as I saddled the other. I guess he had instructions not to let me go out alone. Well no point in getting him in trouble. I smiled and told him I wanted a long ride. He knew my smile was forced and just nodded in agreement.

He rode up a trail to the east, at first he walked then he broke into a steady trot. He kept up a trot for a good half hour. I was deep in thought. Then he brought his horse back to a walk. The trail narrowed and we had to duck under low branches. We came out next to a pool fed by a waterfall.

"We will let the horses rest and drink now," he said, dismounting and loosening his horse's girth.

As the horses drank he pointed to several different birds in the trees around the pool. But he said nothing. He was completely at ease and seemed happy gazing at the plants and birds. What was my problem anyway? People paid thousands of dollars to visit wild and beautiful places like this.

After twenty minutes or so he tightened the girth on his horse's saddle and mounted up. I did the same and followed him down the path. The trail opened up and flattened out as we approached the airstrip.

He said, "I'll race you," then spurred his horse into a gallop. I followed. We raced along the grassy side of the airstrip past the ranch buildings and to the stables. I was a distant second.

He jumped off his horse and with a big smile said, "I win." I smiled back and we both started to laugh.

As we walked, washed, and groomed the horses I realized I felt great, no more black dog. Mood is a strange thing. Life hardly seems worth living one minute and the next the world is a wondrous place. I thanked him and headed back to the guesthouse.

I took a quick swim, showered, and went out on the patio.

Abbey came out. "You look a little better," she said.

It was a beautiful evening. I didn't want to spoil the mood. I asked, "Where is everyone?"

"Dr. Lord and Professor Wang are working. They were deep in conversation when they headed to the workroom. I don't know where Ned is. Wait here."

She went in and was back in a minute with a bottle of white wine, a bowl of nuts, and her iPad. She poured us a glass of wine.

"Cheers. I'm not sure what the hell we are doing here but it's a beautiful evening and I was getting tired of Mongolia."

I asked, "Is your boyfriend still there?"

"He left six weeks ago for New Zealand. He got a grant to work on some endangered bird species there."

She seemed very neutral in her tone as she said this. I decided to change the topic.

Before I could she said, "I've got something to show you."

She picked up her iPad. "I had Gabriela send these." She spun the iPad around and went through a series of photos. My dog Beast sitting on the couch next to Gabriela as she read, one of my cats sleeping on top of Beast in the barn, then Gabriela and her father riding my two horses. Her mother had obviously been the photographer. There were a dozen more. I missed my four-legged family but it was fun and uplifting to see the pictures.

We drank a second glass of wine, made pleasant small talk, and then decided to go to dinner at the canteen.

As we finished dinner Dr. Lord and Professor Wang came in. They were talking animatedly, we said hello and after a brief visit we left.

I went to my suite. I was no longer depressed, just frustrated. We needed a break. We needed something to go on. In archaeology we train ourselves to work slowly and patiently so as not to inadvertently damage something valuable. This wasn't the way I needed to drive our investigation forward, we needed progress. Bad things were going to happen, I could feel it.

I was trying to read. I heard a gentle knock on the door. I opened it and Dr. Lord was standing there with a bottle of wine in her hand and a wry smile on her face. She had definitely slipped into something more comfortable since we said hello at the canteen a few hours ago. I tried not to stare.

"Rob, I thought a glass of wine would be nice and you promised you would tell me more about Abbey."

She handed me the bottle, walked in, and closed the door. I told her to have a seat and walked to the counter to open the wine. Yes my heartbeat had quickened.

She sat on the couch. I poured two glasses of wine and handed her one. When I started to sit in the chair she patted the couch next to her.

"Sit here, I won't bite, well not hard. Cheers. Tell me about Abbey, she obviously adores you and you know how I mean that."

I did. "If I had a daughter I could only hope she had some of the fine qualities Abbey has.

"I first met Abbey when she was a fifteen-year-old freshman. I was her adviser. She stood out even among the many brilliant Cornell students. She had her pick of the top Doctoral programs in the country when she graduated. I was thrilled when she decided to pursue her PhD in archaeology at Cornell.

"You know most of the rest of her academic background from her résumé."

She smiled. I noticed Carol's beautiful smile when I met her but now it lit up the room.

"Rob, Major Campbell didn't seem the least surprised by Abbey's reactions when the poachers shot at us."

I thought back to our first time in Peru.

"I was as shocked as you the first time I saw Abbey under fire. Afterward Major Campbell told her that most of his SAS soldiers couldn't handle themselves that well. Abbey said to him, 'My grandfather was a Marine. He taught me stuff when I was a little girl. I never shot anyone before.' Then tears started streaming down her cheeks. It almost broke my heart.

"Later her grandfather told us the entire story."

Carol reached for the wine bottle, refilled our glasses, and returned it to the table. She then slid her hand gently under my arm.

"When her grandfather retired from the Marines he and his wife decided to move to Plattsburgh to be near their son, daughter-in-law, and Abbey. Unfortunately his wife contracted cancer and she was dead in less than two years. Abbey's parents both worked so when his wife passed, it was his job to watch Abbey. He said he taught her to play chess. But in about two months she could beat him in ten minutes. She was so quick at learning everything. So he started teaching her the only thing he claimed he really knew well, how to be a Marine. A big part of his career was in training. For a number of years he helped train the Corps' elite Force Recon units. The ones the media like to call 'the tip of the spear.' He told me in all his years training he had few if any who learned as fast as Abbey.

"In the winter he would go with her to the shop of a friend who was a gunsmith. Abbey would help repair all sorts of small arms. They took apart every gun in his shop, then cleaned and reassembled it. Abbey could take apart and reassemble almost any gun blindfolded. They shot at the range together. She couldn't seem to learn enough. By the time she was fifteen and able to be on her own after school, her grandfather claimed she knew more about being a Marine than he did.

"She has amazing skills. She saved my life more than once. But I worry about how it might affect her. She probably wouldn't ever use or even remember those skills if it weren't for the places I've taken her. I worry about her."

We were quiet for a while. Finally I said, "Tell me about yourself."

She looked at me, put a hand on my cheek, turned my head slightly, and kissed me full on the mouth.

Chapter 9

The next morning I was up early. I took a quick swim and then headed to my office in the work area.

I heard the squeaking of my chair as I approached my office door. A woman with shoulder-length black hair was working on my computer. She looked up. I said, "Mitch?"

The last time I saw Mitch was in Mongolia. She had platinum blond hair and rode a white Bactrian camel. She had been part of our team when I first worked for Walter in Peru and then she again joined our team in Mongolia.

"I hear you're bopping Dr. Lord. Good for you, Professor, I was beginning to think your ex-wife took your privates with her when she walked out."

I felt red creep up my neck and reminded myself that Mitch had a rough edge to her. She liked getting under people's skin. I wasn't going to take the bait and I certainly wasn't going to tell her that Carol's Olympic-level athletic ability extended beyond the volleyball court. I preferred to think of it as a close and warming relationship that I hoped would deepen into more. Probably everyone knew she was in my room last night.

"You know, Professor, the Asian chick has the hots for you too. You might be in for a multicultural ménage à trois if you play your cards right."

I tried to put that thought out of my mind. "Mitch, great to see you. When did you get here?"

"Yesterday afternoon. Walt said you needed help and flew me down. In Mongolia your plan was shit but at least you had a plan. From what I can see, you don't have any plan."

I sat down in the chair across from my desk. I decided I better change the password on my computer. Not that it would do much good if she wanted to hack in again. "Have you been briefed on what we know?"

Mitch was a brilliant computer engineer. But she hated to be cast in any mold, least of all a nerdy engineer type. Last I knew she was completing her PhD thesis in eastern Asian religions at Princeton. I think Walter's company paid for her PhD studies. He had a way of finding exceptional talent that others overlooked. He also built tremendous loyalty that went both ways.

"Ned filled me in last night. Strange stuff. I figure we got two shots. Either the CDC figures out a lead on the genetically engineered rhinovirus or Ned makes a connection through his poking around on the do-gooder website. The tomb and manuscript robberies happened months ago, maybe we could get a lead on who was involved but I doubt it. They were probably contract jobs.

"If it's OK with you, boss, I'll work the website with Ned. I'm better at that computer shit than he is. I know how some of those weirdos think."

That much I believed. "Sounds great. Mitch, I'm glad to have you here." And I was. "Carol should have something today from the CDC and maybe the CIA has more for us. I'll let you know when I've scheduled a time for all for us to meet."

She stood and started to walk out. "I'm glad to see you old folks can still get it on."

I smiled but that one hurt. "Old folks," I was barely forty. I sat and began checking my emails.

A while later Abbey came in. She was smiling. Abbey was usually smiling but this morning I felt she was grinning about Carol being in my suite last night. I'm probably being paranoid.

I cleared my throat. "Mitch is here, have you seen her yet?"

"No, how is she?"

"She is well, she's Mitch and not a platinum blonde anymore. She has black hair. She's working with Ned doing something on the do-gooder site. She said she knows how weirdos think."

Abbey's smile broadened. "I'll go find her in a little bit. Dr. Lord and Professor Wang have been burning up the wires with the CDC. By the end of the day they may have some interesting stuff for us."

I thought a minute. "Let's meet first thing tomorrow. Tell Mitch and Ned to be prepared to bring us whatever they have. Chad emailed saying he is arriving back late today. He was vague about what he might have found. I hope Carol has a solid lead from the CDC."

I tried not to let my frustration show and went back to reviewing everything on the robberies at archaeological sites. Everyone else seemed hard at work so I figured I had to try and be productive. Nobody likes to work for a lazy boss. I kept at it until late in the evening.

At 9:00AM I walked into the workroom. It was buzzing. There was energy in the group that I hadn't seen before. I liked it.

I tried for my most upbeat professorial tone. "Good morning. Let's get right to it. Chad, welcome back, you start, tell us what else you found out in Bolivia."

He gave me his smirking grin. "There is no record of the two foreign men entering the country legally that we could match to the descriptions we had. They could have come in separately or as part of a bigger group and the authorities wouldn't have spotted them. Some of the villagers claim they came upriver. So they could have crossed into Bolivia from Brazil.

"In the Beni Department of Bolivia there have been several reported vandalisms of archaeological sites in a savanna area known as the Llanos de Mojos. The sites are mound and canals that are thousands of years old and go on for miles. I have all the reports and photos. I'll give them to you, they don't mean much to me. Anyway it appears that whoever did it in came upriver from Brazil."

I was interested and excited. "Yes, it is the area of the pre-Columbian civilization known as the hydraulic culture of Las Lomas, or the hills. These people constructed over 20,000 artificial hills, interconnected by thousands of square miles of aqueducts, channels, embankments, artificial lakes and lagoons as well as terraces."

Only Abbey seemed as excited as I was. "Great, I'll go over what you have when we are done. Anything else?"

"One more thing, the Agency has located the site in Zululand where those poachers were buried. They want a CDC team with them when they exhume the bodies."

"That's progress, Chad. Thanks. Carol, what have you and Mia found?"

She stood and brought up a diagram on the whiteboard. "This is the gene structure of the most common rhinovirus. The structure of what you see in most common colds that people get. If you look at the second diagram of the rhinovirus from our samples in the Bolivian village you will see several differences."

I didn't see anything.

She circled portions of the two diagrams. "The CDC quickly identified the areas that were distinctly different than the ninety-nine known rhinoviruses. Figuring out what they do is another matter. They were stumped until Mia came up with a theory.

"She realized that the gene sequence in this area resembled a bacterial gene sequence and not just any bacterial sequence but that of magnetotactic bacteria or MTB. They are bacteria that orient along the magnetic field lines of Earth's magnetic field. I know this sounds supernatural but Salvatore Bellini first described magnetotactic bacteria in an Italian publication in 1963. In 1975 Richard Blakemore, a microbiologist at the Woods Hole Oceanographic Institute, published the first peer-reviewed article on magnetotactic bacteria in the journal *Science*. These microorganisms were following the direction of Earth's magnetic field, from south to north, and so the term magnetotactic. It is a specialized area of study but quite a lot of work has been done in the area."

Mia spoke up. "Now over forty years later several institutes and pharmaceutical companies are engineering magnetotactic bacterial magnetite particles. They are also introducing these genes into cells, a technology in which magnetosomes are coated with DNA then shot using a particle gun into cells that are difficult to transform using more standard methods.

"These bacteria have been the subjects of many experiments. They have even been aboard the Space Shuttle to examine their magnetotactic properties in the absence of gravity."

She went on for a bit more about what is being done. Finally I interrupted and said, "But I thought we were dealing with a virus not bacteria."

"Yes, that's the exciting part. I haven't heard of it being done with a virus. No reason it can't be. I'm having the research checked now to see if anyone has published something on it."

Abbey cut in. "These magnetic crystals can be preserved in the geological record as magnetofossils. The oldest unambiguous magnetofossils come from the Cretaceous chalk beds of southern England. There are reports of magnetofossils extending to 1.9 billion years old in the Gunflint Chert. There have also been claims of their existence on Mars based on the shape of magnetite particles within the Martian meteorite ALH84001, but these claims are largely disputed.

"But in every case I've read they can only align in a north-south axis with the gravitational field. So how does it keep the virus place-bound? I assume that is what all this is leading to."

Mia said, "You're right about a north-south axis unless an artificial magnetic field is introduced. But what we saw was a viral infection that was limited to a specific area and for a limited time period. Lots we don't know."

Carol joined back in. "CDC is looking at these other distinctly different gene areas. Perhaps one of them is linked to a time factor. Maybe only so many generations of the virus can reproduce. Lots to study but we have people working on it. They should have more for us soon.

"Now another interesting thing. CDC had people check out the schools in Philadelphia and Chicago that are reporting greatly reduced rates of teen pregnancy. Very strange, the pregnancy rate is way down but cases of socially transmitted diseases are not. No increase in the sale of birth control devices can be found. They have been able to get some volunteers to give blood samples. We should get results soon.

"Talk is starting on social media about a right-wing conspiracy to depress the black birth rate. Again, it is early on in their investigation."

Strange but I didn't see how all this fit. "Ned, what have you found on the do-gooder website?"

"Well mostly a whole lot of general stuff that doesn't amount to much. But maybe Professor Wang could help me push the magnetic bacteria angle. That seems pretty specialized, we might get something there.

"I've got some progress on the anti elephant poaching. I probably should have checked with you before I went as far as I did. But you remember agreeing to have me set up sock puppets and well..."

Ned looked nervous. It had to be trouble.

Mitch looked at Ned. "Tell them with no bullshit or I'll break your arm and tell them myself."

"OK. I set up as if I was Abbey on the elephant poaching site and of course I was strongly against poaching. I played up what she did in Mongolia and I got invited to a private chat room. Most of the people there were very passionate about saving the elephants. Many advocated much stronger direct measures. You, well I agreed with them. I posted the video of you shooting on the range that I took with the quadcopter a few days ago. I exaggerated a bit on the number of poachers you have killed.

"There is a big anti elephant poaching donor conference in Johannesburg, and you were invited to be on a panel because you're a famous professor and because of your experience in Mongolia."

He stopped. Mitch said, "Tell them the rest."

"I kind of implied that you thought shooting low-level native poachers wasn't enough, that you would go up the chain and assassinate the ivory dealers and bosses. I implied that if given the identities and locations of the bosses, you would handle the rest."

Everyone was quiet and just looked at Ned.

Abbey said, "I'll go. It's the only lead we have. It's a legitimate donors conference. It'll be in a big fancy hotel with lots of people. Maybe I'll be able to find out something. It is about the only lead we have."

Major Campbell said, "I can arrange for company security in South Africa."

Chad Dillon spoke up. "I'll go with her. We have greater assets in South Africa than Walter's company. I'll make sure Abbey is safe and we have the resources to follow up on anybody who makes contact with her. It could be a big break or it could be just a nutty fringe save-the-elephants group. Either way the Agency will be better off knowing more about them.

"When is the conference?"

"It is in three days. Abbey is all signed up." Ned read our body language. "I figure we could always just cancel."

I wasn't sure how I felt. Abbey was right, of course a conference like this would be at a big hotel with lots of people and media. Whoever that group was, they probably just wanted to talk to Abbey face to face and make sure she was real. She would have CIA protection. I had nothing to worry about.

I looked at Ned. "What else?"

"Nothing else at this point. Things will go faster now that I have Mitch to help. Being a dozen different people at once on the Internet is a lot of work. I'll focus on working with Professor Wang. Abbey, should I keep being you on the chat room?"

"No. I'll read everything in your posted exchanges and then take over myself. I need to learn what you said and get into the flow of the discussion."

Chad said, "I'll get the Agency going on having resources available in Johannesburg."

I said to Chad, "Carol and I will go with you. See if the Agency can arrange for us to examine the site of the dead poachers in Zululand.

"Carol, arrange for the CDC to have their people meet us in Johannesburg.

"Major Campbell, can you arrange for transport to Johannesburg? We don't have a lot of time."

Before he could answer, Chad said, "I'll arrange separate accommodations for you and Dr. Lord away from the convention site. I'll book a room at the same hotel as Abbey."

Major Campbell said, "We will need to leave tomorrow night if we want Abbey to be on time for the conference. I'll get back to you." He got up and left.

I said, "My report on graves and manuscripts doesn't seem very important now. We all have a lot to do before we leave tomorrow. Let's get to it."

I went to my office. Mitch walked in and plopped into a chair. She looked miffed.

"So what do I do, sit on my ass here?"

"Mitch, you were right if we got a break it would probably come from the website. I want you to do two things. Keep Ned and Dr. Wang focused on the biotech aspects of the website and then figure out who is really behind this do-gooder website. I asked Ned to look into this but he ended up spending all his time playing with his sock puppets.

"There has to be a way to figure out the organization or mechanics of this site and who really is involved. All Ned did was give me what anybody might have found with a

Google search. There must be a way to hack into the inner workings of the site.

"If what everybody sees in these chat rooms is just a way to identify people for potential further screening and recruitment, someone must be making these decisions. It is likely some group of people. There is too much going on for just one or two individuals. There has to be a hand-off process for further screening and ultimate recruitment. Probably a system of cells like terrorists use."

I smiled. "I guess these are terrorists." Then I stopped.

Mitch stood. "I'm on it." Then she turned and walked out.

I'd seen that look before, when she grabbed onto something she was like a terrier, she wouldn't let go. A pain in the butt, often foul-mouthed, yes, but she could get things done others couldn't. I was glad to have her on the team.

Things began to move fast. Later in the day I got a text from Major Campbell asking me to bring Abbey and Dr. Lord to the security office the next morning. He also said we would be flying to Lima tomorrow afternoon to get a flight to Johannesburg that night.

I reread everything we had on the Zululand poachers. Abbey was going over all the posts Ned had done in her name. I told her about tomorrow's schedule. Carol was in the workroom on the phone. I held up my phone with the text message from Major Campbell for her to read. She nodded and again focused on her call.

The rest of the day was a blur. The next morning at 9:00, Carol, Abbey, and I walked over to the security office. We were told to go into Major Campbell's office. He hung up the phone as we came in and asked us to have a seat.

"I spoke to Walter last night. He is both pleased and concerned. He asked me to accompany you and Dr. Lord. He agreed with me that Abbey should be safe with Chad and the CIA looking after her."

I didn't like his use of "should be safe." I would have preferred "will be safe."

He went on. "Walter also insisted that the three of you be chipped. He is arranging for a monitoring team to be in Johannesburg when we arrive. We won't see them but they will be there. He also wants me to accompany you and to have a company security response team in place even though the CIA should have everything secured and protected."

I really didn't like this now. I said, "Does Walter know something that we don't? What is he expecting?"

"Rob, I'm not sure. He said he is concerned and there are a lot of moving parts. Perhaps he is just being cautious."

His answer didn't make me feel any better.

Carol was looking back and forth between us. "What is a chip?"

He started to explain. "A radio-frequency identification chip or RFID uses electromagnetic fields to automatically identify and track the object it is attached to."

She cut him off. "Like what they put in dogs."

"It's the same principle but ours are quite a bit more sophisticated. Much of the work we do around the world in the mining and petroleum industry is in somewhat dangerous areas. It gives our employees an added measure of security and peace of mind."

I didn't think Carol was buying it. But Major Campbell went on to explain the technology and process in great detail.

Finally Abbey said, "OK, let's get it over with. We can have them taken out when we get back."

Chapter
10

Johannesburg is the largest city in South Africa. The greater metropolitan area has almost eight million people. The city sits on the mineral-rich Witwatersrand range of hills and is the center of large-scale gold and diamond trade. We landed at the city's main airport recently renamed O.R. Tambo International Airport and taxied to the general aviation area.

The anti elephant poaching donor conference meetings were being held at the Sandton Convention Center. Sandton is an affluent area situated within metro Johannesburg. Chad and Abbey would be staying at the Michelangelo Hotel. Carol and I were staying at the Sandton Sun Hotel with Major Campbell. Both hotels were within walking distance of the convention center.

We took separate cabs. It was about a thirty-minute drive to our hotels. Major Campbell had booked adjoining rooms for Carol and me. He had a room on another floor. I thought about that a minute. I guess there are no secrets at the ranch. Then I wondered why I even cared if people knew I was seeing Carol. Strange.

We had flown all night and it was midmorning in Johannesburg. Major Campbell headed to the company's local office. Carol and I decided to walk around the area and then to the convention center where the donor conference was being held.

I grabbed a brochure on Sandton City Center as we left the hotel lobby. It is called "Africa's richest square mile" and it was easy to see why. The brochure said there was over a million and a half square feet of shopping space. We headed to Nelson Mandela Square, passing by every high-end store I'd ever heard of and many I'd never heard of. In the square there is a fountain with a 60-foot bronze statue of Mandela behind it. It was all very modern with glass-clad skyscrapers all around.

The convention center was huge, twelve stories high and several hundred thousand square feet. We wandered around until we found the area being used for the elephant conference. In the lobby of the floor where most of the conference was taking place there were large display panels. They gave an interesting overview of elephants and their plight.

The first showed African and Asian elephants and said this conference was on African elephants but that Asian elephants were also endangered. There are two extant elephant species in Africa: the African bush elephant and the smaller African forest elephant. It was estimated that in 1979 there were between 1.3 million and 3 million African elephants. By 2012 the estimate was just 440,000. It went on to outline the alarming decline of elephants in various African countries. Poaching was the main cause of the decline but changing land use also was cited as another major factor.

Other panels discussed feeding, mating, and how intelligent elephants were. I was drawn to the panel on war elephants. Although war elephants were mostly used in Asia, the now extinct North African elephant was used in North Africa. These were the famous war elephants used by Carthage in the Punic Wars, their conflict with the Roman Republic. The elephants that crossed the Pyrenees and the Alps with Hannibal in order to invade Italy during the Second Punic War (218-201 BCE) were North African elephants.

We browsed through the displays a while longer and then went to have lunch. Everything we saw looked on the up and up at the convention, just what you would expect. After lunch Carol want to contact her colleagues and find out the details on our trip to Zululand. I decided to read up on the Zulus and Zululand.

The next morning Major Campbell met us for breakfast. We would fly into Ulundi City in Zululand District Municipality, which is one of the 11 district municipalities of the South African Province of KwaZulu-Natal. KwaZulu-Natal is located in the southeast of the country, enjoying a long shoreline beside the Indian Ocean and sharing borders with three other provinces and the countries of Mozambique, Swaziland, and Lesotho.

Zululand District Municipality is part of a larger historical area also known as Zululand. The majority of its 804,456 people speak IsiZulu.

Ulundi was created on September 1, 1873, as the new capital for the Zulu nation when Cetshwayo became king of the Zulus. Ulundi means "the high place" in Zulu. It is about 300 miles by air from Johannesburg.

From there we would head into eMakhosini Ophathe Heritage Park less than ten miles south of Ulundi.

We landed in the early afternoon at Ulundi airport. It was bigger than I expected with two long paved airstrips and large commercial jets parked in front of the terminal. The three of us got into a beat-up old Jeep that served as our taxi. Major Campbell had booked us in the uMuzi Bushcamp. Carol looked a bit apprehensive when she heard the name.

It turned out to be in the grounds of the Ondini Cultural Museum and was simple but quite nice. Each room was a hut and the whole place was laid out in the style of a traditional Zulu village. In the shade of huge marula trees they have recreated a Zulu isibayo or cattle enclosure with the inn's bar forming the centerpiece.

It was luxurious compared to some of the places I'd stayed in Mongolia, but Carol still looked a bit skeptical. It was a big step down from the luxury of Walter's ranch.

Two people from the CDC in Atlanta and a person from the World Health Organization were already there. After checking in, Carol went to meet with them, and Major Campbell went to contact the park rangers who would take us to the site. I decided to check out the museum.

It was set up in three parts. One was Ondini, a reconstructed royal residence of King Cetshwayo. A small site museum provided background to the pre-colonial history of the region with a model explaining the layout of the royal residence and offering displays on the Anglo-Zulu War, King Cetshwayo, the Zulu Monarchy, and the archaeological excavation work done at Ondini. The third part was the KwaZulu Cultural Museum that opened in 1984. It housed a collection of the cultural heritage of KwaZulu Natal, from the earliest inhabitants to the great Zulu Nation.

After wandering around for about an hour and a half I decided to take a nap before dinner.

The next morning we were off. Carol rode in a Range Rover set up as some kind of medical support vehicle and I rode with Major Campbell and the two park rangers in their Jeep. Both rangers had automatic rifles and Major Campbell wore his sidearm. If Abbey were here she could have told me the make and model of each.

The head ranger gave us a description of the park as he drove. He spoke English with that charming South African accent.

The park covers an area of 59,000 acres along the White Umfolozi River. It is set in the valley known as the Valley of Kings. He explained that with the reintroduction of the black rhino into the park and the fencing of the area, over 20,000 hectares of land has been made available for the rhinos again. In addition to the black rhino the wildlife in the park includes buffalo, giraffe, blue wildebeest, and various species of antelope. He told us that there had been several other reports of deaths by what was now being called "The Zulu Curse." Some were outside Zululand and it wasn't clear if they were all true or a spreading rumor. A few of the deaths in Zululand were confirmed. The local authorities were trying to play down the rumors for fear it would hurt the tourist trade.

We drove almost three hours to the spot where the poachers were buried. The Jeeps stopped and the ranger pointed to a spot about 50 yards away where the ground was recently disturbed. The CDC and WHO people opened up boxes. They then began donning biohazard suits.

I said to Major Campbell, "This is as close as we get, right?"

"It's plenty close for me," he replied.

The ranger didn't seem to want to venture closer either.

It was a long, slow, and methodical process for the people putting on the biohazard suits. All suited up, they reminded me of the Ebola workers I saw on the news. The day was pleasant enough but a chill ran down my spine as they walked toward where the poachers were buried, with tools and instruments in hand.

It took about two hours as they sampled, measured, and photographed. The samples were bagged, tagged, and then put in steel biohazard boxes and locked. I noticed how carefully they treated the bodies, with respect for the dead. The CDC workers were trained professionals. I assumed they treated all disease victims with dignity and respect. I doubted the rangers who buried them felt the same way. Each year several rangers are killed by the poachers and they had no love for them.

The decontamination process was even slower than putting on the biohazard suits. They were all drenched in sweat and drinking water when they were finally out of the suits. I couldn't imagine trying to work in those suits.

It was early evening when we arrived back at the inn. After cleaning up we met at the outdoor bar under the marula trees. Major Campbell and I were the first there. We were on our second beer when Carol and the others arrived. They looked somber, even worried.

I said, "I think you folks could use a drink."

Carol made an attempt to smile as they ordered their drinks.

"That bad?" I commented.

"We don't really know yet but from what we saw it looked very much like the plague or the Black Death as it is called. The plague has three forms: bubonic, pneumonic, and septicemic. What we saw resembles septicemic plague, the rarest but most virulent of the three forms. Septicemic plague can cause disseminated intravascular coagulation, and is almost always fatal when untreated. The mortality rate in medieval times was 99 to 100 percent. Early treatment with antibiotics reduces the mortality rate to between 4 and 15 percent.

"It is caused by Yersinia pestis, a gram-negative species of bacterium. Septicemic plague is a life-threatening infection of the blood, most commonly spread by bites from infected fleas. But there is no way a dozen men are bitten by fleas at the exact same time and die while eating dinner. People who die from this form of plague often die on the same day symptoms first appear. Still it seems unlikely they would all die together sitting around the campfire."

I said, "The CIA speculated that they might have been drugged by something they all ate or drank at the same

time. The drug caused them to pass out and then the whatever it was killed them."

Carol said, "Hopefully we will know a lot more once
the lab tests come back. It is scary, none of us have ever
seen or even heard of anything like this before.

"I'd like another glass of wine and a bottle of water." She
smiled. "It is not a good idea to rehydrate with just booze."

I thought about what Ned had told us about the software identifying several references to the plague and
plague gravesites being disturbed. I decided not to bring it
up; they were worried enough as it was.

Major Campbell walked away from the group to talk
on his satellite.

When he returned he said, "We have to go first thing in
the morning. A corporate jet is being sent in tonight and
will be ready to take off first thing in the morning.

"Ned and Mitch have made progress and it looks like
things are happening more quickly now."

I said, "What about Abbey and what things?"

"Abbey can finish up at the conference and Chad can
bring her back to Peru. She'll be fine, the CIA has half a
dozen men covering the conference. As for the things, that
will have to wait until we have secure communications. We
can't do anything from here anyway," he replied.

Carol said, "They don't need me here anymore, my
associates will accompany the samples back to both the
CDC in Atlanta and to the World Health Organization in
Geneva. We took duplicates of all the samples."

After dinner the folks who had worked in the biohazard suits were the first to go to bed. I knew there would be

no visit to my room from Carol tonight.

Major Campbell and I went back to the bar. It had to be an urgent and significant situation to send a corporate jet halfway around the world on short notice. No point in worrying about it now so I asked him about his childhood in Scotland.

Chapter 11

As the jet lifted off the runway from Ulundi I looked out the window. It seemed a waste to come all this way and see so little of the magnificent park below us. I wondered if I'd ever be back. I leaned my seat back. It was definitely nicer flying on Walter's private jets than going through all the hassles of commercial airlines. Plus the food was far superior.

The flight was about 7,000 miles and would take fifteen hours. Ulundi was seven hours ahead of Lima so we should arrive about 4:30PM Lima time.

I was being paid well so I decided to try and earn my pay. I took out my iPad loaded with all the references Ned had given me on the Black Death and the related gravesite robberies, not exactly pleasant reading. After two hours of reading I was even more confused. I went across the aisle to where Carol was working away on her computer.

I sat down and said, "Do mind if I ask you some questions about the plague? You said there are three types of plague. From what I've read about the Black Death and the investigation done on the remains in the graves, it seems like the bubonic plague was the cause of the great pandemics in Eurasia."

She interrupted me. "There are actually more types of plague. Meningeal plague, this form of plague occurs when bacteria cross the blood-brain barrier, leading to infectious meningitis. Pharyngeal plague, this is an uncommon form of plague that resembles tonsillitis, which is found in cases of close contact of patients with other forms of plague. There are a few other rare manifestations of plague, including asymptomatic plague and abortive plague. Cellulocutaneous plague sometimes results in infection of the skin and soft tissue, often around the site of a flea bite."

I said, "So the different names of the plague just refer to what areas of the body are affected but they are all caused by Yersinia pestis?"

"I'm not sure how deep you want me to go into this. The bacteria genus Yersinia includes 11 species: Y. pestis, Y. pseudotuberculosis, Y. enterocolitica, Y. frederiksenii, Y. intermedia, Y. kristensenii, Y. bercovieri, Y. mollaretii, Y. rohdei, Y. aldovae, and Y. ruckeri. Among them, only Y. pestis, Y. pseudotuberculosis, and certain strains of Y. enterocolitica are of pathogenic importance for humans and certain warm-blooded animals. Y. pseudotuberculosis causes Far East scarlet-like fever in humans. Y. enterocolitica infection causes the disease yersiniosis and as you know, Y. pestis causes the plague."

She smiled at me. I said, "OK, I sort of get it. But the Y. pestis is still around today. A sixteen-year-old boy in

Colorado died from the plague in 2015 and Asia still has cases, right?"

She nodded her head. "So you don't need to dig up old graves to get Y. pestis, right? Why would someone bother?"

"Rob, I don't know, it is one of the few thousand questions running through my head now. Also there are several published papers where scientists have analyzed remains from these gravesites and studied the DNA structure of Y. pestis. It would be a lot easier to just read the papers. Scientists study this to understand how the bacteria evolved over time. As I said before, reintroducing a disease that has not been around for a thousand years could be very deadly because there might be no built-up resistance to the disease in the population.

"It is all just speculation until we have more test results. Do you know why we are rushing back?"

I said, "Major Campbell didn't know or didn't want to discuss it until we got back to the ranch."

I looked to where he was sitting. He had been on his satellite phone since we took off. His job did entail a lot more than just babysitting us.

I squeezed her hand and went back to my seat. She wanted to write up her notes from yesterday and draft a report to send to CDC in Atlanta once we got back. Everyone had real work to do but me. I could feel my mood turning black.

I sent Abbey a text and asked how she was doing. "Fine" was what I got back.

I started rereading the summary of everything we thought we knew. They served lunch. After I finished I put my seat back and took a nap. I woke when they brought us warm washcloths and asked if we would like anything to drink.

Finally we began our descent into Jorge Chávez International Airport. It was named after the famous Peruvian aviator Jorge Chávez Dartnell.

Major Campbell collected everyone's passports and customs papers. Our plane taxied to the general aviation section of the airport to a hangar used by Falone Advanced Technologies. As we reached the bottom he handed us our passports and we got in a waiting van. Our luggage was already in the back of the van. What service.

When we arrived at the ranch Carol and I had a quiet dinner. My body wasn't sure what time it was. I sent a text telling everyone to meet at 9:00AM in the workroom to review what was happening. Carol said she was beat and went to her apartment. I poured another glass of wine and went out by the pool.

The next morning I took an early morning swim and went over to my office. I answered some emails. I wanted to gather my thoughts but I really didn't have any, just lots of questions and no answers.

At 8:55 I pasted a smile on my face and walked out of my office through the smaller office Abbey used. To my surprise Walter was sitting there reading documents.

He looked up. "Rob, welcome back. I hope you had a productive trip."

I stammered. "How long have you been here?"

His reply was "About a half hour. I needed to review these documents and I didn't want to disturb you."

An interesting man, I thought. I said, "I wish I had something more important to report. We found where the poachers were buried. The CDC and WHO took samples and photos. They are being delivered to Atlanta and Geneva. I don't know when we will get test results. Carol can probably give us some idea.

"Abbey says she is fine, whatever that means."

We walked into the workroom. It was clear everyone was pleased and a bit surprised to see Walter.

I was supposed to be in charge so I greeted everyone then looked at Mitch and Ned. "I assume one or both of you have progress to report."

Mitch nodded at Ned. Ned said, "Mitch has made unbelievable progress at hacking into the layers of the do-gooder website. She is mapping it out like pieces of a puzzle but I'll let her explain. Dr. Wang has been a great help with the biotech leads on the website."

I wasn't sure if Ned was finally growing up and giving his coworkers appropriate credit or if he was just scared of Mitch.

He went on. "I'll let them report on that. In running the software it appears that we are due for a substantial increase in activities that will demonstrate the technical capabilities of we don't know what or who to another interested party that we also don't know who they are. I've been calling the former the sellers and the latter the buyers for lack of a better label."

I said, "You don't have any more definite information on what might be planned or when?"

"The software indicates it is most closely related to the

rhinovirus outbreak in Bolivia and the dead poachers in Zululand. There are indications of less closely linked association with other events such as the stolen manuscripts, the grave robberies, and the schools in Philadelphia and Chicago that are reporting greatly reduced rates of teen pregnancy.

"I have the software continuously running and alerts set for lots of parameters. If something highly correlated happens we should hear about it."

Walter asked to see the data from those runs after the meeting.

I said, "Wait, I thought you had to feed the information into the software and run it against all the other data in the software."

Ned looked at me as if I was a dimwitted child. I'd seen the look before. He said, "You do, so I programed a dozen news aggregators to feed into the software in real time."

Unable to think of anything less dumb to say, I said, "Good thinking. What else?"

Ned shook his head and Mitch got up. She powered up the large flat-screen TV and began.

"I started by checking out the list of key supporters on the website. An assortment of advocates for animal rights, climate change, save the whales, and so on, much as we suspected. Most of them wealthy, some a bit out there but nothing that I could find indicated serious criminal behavior and nothing relating to terrorism.

"Next I followed up on Ned's idea of the open forum being a screening method to recruit people with more extreme views who are willing to actually take part in marches, boycotts, and various disruptions."

Mitch had a slide up with more than two dozen public forums and chat rooms from the site. She had hacked her way back from the public forums to the invite or members only areas. Most weren't very sinister. She explained the PETA, or People for the Ethical Treatment of Animals, forum. It showed PETA's four core issues: opposition to factory farming, fur farming, animal testing, and animals in entertainment. It also campaigns against eating meat, fishing, the killing of animals regarded as pests, the keeping of chained backyard dogs, cock fighting, dog fighting, and bullfighting. There were extensive debates and discussions around these topics and some offshoot topics. A bit nutty, many people might think, but not evil or dangerous. The closed or private forums discussed planning for upcoming protests, fund raising, and administration matters. Just what one would expect for this type of organization.

The next example was ALF, the Animal Liberation Front, an international, clandestine resistance that engages in illegal direct action in pursuit of animal rights. They seem to say acts of vandalism causing economic damage to their victims are fine as long as all reasonable precautions are taken not to harm human or non-human life. Mitch explained that ALF was included in a United States Department of Homeland Security planning document listing a number of domestic terrorist threats on which the US government expected to focus resources.

Mitch went on to explain that ALF is active in over 40 countries; its cells operate clandestinely and independently making the movement difficult for the authorities to monitor. She had hacked into over thirty cells.

Walter interrupted her. "Quite an impressive job of hacking but they don't seem like what we are looking for. When we are done review all your material with Major Campbell and turn over to Homeland Security anything you two think they might be interested in that doesn't relate directly to our work."

Mitch skipped ahead through several slides. As she did I thought about the way Walter said "that doesn't relate to our work." So he didn't want them to know what progress we were making. I would have to think about what that meant.

Mitch stopped at a slide that showed numerous forums and chat rooms leading back through several layers to three websites. Each was funnel shaped with lots of chat rooms and forums at the public level and ending in one of the three websites. There were a total of five levels.

She said confidently, "In all that clatter on the do-gooder website this is what we are looking for."

Quite a statement I thought.

She continued. "There are three broad themes that cover all these forums and chat rooms. Stopping poaching of endangered and exotic species, human population control, and bioengineering.

"The communication follows the levels so the second level is the only one communicating with the public chat rooms and forums. The second level then communicates with the third level. The third level encrypts messages to the fourth level and for communication between other third-level sites. The fourth level uses a separate encryption system to communicate between fourth-level sites and to the fifth level. There has been no communication

144

between the three fifth-level sites during the time I've been monitoring them.

"Communication between the four top levels is often in real time as a back and forth conversation. There hasn't been any real-time communication between the fourth and fifth levels that I could find. That indicates there is a totally different communication process between the fifth level and whoever is coordinating the three fifth-level sites. The time delay between when a message is sent from level four to level five and when a response is sent varies greatly.

"The encryption software appears to be top-quality commercially available software. The type a security conscious Fortune 500 firm would use. We haven't been able to crack it so we only know what is being said from levels one to two and two to three."

Mitch then reviewed the items in each of the three groups of forums and chat rooms she thought were relevant. She assigned a priority number to each based on some computer algorithm she developed. I was lost, other than the three main themes she identified at the beginning I couldn't see any meaningful pattern.

Walter seemed pleased with her work. He said, "Keep monitoring and compiling the data from the communications. Useful patterns and information should emerge over time." Then he looked at me.

I said, "Mia, anything to report?" She said no. "Carol?"

She began. "We will have the first test results from the sample we took in Zululand in a few days. Some of the tests take longer and it could be a couple of weeks depending on how busy the labs are.

"Nothing new on the bioengineered rhinovirus. The scientists studying it are quite amazed and puzzled.

"Abbey was correct that something strange is going on in the five high schools that have reported the dramatic drop in pregnancy rates. There continue to be essentially zero pregnancies in these five schools. Of few pregnancies that did occur, most turned out to be young women who became pregnant before transferring into these schools. Several teachers have become pregnant. In interviews most stated that they were planning to have these babies."

Before really thinking I said, "Check the ages of the women who became pregnant."

Carol looked at me. "Why?"

"I don't know, just that students tend to be young and teachers tend to be older," I said.

"OK, I will. Here is what else they found out from the blood and other tests. The students tested all had abnormal thickening of the cervical mucus. There are two types of oral birth control pills, one contains both estrogen and a progestogen and the other only contains progestogen. Both types of birth control pills prevent fertilization mainly by inhibiting ovulation and thickening cervical mucus. Confirming inhibited ovulation requires different tests. CDC is seeking parental permission to perform these tests on some of the students. Needless to say this is a sensitive topic and there is a great deal of controversy around the whole investigation."

I interrupted Carol again. "Did they do any blood tests on the male students?" Now everyone was staring at me. I went on. "The female students must have come in contact with some kind of birth control substance. None of the students say they knowingly did so. Therefore they unknowingly ate, drank, or breathed it in or perhaps it was applied to toilet seats and they got it transdermally. I'm just saying if it were in the air, water, or food, the boys would have also ingested it and it may show up in blood tests. They test Olympic athletes for all sorts of compounds. Have the CDC run a few tests on some of the boys."

Carol said, "OK, that is easy to do. But they tested the water and air, and took a variety of samples in the cafeteria and found nothing."

I asked, "If there was only one dose or doses over a period of weeks of some type of birth control pill, how long would the effects last?"

"The existing birth control pills would wear off in a matter of days when stopped. I see what you are saying, Rob. We can look more closely at the timeline. I'll get back to my colleges at CDC and see what else they can find out.

"That is about all I have at this point."

It didn't seem like much. I felt at a loss and wasn't sure what to do next. Everyone was looking to me for guidance.

Sensing the mood Walter spoke up. "Fascinating. You have made great progress in a short period of time. Keep digging. My experience is once a few pieces fall in place the pace of progress will accelerate.

"Ned, I'd like to review your raw data before I have to leave. Thank you all."

And that ended the meeting less than half an hour after it started. I had the feeling Walter was just being supportive and encouraging. I didn't see much progress.

Walter followed Ned to a bank of computer screens. Mitch went with them. Carol left to call her office in Atlanta.

I looked at Mia Wang. "How are you doing, Mia?"

She looked like she was going to give me an earful then her look softened and she said, "How I'm doing is OK. What am I doing? That is the real question. I'm a research genetic biologist but other than answer about a million questions for Ned I haven't done much of anything."

"What are your thoughts on the rhinovirus and the dead poachers?" I said.

"All fascinating but I don't have any access to the samples or know the test methods used. All I get is a general summary of the results."

I thought for a moment and said, "Yes, I understand. How about you go to Geneva and oversee the World Health Organization testing of the sample we sent? You can see exactly what they are doing and suggest additional tests or alternate methods that you think are required. Carol is working closely with the CDC so hopefully they will be following up on everything."

Mia asked, "We can do that?"

I wasn't sure but I said, "I'll clear it with Walter. He has a way of opening many doors and then I'll have Major Campbell arrange transport for you today. Talk to Carol so you can learn as much as you can about what CDC is doing and then pack a bag. I'll be back to you shortly."

I briefly interrupted Walter and told him what I wanted to do. He told me it was a great idea and he would make a few calls. Then he was back deep in discussion with Ned and Mitch. I knew it was a so-so idea at best but Walter was trying to keep us motivated.

I went to find Major Campbell. He told me to have Mia at the airstrip in an hour and he would fly her to Lima. He had to go to the company office there and he'd arrange flights to Geneva. He also told me Abbey and Chad Dillon were on the way back.

He seemed busy and distracted. Everyone was busy. Good. I sent a text to Mia and went to my office. First I reviewed each of Mitch's PowerPoint slides, not just the ones she highlighted. Next I went back to everything we knew about the stolen manuscripts. Laura O'Hara sent me copies of the few manuscripts that had been digitized before they were stolen. A couple had English translation but most were in their original language. I worked my way through them as best I could until 4:00PM then I went to go riding.

I still wasn't allowed to ride alone. My usual stable hand came with me. I didn't mind and he liked the break from mucking stalls and his other duties. He kept telling me to call ahead and he would have the horses ready. But I liked brushing and tacking the horse it, was how I intro-duced myself to the horse. My Spanish was good and he spoke a little English but we didn't talk. We rode in silence for two hours enjoying the scenery.

The next day I continued going through the digital copies of the manuscripts. Carol seemed distracted and distant. There were no late night visits to my room. I didn't push the issue as it was a bit awkward. I'd trained myself to spend hours going through ancient texts trying to find the buried information that might help my research. However by 4:00PM I'd had my fill and went riding again.

After riding I showered and took a beer out by the pool. It was a beautiful place but I felt frustrated. I wasn't sure we were making any progress and I knew I was making none.

I heard, "Drinking alone these days?"

It was Abbey casually dressed with her red hair pulled back and a radiant smile on her face. I jumped up and gave her a hug and kiss on the cheek.

"How about buying a girl a drink?"

I said, "With pleasure. It will be the most productive thing I've done in days."

As I went in to get a bottle of wine I thought about how relieved I was to have her safely back. She was sitting with her legs tucked up under her when I returned. I poured two glasses of wine.

"Cheers," I said.

I sipped my wine and waited for her to start the conversation. I had lots of questions but I thought it better for her to tell me at her own pace and in the order she wanted.

After a moment she said, "Our cover was blown. I'm not sure if they spotted Chad as CIA or if it was something I said or did. Chad said it wasn't me. He believes someone tipped them off that we were Agency. The contact person who began asking me probing questions just vanished. After my panel discussion I was just another conference attendee."

I said, "They may have been on guard because of the hacking Mitch has been doing. I'm not sure you can do everything she did in a short period of time without the other side noticing."

I went on to explain what Mitch and Ned had done while she was away.

She poured me more wine and said, "How is your black dog?"

"He's lurking in the shadows ready to pounce."

Shaking her head she said, "You can spend days sifting through dirt on a dig site looking for small bits of pottery and never get frustrated or depressed. Yet..."

All I could think to say was "That's different."

I continued. "I've spent the last few days reviewing the stolen manuscripts. They are in several languages, some so ancient that only a handful of scholars can read them. They cover about a thousand years and all they have in common is generally referring to disease and medicine. I don't see how they could be that valuable to someone trying to bioengineer a weapon or whatever. You would need dozens of scholars versed in many different languages and time periods to go through them to find what you were looking for."

Abbey said, "Walter isn't the only one who has amazing artificial intelligence software. Someone may have AI software designed to do just that. But I see your point, it is a lot of work for a questionable outcome.

"Let's go get dinner."

We headed over to the dining room. As we were finishing dinner Chad Dillon walked in and headed to our table.

"Someone tipped them off. It had to be."

He looked mad. I said, "Hi Chad, welcome home, how are you?"

I went on to tell him about Mitch's hacking.

"No," he said. "That's not it. Someone told them who we were. One minute the guy is grilling Abbey, the next he gets a text and bolts.

"The Johannesburg chief of station is pissed. He's digging into this. He considers it his operation that was blown. I'll find out more from him in a day or two. I need a drink."

I said, "Maybe we kicked the hornets' nest and have stirred things up? Ned told us the software is indicating an increase in activity."

"Maybe," he said. "But maybe they will pull back and be much more careful."

Abbey said she was going to find Mitch. I went with Chad to the bar. He was usually so cocksure. I'd seen him kill people without showing any remorse. Now he was mad. It surprised me. We drank our drinks and made small talk but I could tell it was still gnawing at him.

Then things began to happen fast. Ned rushed in and came straight over to us. He was out of breath like he had run over here.

He looked around and lowered his voice. "I got a hit, it's a big-time disease outbreak in the US."

I put my hand on his shoulder. "Let's go over to the workroom and see what you've got."

Chad paid for our drinks and we left.

Ned was worked up. "Professor, I knew something was coming. I told you that in our meeting. I was right or our software was right.

"There is an outbreak of the vomiting bug at the super-max prison ADX Florence in Fremont County,

Colorado. They call it the Alcatraz of the Rockies. It is where the super bad dudes go like Larry Hoover of the Gangster Disciples, and Barry Mills and Tyler Bingham of the Aryan Brotherhood. Also foreign terrorists including Zacarias Moussaoui of the September 11 attacks; Faisal Shahzad, perpetrator of the 2010 Times Square car bombing attempt; Ramzi Yousef, mastermind of the 1993 World Trade Center bombing; and Dzhokhar Tsarnaev, perpetrator of the Boston Marathon bombing. Former Bonanno crime family boss Vincent Basciano is currently serving time there, too.

"Well they are all heaving their guts out and shitting their pants right now."

When we got to the workroom Ned really didn't have much, only a brief news wire report. It stated that the United States Penitentiary, Administrative Maximum Facility (ADX), a federal super-max prison for male inmates located in Fremont County, Colorado, was on lockdown due to an outbreak suspected to be norovirus, sometimes known as winter vomiting bug. It went on to say the prison was unofficially known as ADX Florence and the super-max unit houses about 410 inmates.

I said, "That's it? Nothing more?"

Ned was disappointed I didn't share his enthusiasm. He said, "It's highly correlated. It's not winter. You wait and see, this isn't just some routine stomach bug."

He could be right so I said a few encouraging words and told him to see if he could find out more by the morning. I told him to forward the wire report to Carol and I sent her a text asking if she could check in with the CDC.

Chad spoke up. "I'll check with the Agency but I doubt they know anything more than the CDC does. I've been traveling all day. I'm beat."

I sent a text to the whole team to meet in the workroom at 9:00 tomorrow and headed back to the guesthouse. I felt drained, frustrated, and I didn't know what. None of it seemed to be getting us anywhere.

Less than an hour later in my apartment in the guesthouse I got a message from Ned. "Read this."

It was another news wire report. "Her Majesty's Prison Long Lartin is closed to all visitors and is on special lockdown due to a massive outbreak of a flu-like epidemic among the inmates. HM Prison Long Lartin is a Category A or maximum-security men's prison, located in the village of South Littleton in Worcestershire, England. It is operated by Her Majesty's Prison Service and has 615 prisoners. No more information is available at this time."

I told Ned to send it on to Carol and Chad. I read for a while and went to bed.

When I checked my phone in the morning I had another message from Ned.

"Pollsmoor Prison is closed to all outsiders except emergency medical personnel because of a mystery disease. Pollsmoor Maximum Security Prison in the Cape Town suburb of Tokai in South Africa is reporting a widespread outbreak of a yet to be determined disease. More than half of the 7,000 inmates and an unknown number of the 1,200 prison staff are affected. Some of South Africa's most dangerous criminals are held in Pollsmoor Prison. Nelson Mandela was the most famous inmate of the prison."

I sent a text to Ned asking him to forward the article to Carol and to send this article and the one from the UK to Mia in Geneva. I hoped the World Health Organization could get some information on those outbreaks.

I took a swim then made coffee and took it out by the pool. I wasn't sure what to think. I'd read that norovirus spreads especially quickly in close quarters such as in hospitals, nursing homes, schools, and cruise ships. Prisons are similar in that they are close quarters and there must be thousands of prisons around the world, so what if three had outbreaks?

Abbey came out and said, "You look like you're carrying the weight of the world."

I started to tell her about the prison outbreaks but she said Mitch already filled her in. Then she headed off for a morning run.

I got another cup of coffee and headed to the workroom. Mitch was hard at work with four computer screens powered up in front of her.

"Good morning, Mitch. What did Walter have to say when he reviewed Ned's data?"

"Not much." She didn't look up or stop typing. "He went through it all in a couple of minutes. He asked a few questions, made some suggestions, and told us we were doing a good job and to keep digging. For an old guy he knows his shit."

From Mitch that was high praise. I left her to her work and went to my office.

At 9:00 I went back to the workroom. Today it was just Mitch, Ned, Chad, Abbey, and Carol with me.

I asked Ned to read the three news wire reports so we were all on the same page. Then I looked at Carol.

She said, "What we know so far is that the cause of the outbreak at ADX Florence prison in Colorado is norovirus. Now norovirus is a very nasty bug. The main risk of the virus is dehydration and most people recover after a few days. It spreads especially quickly in close quarters like a prison. In 60 percent of cases it is spread through direct contact or touching a contaminated surface. The incubation period is usually 24 to 48 hours and symptoms typically last two to three days. Those infected continue to shed the virus for days and possibly weeks afterward.

"It is also a hardy virus. Studies have detected the virus on surfaces three to four weeks after it was put there. Other studies have found that the virus survived in water at room temperature for two months and could still cause infection.

"People are generally most contagious when they are ill and the first few days after they feel better. Worldwide it is responsible for about ten million hospitalizations and two million deaths a year. All in all a rather nasty bug."

I asked, "Is there any indication it is an engineered bug like we saw in Bolivia?"

"We don't know. There is a CDC team there now so we will get samples. I understand they have really bad people there so it won't be the easiest place to work. The Federal Bureau of Prisons is bringing in additional guards and medical staff from all around the country. They need to contain the outbreak while trying to treat the inmates and staff that are sick, not an easy thing to do in a maximum-security prison. I'll let you know when I hear more."

I said, "Does CDC know anything about the prison outbreaks in the UK and South Africa?"

"Not that I know of. The only word I've gotten is that the testing of the sample from the dead poachers in Zululand indicates it is a modified form of Yersinia pestis, the bacterium responsible for septicemic plague. The samples had no live bacterium so it will be hard to understand how it behaves. They are trying to determine how it killed them so quickly. As I've said, people who die from this form of plague often die on the same day symptoms first appear. However it appears that all of these people died in a matter of hours or even minutes."

I thanked her and said, "Mitch, any update?"

"Well the operators of the forums and chat rooms I've identified seem to know that someone is attempting to hack into their sites. They have changed encryption types between the fourth level and the fifth-level sites."

I asked, "Can they trace it back to you here?"

"I doubt it. I've been working through a dozen different intermediate servers. Plus the company has good defensive software. I'll know if they are getting close."

"OK. Anybody else have anything to add?"

Ned said, "The software indicates more related events are imminent."

Chad spoke up. "I heard from the Johannesburg chief of station that using the photos we got of the man who approached Abbey they were able to get a match. He is Jacob Willemsen traveling with a Dutch passport. The same day he broke off contact with Abbey he boarded a flight from Johannesburg to Paris. We don't know where he went from there. They are checking with the Netherlands and I'll let you know what they find out."

Abbey spoke up. "When we were in Bolivia interviewing the villagers they mentioned a foreigner who spoke Spanish but not like a native and spoke English but not like an American. Perhaps he was a Dutchman."

Chad said, "Good idea. I'll have his photo sent to our embassy in La Paz. They can send someone to the village and see if anyone recognizes him. They can also ask the Bolivian government to check their customs records for a Jacob Willemsen."

"Anything else?" I said.

Abbey said, "I'm going to start trying to find any leads on Justin Barry. I know Mia said he didn't have any close friends at Cornell but it is unlikely he is totally off the Internet and out of communication with everybody."

Then everybody went back to work.

I decided to go and see Walter. As I walked up the steps of the main house the door opened and Mrs. Lopez was there. The security cameras alert them when someone approaches the house. I'd gotten used to it but the first few times it was spooky to have the door open just before you knock.

"Good morning, Mrs. Lopez. Have you heard from your niece? How are they doing in Ithaca?"

"Gabriela is doing well in school and loves your animals. Beast sleeps next to her bed each night and the cats sleep in the bed with her. Sofia and Carlos have made friends. For a small city they find Ithaca has quite an international mix of people.

"But I'm sure you're here for more than checking on my niece."

"I was hoping to have a brief talk with Walter."

"I'm sorry, Professor, he left early this morning for Canada. You can email him."

I said, "I know, he is good at getting back to me." I thanked her and left.

I'd wanted to get a feel for how he felt and what he was thinking. I needed to get my head around the big picture. Perhaps he could help focus our efforts. I knew Ned was forwarding everything we knew to Major Campbell. He would keep Walter updated.

My phone vibrated. It was a text from Ned saying he needed to see me. I headed back to my office. Ned was waiting there when I arrived.

"What's up?" I said.

"It's the Zulu curse, the one we saw in the video. That's what is killing them in Pollsmoor Prison in Cape Town. No word in the media but I got photos from an online source. It looks like the government is not telling anyone in the media. All they say is an unknown illness.

"Look at these photos."

He turned his laptop around and ran through them. It looked like they were cellphone photos. It showed prisoners in what I took to be a prison infirmary. They had the same black nose, lips, and fingers as the poachers. I was worried.

"Let's go find Carol and Chad."

Carol was in the workroom and I sent Chad a text. Then we showed Carol the photos.

She looked alarmed. That greatly increased my worry.

Ned explained what the photos were and how he got them.

Carol said, "We have no idea how this disease is transmitted, how contagious it is, or if there are any preventions or effective treatments. Those poachers were out in the middle of nowhere, it was days before they were found and then buried. In the close quarters of an overcrowded prison we have no idea what could happen or what we are dealing with."

Chad arrived as Carol was talking. He went through the photos.

I said, "Do we know if the photos are real?"

Chad said, "I'll send then to Langley and to our people in South Africa. Ned, please forward them to me."

Carol asked, "Should I call CDC or wait for some confirmation that the photos are real?"

Chad said, "You better call them and the World Health Organization. Tell them everything you know. They've been analyzing the samples from the poachers, that may give us a start. If this thing is highly contagious, hours and days may make a big difference. I'll try to confirm what is going on in the prison. The Agency may already know. Now I need to make some calls."

Chad headed to his office. He was dialing his phone as he walked.

I turned to Ned. "What do you have on the other two prison outbreaks?"

"ADX Florence in Colorado is still reporting it as a norovirus outbreak. I'll check on the HM Prison Long Lartin."

Carol said, "CDC seems to believe it is a norovirus strain. There is no word yet if it appears to be genetically modified. If it were anything like those photos I'd know about it and the whole response would be different. If those pictures are accurate South Africa has a whole different problem than the US."

I thought for a minute. "Is there any chance a poacher or other criminal came into contact with the poachers you exhumed and later was imprisoned, starting the outbreak in Pollsmoor Prison?"

Carol shook her head. "The timeline doesn't make sense. Cape Town is hundreds of miles from where the poachers died. Plus if that person existed he would come in contact with dozens of people before ending up in that maximum-security prison."

I must have looked dejected. Carol said, "You have some good ideas. The males tested in those five schools all had elevated levels of estrogen and progestogen. They're doing more tests. Now I need to make those calls."

Ned was bouncing from his toes to his heels and back again. "This is way cool. I knew things were going to start to rock and the software says there is more to come. We'll out these bad guys and Chad's boys will take them down."

I had to smile. "Go see what you can find out about the UK prison and keep me posted on anything new."

I had a bad feeling about all this. Assuming they were connected, who was capable of doing this and why?

I stopped in Abbey's office and told her what was going on. She asked if I wanted her to help in some way. I told her to keep working on finding any leads on Justin Barry. He seemed to be somehow in the middle of all this.

Next I went to my office and sent an email to Major Campbell informing him of what I knew and what people were doing.

After sitting awhile and trying to take it all in I got up to go find Mitch.

"Mitch, I'd like to get some help from you."

She stopped typing away on one of several keyboards on her desk. "Sure."

"I'm having trouble getting my head around this and I've got a couple of half formed ideas."

"No problem. Some of your dumbass ideas actually worked out in the past. What do you need?"

"I need some simple way to see how the events are related and how high the correlation is between each. I need to be able to visualize it and try to see how it ties together. But the output from the software overwhelms me."

Mitch said, "I'll dumb it down for you. Let me close out what I'm doing and I'll have it in an hour or so. I tutored kids with learning disabilities one summer, I know how to do this."

I think she was smiling when she said that.

We were just watching events unfold. We didn't know what they meant. Let alone what to do about it. My frustration was building, I want to drive the process forward but felt I was spinning my wheels. So I went for a walk and then to have lunch.

When I got back to my office there was a folder on my desk from Mitch.

It was really quite ingenious. She developed three sheets. Each sheet had a matrix. The events were the same but the correlations were shown differently. On one matrix it showed the probable correlation with every other event as a percentage in a table. In the next the correlations were shown as colored lines with the thickness of the line indicating the level of correlation. The third sheet was a 3-D computer rendering graphically showing the relationships of events.

I read each one carefully in the order she had them in the folder. Then I read then again. I made copies of each sheet and then cut the copies up into sections. I began moving the sections around on my desk, mixing and remixing.

I'd been doing this for several hours when I looked up and saw Abbey standing there. I explained what I was doing. She sat down. First she looked at Mitch's three original sheets. Then she studied my final arrangement on my desk. She looked over the entire arrangement several times. Finally she moved just three of my cut-up sections.

Yes, that was it. The best visualization of what was happening.

I looked at her and said, "It's like coming in at the end and putting the last three pieces of the jigsaw puzzle in place." But I knew she had seen something I missed in my hours of work.

Then I said, "I need a drink."

She said, "Let's go riding first."

Chapter 12

I told everyone to keep working for the next two days. By then I hoped we would have enough additional information to hold a productive meeting.

Ned stopped in to tell me it appeared that the outbreak at HM Prison Long Lartin was now being treated as a cholera epidemic. All prison staff and medical workers at the prison were being vaccinated for cholera and the affected prisoners and staffs were being given the standard cholera treatment of fluids, electrolytes, antibiotics, and zinc supplements.

I asked Ned to let Carol know and he said he already did.

He also said, "There was a report of a big-time gangland style massacre in Haiphong, Vietnam, that the software shows is highly correlated. Big shootout, dozens killed, and buildings blown up. I told you things were going to start hopping. This is getting way cool and there will be more."

I wasn't sure I agreed with Ned that the killing of dozens, even if they were gangsters, was way cool. I said, "Ask

Chad to see what the CIA knows about it."

More disturbing, I received a call from Elizabeth, the company's Chief Technology Officer. She told me that unidentified hackers were now repeatedly probing the company server systems in Peru. These hackers were different than the usual ones that routinely tried to steal company secrets.

I asked, "Were they a result of Mitch's penetrating the do-gooder website?"

"No, at least not directly. Mitch routed her work through a dozen servers around the world. Whoever it is knows about your efforts from some other source," she said.

"Are they doing any damage or making progress?"

"No, we have them boxed in a dead end and are monitoring them. We will work on tracing them back to the source but I doubt we will find them. They seem quite sophisticated. Just follow the company's security procedures and I'll let you know if the situation changes."

I spent the rest of that day and the next continuing to plow through the information on the stolen manuscripts and grave robberies. I finally concluded this wasn't going to get us anywhere. So I asked Mitch to add Ned's new information to the matrixes she made for me and went back to studying that.

The next day we assembled at 9:00 to review what we had. Major Campbell joined our little group.

I said, "Who wants to start?"

Chad spoke up. "The Agency made some progress. The address on the Dutchman's passport was to a rooming house in Amsterdam. No one of that name is currently registered there. The last person of that name registered at the rooming house died seven years ago. It appears to be a fake address and it seems Jacob Willemsen is about as common in the Netherlands as John Smith in the US.

"Several people questioned in the village in Bolivia think the photos matched the person they saw. However Bolivian customs has no Jacob Willemsen entering the country during that time period."

I said, "Didn't some people we questioned there say they thought he came upriver?"

"I can have the Agency check with Brazilian customs.

"What the Agency said they know about the gang-style killing in Haiphong is interesting. As you probably know, Haiphong is North Vietnam's most important seaport. It also happens to be one of the country's biggest smuggling ports. There are many gangs and criminal organizations operating in the city. Some cooperate and some compete quite violently.

"Both the victim gang and the assaulting gang were what we classify as Chinese Triad. A triad is one of many Chinese transnational organized crime syndicates. Their main bases are in China, Hong Kong, Macau, Taiwan, and also in countries with large Chinese populations, such as Vietnam, Korea, Japan, Singapore, Philippines, Indonesia, Malaysia, Thailand, the United Kingdom, Belgium, Netherlands, France, Spain, South Africa, Australia, New Zealand, including the United States, and Canada.

"There are almost fifty triads based in Hong Kong. But there are seven that are true international powers. The gang that was attacked was the Sun Yee On. It is the leading triad in Hong Kong and China. It has more than 55,000 members worldwide. Its criminal activities include racketeering, counterfeiting, extortion, drug trafficking, human trafficking, smuggling, money laundering, murder, illegal gambling, and prostitution.

"The initial speculation was that this was the work of either the 14K or the Wo Shing Wo, both of which are archrivals of the Sun Yee On. The Sun Yee On along with their close allies the Wo Hop To, which is based in Wanchai, Hong Kong, and the Wah Ching based in San Francisco are continually battling over turf with the 14K and Wo Shing Wo.

"It now appears that on the killing side it was the Bamboo Union. It is the largest of the dozens of triads in Taiwan with about 10,000 members. Now this is an interesting group. They simply call themselves businessmen and don't view themselves as criminals, but instead they view themselves as patriots.

"The Bamboo Union developed close links with Taiwanese military intelligence and security agencies by using their contacts in Mainland China to gather information for them. In Taiwan their activities include security services, debt collection, loan sharking, gambling dens, hostess clubs, restaurants, and running small businesses. They are involved in the really nasty stuff like drugs, human trafficking, murder for hire, etc., only overseas. Therefore the security services overlook much of what they do in Taiwan.

"Their current leader Chang An-Lo, known as 'White Wolf,' moved to Las Vegas in 1968 to study and keep order in the Bamboo Union's expanding empire in the US. He took over as the leader in 1995 when the longtime leader

'King Duck' Chen Chi-li died. Under Chang An-Lo they have become the most powerful gang in Taiwan.

"Outside Taiwan they will do just about anything for anyone who is capable of paying for the gang's services. They have the reputation of being able to get the job done.

"Now as to what happened, the Sun Yee On warehouse and major staging area in the Dinh Vu docks area was blown up. There are three main dock areas in the Port of Haiphong on the Cấm River. Dinh Vu is the furthest downstream to the east and the most remote.

"As Sun Yee On members ran out of the building they were gunned down. It is reported that several top Red Poles, or enforcers were killed along with regular gang members.

"The warehouse that burned down after the explosion is believed to be where Sun Yee On gathered ivory and rhino horns for sale to China and other Asian countries. The stockpile of tusks was believed to be abnormally large because of Beijing's recent closing of all the country's ivory carving factories and workshops. Many millions of dollars of tusks and horns were destroyed in the fire.

"The Agency and various Homeland Security experts are debating if this is a move by the Bamboo Union to try to take over the ivory and rhino horn trade, to generally expand in Vietnam at the expense of the Sun Yee On, or was the Bamboo Union hired to make the hit?

"There is no love between these gangs and they have had minor turf clashes before but since the Sun Yee On gang is much larger and very well entrenched in Vietnam, the analysts are leaning towards a hit for hire. If so there had to be a really big payoff for the Bamboo Union to do this knowing that the Sun Yee On will strike back."

I said, "Follow the money. If it required that large a payoff, can the Agency or Treasury or someone spot it?"

Chad thought for a moment. "Perhaps, but it could be a rival Chinese gang that didn't want to hit Sun Yee On directly and all payment will be transacted in China, or the payment might be a piece of some illegal trade with no cash changing hands."

I asked, "If that's the case, why did the company software show such a high correlation?"

He said, "I'll ask. The Agency believes the photos of the disease victims at Pollsmoor Prison in Cape Town are real and additional information leaking out seems to confirm it. The South African government is still not saying anything officially. That's all I've got. Carol probably knows more."

"Carol, what have you been able to find out?" I said.

"Quite a bit and most of it is bad. The World Health Organization also believes it is the same septicemic plague type disease. They have people on site and hope to get live samples of the bacterium. The samples from the poachers confirmed that it is a bioengineered bacterium. Someone bioengineered this plague and deliberately introduced it to the Pollsmoor Prison. With a live sample they should be able to find out much more about it. I don't have a count on the death toll but it will be in the hundreds at the very least.

"CDC has confirmed that the norovirus at prison ADX Florence in Fremont County, Colorado, was a bioengineered virus. Again they are studying it as we speak. No reported deaths.

"The WHO and the UK *Department of Health* both agree that the cholera at HM Prison Long Lartin is bioengineered. There are a few deaths reported from prisoners with compromised immune systems.

"Having Mia in Geneva at the WHO has really helped. She has impressed them with how serious this could be. Between her being there and these new prison outbreaks they are now giving it top priority.

"We have two bioengineered viruses, the rhinovirus in Bolivia and the norovirus at ADX Florence. Then we have two different bioengineered bacteria in the UK and South African prisons. Plus the introduction of an unknown type to birth control drugs in five US high schools. This is setting off major alarm bells all over the health community. Someone can engineer these and is willing to deploy them. Very scary."

I asked Mitch what she had.

"There is already a lot of buzz in the chat rooms of the do-gooder website about the burning of tons of ivory in Haiphong. Haiphong is known as one of the main hubs of the illegal ivory trade. There is also much chatter that the same burning of illegal stockpiles of ivory should be carried out in Mong Cai and Da Nang, both of which have a major role in the illegal ivory trade.

"I've been hacking my way back through server centers trying to find out where the three level-five sites are located without much success."

I looked to Abbey. She said, "I'm just getting started trying to find some trace of Justin. Plus I've had no contact from the forum that arranged for me to speak in South

Africa. Somehow my cover was blown there and that's it."

Ned jumped in. "There is more to come and if it weren't for us the CDC and WHO wouldn't even know these are all connected. Elizabeth's software works and the company should be getting a billion dollars from the government for it. We are going to out these guys. We are cyber warrior kings and the white knights of the Internet."

He was about to go on when Mitch poked him in the stomach.

"Ouch. I'm just saying we're making progress."

I said, "I agree we are making progress and what we are seeing is two different things that the software indicated are related. One, we are seeing someone go after the illegal trade in ivory and rhino horns. Two, we are seeing the same or a different group that is demonstrating that they have developed some very powerful bioengineering processes that can produce both customized virus and bacteria in ways that would make them powerful weapons. I'm not sure how the five high schools fit into this.

"I'm thinking demonstration because if they just wanted to test their capabilities they could do that in a lab. So who are they trying to impress and why?"

Abbey said, "Again, Prof, as you said, follow the money. It has to be expensive to do all this so maybe they are trying to show buyers just how powerful their work is to maximize the price they get."

I said, "Commercially this technology has to be worth billions. Why not just patent it and then sell?"

Carol said, "There are lots of regulations around bioengineering not even considering the ethical questions.

They may have broken enough laws that they know they can't sell their technology legally."

"So who would the buyers be: terrorists, rogue governments, others?" I said.

Chad said, "Governments have a lot more money than terrorists and it doesn't have to be someone like North Korea. Many government militaries try to be the first to control new technologies with military applications. I'll talk to the Agency."

Mitch was looking off into space. I'd seen that look before. "What is it, Mitch?"

"Nothing. I just had an idea. Probably nothing."

I looked around the room. "Anything else?"

Major Campbell said, "Walter asked me to increase security here at the ranch."

"Was he talking about cyber security?"

"We've already done that. He was talking about physical security."

"Did he say why?"

"He told me it was a precaution."

I wondered what Walter knew that we didn't. "Did he say when he was coming here?"

"He said as soon as he could, and tell everyone they were doing a good job."

"OK," I said. "Let's keep digging. Let me know if you find anything else and we'll meet in a few days."

I went back to my office frustrated. When Abbey settled in her office I went in and sat down. She just looked at me.

"I don't think that looking at the grave robberies or studying what was in the stolen manuscripts will get us anywhere. That means the only areas that have anything to do with archaeology are totally unimportant to what is going on. So what is the point of us being here?"

She said, "Walter must have his reasons. We were here when Elizabeth developed her super software. We understand it and were the first to use it. Ned, Mitch, and Major Campbell were all involved so they understand it. Maybe it's your sunny personality.

"Go take a walk or something I've got work to do."

"Thanks, Abbey, that clears it all up."

I got up to go and Abbey stuck her tongue out then smiled.

I smiled back but didn't feel much better. I walked over to the security office to talk to Major Campbell.

I went in and asked, "Is Ian free?"

"He's at the airfield."

As I walked to the airfield I heard a plane. I watched as the plane lined up to land. It was the Britten-Norman Defender 4000. Major Campbell told me last time I was here it is an enhanced version of the BN-2T Defender intended for the aerial surveillance role. The nose structure is capable of accommodating a FLIR turret or radar, and an increased payload. The forward-looking infrared (FLIR) cameras were supposedly the best in the world. The airstrip was only 1,200 feet long so the plane had been modified for short field takeoffs and landings. It was the largest plane that flew to the ranch.

I went to the main hangar as the plane taxied up. Major Campbell was there. He waved to me as the plane cut its engines. Eight men got off and started unloading duffel bags.

I went over to Major Campbell. "I see the cavalry has arrived." The men all had a hard, fit military look.

Major Campbell said, "Walter usually has good reasons for what he wants. If he thinks security needs to be beefed up I'd rather have too much than too little."

I didn't like the sounds of that and I wondered again what Walter knew that we didn't.

Major Campbell went over to talk to the new arrivals. So I went into the hangar to look around. I heard whistling towards the back of the hangar and headed that way. It was Peter Frank, another employee who seemed always to enjoy his work.

"Hi Peter." He had his head inside the big IAI Heron drone. It has a 54-foot wingspan, is 28 feet long, and was developed by a division of Israel Aerospace Industries.

"Hello Rob. What brings you up here?"

I said, "I wanted to speak to Major Campbell but he is busy at the moment. Have you heard anything about the increasing of security at the ranch?"

"No but I'm just here for a day or two to install a few new sensors in this drone. Let me show you what came of your brilliant idea."

I couldn't remember any brilliant ideas I'd had in a long, long time. About now I'd love a few good or even OK ideas. I followed him to a workbench all the way at the back of the hangar.

"Here it is, your brilliant idea. I can't believe I didn't think of it given all the time I spend fixing drones and remote sensing land machines."

It all came back to me now. When I was playing with

his hex-bug, the six-legged thing that could crawl over most terrain and right itself if it tipped over, Peter said he needed one that could crawl like this when it needed to and fly like a drone when it needed to. I told him to stick some rotors from a small drone on the hex-bug and pointed to where I thought they should go.

He held it out for me to look at. Peter had done the opposite of what I suggested. He started with a drone and added six spider-like mechanical legs. It was the size of the drone you can buy online and you see people flying around.

He said, "Let me show you."

He put it on the workbench and picked up an iPad. It started to crawl across the bench over tools and small items. At the edge of the bench the rotors started and it lifted off and landed on the floor about ten feet from the bench and started crawling again. It crawled into a wall and tried to climb it. It flipped on its back, then the rotors started and it righted itself, then backed up and turned away from the wall. Next it took off and flew back to the bench.

Peter was all smiles. "Isn't that great? This is just a prototype, a toy really, but prototype sounds better. Next I want to get some time and a few bucks to build a real commercial-grade one that can work in harsh environments and has sophisticated AI. I call it a drone bug and it is all thanks to your bright idea."

I wondered if it was true what many said: that it take someone outside a field to see the obvious or break through new combinations that the experts miss.

"Maybe you can have a bright idea about what I should be doing."

"Not likely but if you have any broken equipment I can probably fix it."

I liked Peter. I let him get back to work and went out to see if Major Campbell was free.

"Ian," I said. "Any word from Walter on when he will be here? You communicate with him regularly. I could use some direction."

"No. He wasn't specific, he just said as soon as he could. Tell Abbey if she is free I'd like to have her join us at the range at 4:00 today."

I said, "Are you going to win some money from your new men?"

"It's more I just want to show them they're not as good as they think they are. Some of them can get a bit cocky."

"I'll tell her." I headed back to the research facility.

Ned was in my office and looked wound up.

"The Zulu Curse is all over the web in South Africa. There was some low-level buzz about it before but now with the Pollsmoor Prison outbreak it is exploding. A Cape Town blogger with a big following released the names of about a dozen known poachers who are in Pollsmoor Prison. He claims they brought the Zulu Curse to the prison and it spread from them to other prisoners and staff. The speculation is starting to go crazy.

"In a small village near Kruger National Park two known poachers were beaten to death by villagers then doused in gas and burned. The Internet buzz is claiming the only way to keep the curse from spreading is to burn poachers' bodies."

I said, "What is the South African government saying?"

"They aren't saying much, just that the outbreak is contained in the prison. Which seems to be true at least so far."

"OK, let me know if anything else breaks." Ned nodded and walked out of my office mumbling something like "if Mitch leaves me any server capacity."

Abbey looked busy when I went to her office so I told her what Major Campbell said about practice on the range and let her get back to work.

Next I walked into the workroom. The only one there was Mitch. She had all six of her computer screens going and was typing away then looking from screen to screen.

She looked up at me shaking her head and said, "Zipf's law, why didn't I think of that sooner?" She shook her head some more and went back to typing.

It looked like the best thing I could do was stay out of everybody's way so I went to the canteen to get lunch. I ate alone and then went over the charts Mitch made for me again. I knew I must be missing something but nothing came to me. Perhaps a nap would help.

At 2:00 I went to the stables. As I rode with my usual stable hand I noticed Major Campbell's men were installing additional cameras and sensors at various places. As we rode past the airstrip I saw they had set up two Scan Eagle drones on their catapult launchers. The Scan Eagle was a surveillance drone about four and a half feet long with a ten-foot wingspan.

My riding mate said, "We may have trouble again, no?"

I didn't think he was here when I was here before but I'm sure he heard what happened. "Let's hope not" was all I could think to say.

The Zulu Curse

We rode for about an hour, then cooled, washed, and fed the horses. Still feeling aimless and unsettled I decided to walk up to the gun range. A few of the security men were setting up targets. They seemed close so I assumed they were for pistol practice. As I watched more people came.

Some of the security men were wearing their sidearms but most had them in locked metal boxes. Yes, they were all men. Major Campbell arrived in a Range Rover. He got out and said, "I thought we'd start with a little competition and then go through our regular practice."

He went on to explain the rules. They would start with pistols. Everyone would get three shots in the first round. The eight highest scorers would go on to the next round at an increased distance. The four highest would advance to the third round and then the two highest to the final round, again moving the targets back on each round.

Chad wandered in but there was no sign of Abbey. The men were opening their gun cases and checking the guns. I saw Chad had his own gun, not the one Major Campbell issued him.

Peter Frank came down from the airfield and stood by me. He said, "Do you shoot?"

I shook my head and said, "I don't even like the noise."

"Me either," he replied.

Major Campbell shouted over to us. "You two look like honest men. I'm appointing you as judges."

We walked over and he explained what we were to do. Still no Abbey, I looked around and then saw her walking towards us with big purposeful strides, her long red hair flowing behind her shoulders.

"Sorry, I lost track of time," she said to Major Campbell. He explained the rules to her and told her to select a pistol from the ones in the Range Rover.

The pistol range was set up so four people could fire at once. There were fifteen and they drew lots out of a baseball cap to see who would go first. Major Campbell told the first four to start. They put on ear protectors and began to fire.

Peter and I stood back by the Range Rover. They brought us the targets from the first group and then the next. We added up the number from the paper targets. The targets were standard ring-shaped targets, the closer the ring to the bull's-eye, the more points. If we had a tie on points we would measure to see which shot was closest to the next ring in.

We announced the eight that would go on. I noticed that more people were arriving to watch. We announced the four semifinalists, Abbey, Chad Dillon, Major Campbell and one of the new arrivals. There was a lot of head shaking from the eliminated shooters.

The four took up their firing positions and began shooting. When the targets came in, it was Major Campbell and Chad Dillon who went to the final round.

Abbey walked over to the Range Rover and gave me a wink and a big smile. She double-checked to make sure the safety was on and ejected the clip, laying both down on a cloth in the Jeep. I knew she would strip, clean, and reassemble the gun before returning it to Major Campbell. She was fond of the Marine saying "take care of your equipment and your equipment will take care of you."

For the final round they agreed to alternate shots. When we scored the target much to my disappointment Chad won. I expected him to be cocky but much to my surprise he was humble and a very good sport.

Next came the long-range rifle contest. Major Campbell explained that everyone would use the same rifle. It was the M40, a bolt-action sniper rifle used by the United States Marine Corps. Each M40 is built from a Remington 700 **bolt-action rifle** and is modified by USMC armorers at Marine Corps Base Quantico. It wasn't clear to me if it was an actual Marine modified M40 or if some other gunsmith had modified it to the M40 specifications.

He went on to explain that since we were shooting one at a time the first round would eliminate all but the four top shooters. Then the finalists would be the top two from the second round. They would start with the targets at 300 yards, then 500 yards, and the finals would be at 700 yards. Again three shots each and they would go in the same order as the pistol contest.

Chad was cleaning his pistol and putting it back in the metal box. He looked like he was getting ready to leave.

I said, "Aren't you going to compete?"

"It's not really my thing. Oh what the hell, I'll give it a try."

They moved the target to 300 yards. The man retrieving the target now rode a four-wheeler. The first shooter selected and examined each of the three bullets he took from the box. I wasn't sure if it was for luck or if they could tell the difference between bullets. They all looked the same to me.

After carefully aiming and firing three shots, the first shooter set down the gun. Then a new target was put in place. A man riding a four-wheeler delivered the first target to us.

The next shooter quickly checked and cleaned the barrel of the M-40. He went through the same routine, carefully picking three bullets. So the process went and we scored the targets as they were delivered to us. When Abbey's target arrived Peter looked at me and mouthed "wow." It was the best score yet.

The crowd of spectators kept growing. I saw my riding mate from the stables with a group of ranch hands.

We announced the four first-round winners but didn't reveal the scores. Abbey, Major Campbell, and two of the new arrivals would go on to the second round. I looked at Chad's score, he finished eighth out of the fifteen, not bad considering it wasn't his thing. I still wouldn't want him shooting at me.

The second round went quickly once they moved the target to 500 yards. The crowd kept growing. I saw the bartender and cook from the canteen among the now large group of spectators. Not much work was getting done at the ranch now.

It was a good thing all Peter and I had to do was add up the numerical scores because we were both rooting for Abbey. She fired first. When we got the target it was a lower score than before. I guessed that made sense, the target was 200 yards farther away.

The second target arrived and the shooter had outscored Abbey by one point. I looked back at the first-round scores. Abbey beat his score in the first round but just barely. The third shooter scored lower than Abbey so he was out. The last to shoot was Major Campbell. I held my breath as they handed me the target. Peter was looking over my shoulder as we quickly did the math. I let my breath out. It would be Abbey and the second shooter in the final round.

I announced the second shooter first, then Abbey. The crowd began to clap and cheer. I spotted Mrs. Lopez, even she was clapping.

They moved the targets to 700 yards. I was amazed anybody could even hit the target at that distance. The other shooter made a big show of letting Abbey go first. She just smiled and began to check the rifle.

After she shot, they changed targets but didn't bring in Abbey's. When the second shooter finished both targets were delivered. Peter and I scored them and both of us agreed to show no expression.

Abbey won by a comfortable margin. When I announced it in my most professorial voice the crowd erupted into cheers. The eight newly arrived security men were a bit stunned. I saw Chad Dillon going among them collecting money. He had on his Cheshire cat shit-eating grin. Today I rather enjoyed seeing that grin.

Major Campbell thanked everyone and told his people to get back to work. Several people congratulated Abbey as she made her way to the Range Rover.

I said to her, "Just the result Major Campbell wanted. He told me some of these folks were a bit too cocky." I had another thought but kept it to myself. I'd check it out later.

She didn't look unhappy but she wasn't overly excited or gloating.

She said, "Lots of very good marksmen in that group." Then she began stripping and cleaning the pistol she used earlier.

I said, "He outscored you in the second round."

"I thought as much. A puff of wind came up as I fired my third shot."

I had the feeling she really didn't care one way or another. Well I was happy for her. Carol came over and congratulated Abbey. She liked seeing a woman beat all those macho men.

She said, "Annie Oakley, girl, you can shot! I've never seen anything like that."

I said, "Do you want to try?"

"I will if you will."

I shook my head no.

After we waited for Abbey to reassemble the pistol, the three of us walked back to the guesthouse. Abbey said, "Let's have a drink by the pool and eat at the guesthouse tonight. I don't want to deal with the crowd that will be at the canteen."

We agreed.

Chapter 13

The next morning I took an early morning swim and thought about last night. After dinner Abbey excused herself and went to her apartment. Carol took the rest of the bottle of wine and led me to my apartment. Making love to Carol seemed more like an athletic contest than a romantic experience. I wasn't sure how I felt about that. The sex was great but a bit forced. I decided not to think about it. I finished my swim, showered, dressed, poured a mug of coffee, and headed over to the workroom.

Mitch was there in front of her bank of screens. I wasn't sure if she was still here from yesterday or was back at it again. It did look like she had on the same clothes as yesterday.

She looked up. "Are you back again?"

I said, "It's tomorrow, Mitch. Have you been working all night?"

She punched a few keys and said, "Shit, it's 7:30. You're up early.

"This run will take a few hours, then hopefully I'll have something for you. I better go take a shower and get some sleep."

She punched a few more keys, slipped on her sandals, and got up.

I said, "Abbey won the rifle contest yesterday."

"I know, Ned stopped in with some food and told me. She's pretty fucking good. Put those meatheads in their place."

Then she walked out, I went into my office and began to check my email. There was one from my favorite research librarian Laura O'Hara. Laura said she'd heard from a researcher she knew at the Wereld museum in Rotterdam that rumors were spreading that rare ancient texts relating to diseases and their treatments were being offered on the black market. This acquaintance remembered she'd been inquiring about stolen medical texts so she emailed Laura.

I knew the Wereld museum it is an ethnographic museum located in the Willemskade area of Rotterdam. It displays more than 1,800 ethnographic objects from various cultures in Asia, Oceania, Africa, the Americas and the Islamic heritage. I sent her a thank-you email and asked her to let me know if she heard anything else. Next I sent Chad a text and asked him to check with the Agency to see if they knew anything.

Abbey came in a while later. I stuck my head in her office and said, "Any luck tracking down Justin Barry on the web?"

"No, it's like he just fell off the earth. I found a few Facebook posts by people asking friends if anyone had seen him. No one had. I need to do something else. Any bright ideas for me?"

I said, "Do you know what Mitch is doing? I got an email from Elizabeth wondering why she was hogging so much server capacity. Other employees were beginning to complain."

She just shook her head no.

I continued. "Mitch was muttering something about Zipf's law and was up all night doing something with all that server capacity."

Abbey was staring at me. "Prof, you don't know what that is, do you? Want me to explain it to you?"

"No, I'll go look it up. You check on Ned. I always worry when we haven't seen him for a while. God knows what he could be up to. Then schedule a group meeting for tomorrow morning."

I went back to my office and composed an email to Walter with a quick recap of what we were doing and ended by admitting we were floundering and needed more direction. Next I looked up Zipf's law.

After lunch I went back and reviewed everything we had. I re-watched the video footage we had and re-read all the reports. Finally I gave up. I decided to check my email before I left. There was a short email from Walter. "You're doing fine, keep it up. More later." Not much help there so I walked over to the stables to go riding.

The next morning I went into the workroom at 9:00 for our meeting. I tried to be positive and upbeat. I really had no plan so I started with Ned.

"Ned, give us the latest of what you know."

"Well all hell is breaking loose in South Africa. The death toll in Pollsmoor Prison is approaching a thousand and that is just what the government is saying. The web reports claim much higher numbers. Vigilante-style murders of suspected poachers are occurring all around the parks that have elephants and rhinos. A whole family was burned to death in their home by a mob at the edge of Addo Elephant National Park in the eastern cape region near Port Elizabeth. That is a long ways from Zululand.

"Rumors about the Zulu Curse are spreading like wildfire on the web. But poaching of elephants and rhinos is way down. So I guess the curse is working.

"Well in the US at ADX Florence prison in Colorado things seem to be under control but Carol probably knows more about.

"In the UK at Her Majesty's Prison Long Lartin things also seem to be settling down. The government hasn't mentioned anything about a bioengineered bug.

"My guess is we will see some retaliation from the Sun Yee On gang. They aren't going to let slide the blowing up of their warehouse and killing of their people. Not to mention losing millions of dollars' worth of tusks.

"That's about it, Professor."

"Carol, what do you have from the CDC?"

She looked like she wasn't sure where to start. "Well it is very likely a bioengineered bug at Her Majesty's Prison Long Lartin. Specifically it is some strain of the bacterium Vibrio cholerae that has never been seen before. That is the family of bacteria that causes cholera. My guess is that they know that but are just calling it a previously unknown strain. It seems the authorities have it under control at least in the prison.

"At ADX Florence prison in Colorado the norovirus outbreak is also under control. That is definitely a bioengineered virus. We know from our analysis of the poachers that the plague bacterium in South Africa is bioengineered. Now CDC, the World Health Organization, and others are working hard to understand how they were created, their characters, and how to prevent and treat them. I should mention that there are no reports of these diseases spreading outside the prisons.

"The health officials and scientists who know what is going on are scared."

I thought a minute. "They should be scared. Someone has demonstrated that they can genetically modify both virus and bacteria that cause human diseases, which are as mild or deadly as they choose. They can introduce them into populations in a variety of places seemingly at will. Including secure places such as a maximum-security prisons. It also appears that they can limit their spread to the desired target areas and no one knows who they are or why they chose the place they did to demonstrate what they can do."

Ned jumped in. "But they are all tied to the do-gooder web site."

"OK. Mitch."

She stood, waved her hands as if summoning the power of the universe, and said, "Zipf's law."

I interrupted her. "Oh yes, the empirical law formulated by American linguist George Kingsley Zipf that states that given some corpus of natural language utterances, the frequency of any word is inversely proportional to its rank in the frequency table.

"Go on, I did not mean to interrupt." I'd just looked it up yesterday. I couldn't help myself; perhaps it was the theatrical way Mitch did her hand waving.

She tried not to look miffed. "Right, Professor. So according to Zipf's law the most frequent word will occur approximately twice as often as the second most frequent word, three times as often as the third most frequent word, etc. Although Zipf's law holds for hundreds of languages, even for non-natural languages like Esperanto, the reason is still not well understood but that doesn't matter for what I did.

"First I loaded the probability mass function and the cumulative distribution function of Zipf's law for the thirty-six currently spoken languages. Then I loaded the distribution patterns from all the encrypted messages I had between levels four and five from the do-gooder website. I then modified one of the company's AI pattern recognition programs to rank them in order of their probable correlation.

"Do you know what I found?"

I said, "You found the highest correlation was with the Dutch language." It was a guess of course but the man who approached Abbey at the conference traveled on a Dutch passport and Laura just told me that some of the stolen ancient texts were being sold on the black market in Rotterdam.

Mitch's jaw dropped but she quickly regained her composure. "Correct, so now I'm trying something different.

I'm working on hacking the major server centers in the Netherlands. It is the only real location lead we have."

I said, "Very ingenious, Mitch, you are truly amazing. Can you crack the encryption?"

"No. What I have done doesn't do that but it should help that we know what language we are trying to understand. Chad's people have way more capability than we do."

"Chad, can you have them take a run at it?"

"I can ask" was all he said.

"Chad, anything more from the Agency?"

"I think they are making headway on getting the Taiwanese military intelligence and security agencies to look into payments to the Bamboo Union or other information related to the warehouse attack in Haiphong. The Agency had to share the terror angle of the bioengineered attacks at the three prisons before they showed any sense of urgency.

"Knowing about the Netherlands should help. They can focus on that as a potential departure point for the money trail.

"No word from the Agency on a Sun Yee On gang revenge attack."

"Anything else?"

"Not that they're telling me," he said.

Abbey spoke up. "Prof, let's go to Rotterdam. We can try and get a line on the manuscripts being offered on the black market. We are expert enough to be working for some rich collector to authenticate the volumes. Walter is a rich collector. Can we use him as our cover?"

I thought about that. My decision was based more on

being bored here than thinking it would be much help. "I'll ask Walter. He may not want it spread around that he is buying on the black market."

"I'd like to go," Carol said. "I want to spend some time at the World Health Organization. I look at the data a bit differently than Mia and we can compare notes. I'll take a flight or train to Geneva."

Chad jumped in. "I'll go and see if I can stir our people to action over there. It's harder to just give you lip service when you are in their face. Plus black market dealers aren't always the nicest people."

"OK, I'll go see Major Campbell about arrangements and contact Walter."

Mitch said, "I know it makes more sense for Ned and me to stay here but I don't like it."

We ended the meeting and I went to Major Campbell's office and explained what I wanted to do.

He listened, asked a few questions, looked at his watch, and then hit the speed dial on his phone. Much to my surprise Walter answered the phone. Ian put it on speaker.

I gave him a quick update and then explained what we wanted to do. He asked only a few questions then said he would make some phone calls and get back to us. He told me we were doing well and then hung up.

Ian said, "I'll look into the logistical and security issues so we are ready to move when Walter gets back to us."

"When will that be?" I said.

He put his palms up and shook his head.

I said, "You didn't by chance let Abbey outshoot you to take your men down a peg?"

"Rob, doing that wouldn't be sporting."

Not a definite answer but I dropped it and let him get back to work.

Abbey was in her office when I returned. I told her about the call to Walter.

She said. "Cheer up. It will be fun. I've never been to the Netherlands and we might actually accomplish something."

"I'm going to contact Laura and find out whatever I can about the manuscript and then see what else I can dig up that might be helpful," I said.

"Another thing, remember the list of countries that the Sun Yee On gang operated in? It included the Netherlands."

I said, "Yes but the Sun Yee On has about 55,000 members in about two dozen countries. Still it's one more possible link to the Netherlands. I don't remember hearing that the Bamboo Union gang was operating in the Netherlands."

Everyone seemed busy so I decided to stay out of the way and went to read about Rotterdam.

Much to my surprise, the next morning, Major Campbell walked into my office shortly after I got there to tell me Walter approved our trip to Rotterdam.

He said, "Walter agreed it was the best lead we had. He talked to Ned, I was on the phone with them and Walter reviewed some of Ned's latest runs with the software. I didn't follow it all but the impression I got is that things are going to get worse and very soon. He suggested some modifications for another run and asked Ned to send the results as soon as he had them.

"Walter has arranged for you to meet with Europol agents that deal with stolen antiquities."

I said, "Stop. Is Europol what it sounds like? The European police."

He said, "Sort of. It is the law enforcement agency of the European Union that handles criminal intelligence mostly involving terrorism and serious international organized crime. They don't do the actual police work. The individual countries do that. Europol provides intelligence analysis, expertise, and training. They also facilitate the exchange of information between EU countries.

"Walter is having you meet the people who track movement and sale of illicit antiquities. With the wars in Syria, Iraq, and Yemen that business is booming.

"Our company has offices there. The Netherlands is a large producer of natural gas, about half of it offshore in the North Sea, and as you know, a major part of the company's business is helping them find it. Rotterdam is the largest port in Europe and the list of top companies there is as long as your arm. Well my point is that we have a good-size facility there with good security and Walter wants you to stay there."

I said, "Won't that hurt our cover as experts who deal in stolen manuscripts?"

"On the contrary, it will fit right in with Walter being a rich collector willing to deal in the gray area of the antique business. Let's find Abbey, Carol, and Chad so I can go over arrangements," he said.

Abbey was in the adjacent office so I asked her to text Carol and Chad.

Everyone was in my office within ten minutes.

Major Campbell was brief. Pack a bag and be up at the airfield at 1:00PM.

We flew in the Cessna SkyMaster for the short flight to Lima. As we approached the city I could see the bright colors of the hang gliders of the seaside cliffs of Costa Verde. We landed and taxied to the general aviation area of the airport.

Major Campbell pulled up next to a midsized company jet. Four of the newly arrived security men from the ranch were there. They must have driven down this morning. Their gear was being loaded on the plane. I recognized the one who was in the rifle shooting contest finals with Abbey. If I remembered right, the other three all finished near the top of the both the rifle and pistol contests. Fit, hard men with an ex-military look, not cybersecurity or analysts but shooters. Abbey's grandfather called them the tip of the spear.

I pointed to the men and said to Major Campbell, "Walter's idea to take them with us?"

He nodded and started unloading our bags.

First Walter beefs up security at the ranch and now he sends the four top gun men with us. He was worried about something and he wasn't letting us in on what it was.

Major Campbell signaled one of the men over. It was the one who lost to Abbey. Major Campbell said, "Rob, you remember Sean O'Connor from the contest the other day. He will head up security for your trip."

I didn't remember his name but I smiled and shook his hand.

He continued. "Sean served with me in the SAS. One of Her Majesty's finest. I've briefed Sean on each of your positions."

I wasn't sure what that meant. Did he now report to me or was he my babysitter? I guess he filled him in on who Chad was.

He then introduced Sean to Carol. Both Abbey and Chad greeted him.

He continued, "Chad, you and my security men will leave your sidearms with me and you'll be issued new ones in Rotterdam at our facility. The guns will be EU permitted. They are rather fussy about guns there these days with all the terrorist activity."

A male steward came over and asked us to board the plane.

Chapter 14

I took my seat, fastened my seatbelt, put my head back, and closed my eyes. The steward woke me and handed me a meal. An omelet, sausage, and toast. I guess it was breakfast time. Abbey sat down next to me.

I said. "Not eating?"

"I just finished. Major Campbell sent some heavy hitters with us. Was that Walter's idea?"

"I'm not sure, probably. This and the increased ranch security, there must be something up. I feel like it is all swirling around us and we can't see it."

Then we were quiet and I ate my omelet.

We started our descent into the Rotterdam The Hague airport. I'd read the runway was fifteen feet below sea level. I figured about half the country was below sea level. We flew over open land then acres of flat roofs that looked like very large distribution warehouses. As we landed I looked out at the red and white striped control tower featured in all the tour books' section on the airport.

Once we stopped we went into a modern-looking building in the general aviation section of the airport. Chad stood next to me while we were having our passports checked.

I said, "What do you think about our security detail?

He looked over at them and then at me. "Well at least we know they can shoot."

Not much of an answer so I let it drop. Once we were done with passport control Sean O'Connor directed us out to a half-sized Mercedes bus. One of O'Connor's men took Carol and her bags to a waiting car; they were going to the main terminal to catch a flight to Geneva.

Carol would stay with Mia at a hotel near the World Health Organization. I hoped they didn't need the man that went with them. I wished I were going with her.

Our bus driver spoke excellent English with a charming accent. He told us the drive was under a half hour.

Abbey said, "I've never been here."

"I'll give you a little tour if that is OK," the driver said. I said, "Sure."

No one else seemed to care. The driver started out south on A13. First he pointed out the Rotterdam Zoo and then something called Miniworld Rotterdam, the largest indoor miniature world in the Benelux. He said the mini landscapes, mini residents, mini trains, and a mini Rotterdam would amaze us. I decided I'd pass on that one.

Next he pointed out the Museum Boijmans Van Beuningen that he said is one of the oldest museums in the Netherlands. The museum has paintings, sculptures, and objects, as well as an important collection of drawings and etchings. It features many major Dutch and European works spanning the period from the early middle ages to the twenty-first century, from Bosch to Rembrandt, and from Van Gogh to Dalí.

He then rattled off the names of about a dozen museums. There were the ones you would expect such as natural history, World War II, maritime, modern art, but then there were a few odd ones. One was the museum of tax and customs, another with just chess pieces, and one for rock art.

My first museum visit would be Wereld museum to talk the woman who told Laura O'Hara about rumors of ancient medical manuscripts being offered on the black market.

He drove around for another half hour pointing out sites. I'll admit there is some very impressive architecture. We saw the Kijk-Kubus or Cube Houses. They are tipped to one side, making three sides face the ground and three face the sky. Cool to look at but I wouldn't want to live in one.

Rotterdam's Markthal looks like a row of giant horseshoes standing on end. The driver told us apartments are draped over the food market in this horseshoe configuration. It has about 100 fresh food stands, 15 food shops, and various restaurants, with a supermarket and a four-level underground parking lot below. He claimed that looking up to enjoy the massive artwork sprawling across the ceiling, you feel as if you are in the Dutch version of the Sistine Chapel. I wasn't sure if it was cool or just weird.

We also saw the Euromast observation tower, the highest watchtower in the Netherlands; the 800-meter long Erasmus Bridge which spans the Maas River and links the northern and southern parts of Rotterdam; the Central Station Rotterdam; and several more.

Finally he headed to the port area. It was huge. We went through a security gate to get into the port area and a second security gate into the Falone Advanced Technologies facility. There were two buildings. One looked like a warehouse and the other an office building. The architecture was modern but not way out like we saw on our tour.

The driver explained that company employees who were here for a short period often stayed in the facilities here and long-term employees lived in the city. He pulled up at the front entrance to the office building.

Sean instructed his men to get everyone's bags. We thanked the driver and went in. Sean took our company badges and we went to a reception desk. Each badge was put in a scanner device and then the receptionist typed into her computer. All the same except when they got to Chad's. Sean gave her specific instructions. She seemed puzzled, checked something on her computer, and then continued.

Sean gave Abbey and me our badges and said, "You are in the system to use the retinal or fingerprint scanners to get into any areas you are authorized to enter. Chad, you will need to run your ID card through the scanner at each entrance. So don't lose it."

Spook stuff. I remembered Major Campbell saying they wouldn't use Chad's retinal image or fingerprints for his security ID.

Sean seemed to know the place, he led us to an elevator and put his hand on the optical fingerprint reader. We went to the top floor. It looked like a small all-suites hotel. Each of our rooms was already coded to our fingers.

I dumped my bag, washed up, and decided to see what facilities the floor had. As I went out of my room I saw everyone else getting ready to get on the elevators.

"Where is everyone going?" I said.

Chad said, "You can come but no toys for you."

Sean just shrugged his shoulders. I took that for yes so I got in the elevator. I gave Abbey a "what's up" look but she just smiled at me. So I kept quiet. We walked outside and over to the warehouse building. We were met by another person from security and walked into the cavernous warehouse. After going through three more locked doors we ended in a room with a glass wall that looked onto a pistol range.

Sean opened a double door that revealed a large metal door. It reminded me of the doors you see in banks to go into the safety deposit box area. Sean used the retinal scanner to release the lock on the door. The inside looked like a small gun store, with rifles individually locked in racks. He pulled open a drawer. There were two rows of pistols. The top row looked like the big brother of the bottom row. I took a step closer.

Abbey said, "The top row is SIG Sauer P226s. It is a full-sized, military-type pistol made by SIG Sauer. The bottom row contains the P229s, a compact variant of the P226. The smaller P229 is preferred for concealed carry. The British SAS uses both plus just about every branch of the US military including our Navy SEALs. Great German engineering."

Sean handed a P229 to each of his men and put another to the side for himself. His two men moved away to a bench and began to disassemble the pistols.

He said to Chad, "Do you want one of these?"

"What else do you have?"

Sean opened the next drawer. Again two rows of pistols.

Abbey said, "The top row is Glock 17Ms, introduced in 2016, in response to an FBI solicitation for a new 9mm pistol. On the left side of the next row are Glock 19s, a reduced-size Glock 17 considered a compact pistol. On the right side are the Glock 26s, a subcompact variant designed for the civilian market. Both the Brits and the US military and police use the 17 and the 19."

Chad said, "No Glock 18?"

Sean shook his head and Abbey smiled. I didn't get the joke.

Chad said, "SIG Sauer P229. If it's good enough for your boys it's good enough for me. What about you, Abbey?"

He pointed to the smaller Glock 26. I looked at Abbey and then Sean. They had to be kidding. She is a great shot but...

Sean said, "I have something else I want you to look at."

He opened another drawer that had an assortment of handguns.

"The Beretta Nano is a compact handgun developed for concealed carry. It has a technopolymer frame and a Pronox finished slide. The sights on the Nano are low-profile 3-dot sights. This one is the 9mm version. It holds 6 rounds of ammunition in a single-column box magazine, for a total capacity of 7 if the pistol is chambered.

"The Beretta Nano is a great little carry gun with absolutely nothing that will ever get stuck in a holster or purse.

There is no external safety lever, teardown lever, or slide lock to get stuck anywhere. The size and weight of the Beretta Nano makes it a perfect handgun for concealed carry — and the 9mm round can stop just about any threat."

Abbey took the gun. I liked this less and less. I said, "Does she really need that?"

Sean said, "Major Campbell told me to arm her. I don't much like the idea either; it's usually trouble when civilians have guns. Just because someone can hit a paper target doesn't make them a soldier or mean they know how to react under fire."

I saw Chad smile and shake his head slightly. Abbey said nothing.

"I'm not worried about Abbey's competence, it's the fact that Major Campbell thinks she might need it that scares me." I was going to go on about why weren't his men good enough to protect us when Abbey put her hand on my arm.

"It's OK, Prof, Walter texted me and we agreed it would be a good idea," she said.

Again it was clear Walter knew more than he was telling us. I let it drop and Abbey picked up the Beretta.

I watched them check and load the pistols.

I said, "They use the same type bullets. Isn't that nice you can all share." Then I walked out.

As I walked down the hall I heard someone following me. I turned. It was Chad.

I said, "Don't you need to practice?" My tone was rude and snotty; I wondered why I was taking it out on him.

He didn't seem offended and said, "I've got work to

do. I want to see what the Agency people here know and set up our meeting with Europol.

"If I were you I'd sleep better knowing Abbey is armed. I know I will and if you haven't figured it out yet we are into some deep shit here."

He was smiling. He liked this. I didn't.

We walked back to the other building. People were coming and going, it was a normal workday for them. Chad went to the receptionist and asked her to order him a taxi.

As I headed to the elevator I said, "Let me know as soon as you can when we can meet with Europol. Then I'll set up our meeting at the Wereld museum."

I changed and went to the small workout room. It was like any hotel fitness center. I got on the treadmill and tried to clear my head.

I was in my room showered and reading after my workout when Abbey called.

"Meet me in the bar at 6:00. I have a plan," she said and hung up.

I looked at my watch, twenty minutes. I changed and went to the bar. Call me old-fashioned but I believe a man should arrive first and not leave a woman alone waiting in a bar. Plus I wanted a drink.

There were only a few people in the bar when Abbey walked in but the men all looked in her direction. For work especially in the field Abbey usually wore jeans and sweatshirts. Tonight she had on black pleated silk pants and a white shirt open at the neck with a necklace of emerald-colored stone and matching earrings. Her red hair was pulled back with an emerald-studded hair clip. It was stunning, her red hair, green eyes, and emerald jewelry offset her white blouse and pale skin.

She walked over, kissed my cheek, and sat down.

I said, "Wow."

She replied, "I don't always have dirt under my nails from digging in caves."

She picked up the wine list and I signaled the waiter.

I had no desire to talk about her afternoon at the gun range but I did wonder where she concealed that Beretta. When our drinks came I said, "You have a plan?"

"Yes, we are going to Zeezout."

I had a questioning look on my face and she went on.

"It is one of Rotterdam's finest seafood restaurants. It's just south of the city center near the Nieuwe Maas River. It is very expensive."

I cut her off, raising my glass. "Walter buying us our last super. That seems fitting. Will we be allowed to go without our guards?"

"Sean said no."

"I bet they are drawing straws to see who goes," I said.

A minute later I pointed my glass to the door as Sean came in dressed in gray slacks, a black blazer, and a white shirt but no tie. I didn't see a bulge from his gun but I was sure he wore it.

"He probably pulled rank when you told him where we were going. What about Chad?"

Not that I really cared.

"I sent him a text," she answered.

After a quick greeting Sean ordered a beer in what sounded to me like fluent Dutch. Well that could be helpful.

It was nice to know he could do more than shoot people.

When his beer came I asked, "What did Major Campbell tell you about what we are doing?"

Sean hesitated a minute and said, "He told me you were doing important work and reporting directly to Walter, that you all had top-level company and government clearances. Anything I or my men heard was to be treated as totally confidential."

I waited and looked at him.

He continued. "He said there was the possibility of trouble and I was to exercise extreme care."

I let it go at that. We drank and made small talk. He said he tried to get his men to bet they could outshoot Abbey at the gun range today but they wouldn't take the bet.

Abbey said, "Let's go. I'm hungry."

When we walked out, a car was waiting. We got in and drove a short distance to a set of docks. I followed Abbey to a waiting water taxi.

"Let's see some of the famous Rotterdam waterfront sights on the way to our last supper," Abbey said.

After fifteen minutes or so the water taxi deposited us at a riverside dock and a boatman spoke to Sean in Dutch as he paid.

"Just one block, this way to Westerkade 11b. The boatman said Zeezout is one of Rotterdam's best restaurants. It has been in business nineteen years and he recommended the mackerel ceviche."

We walked one block in from the river. Zeezout's was on the end of a triangle-shaped building. It reminded me a little of the Flatiron Building in New York City. There were gray awnings over each window with an outside table under each. We went inside. The décor was modern, lots of chrome and glass. The tables had white tablecloths, the chairs were all upholstered in gray matching the outside awnings.

Chad was waiting for us. He said, "Nice place. The dishes look better than the boiled potatoes and mutton we eat in Mongolia."

I looked at the dishes being served. Each one looked like a work of art. The plates were custom selected to match each dish. I saw onion soup served in a bowl carved from a fresh onion; Thai chicken coconut soup, Tom Kha Gai, was served in a coconut shell; and many of the fish dishes had the heads on and the eyes seemed to be staring at me.

We sat, the waiter came, and Sean asked in Dutch to see the wine menu. He said, "Do you mind if I suggest wines for this evening?"

Abbey said, "I guess if we trust you with our lives we can trust you to order a palatable wine."

I said, "OK, I'm sorry I started it. No more 'Walter's last supper' jokes. I want to focus on our dinner." I was still eyeing each dish as it went by.

First came four glasses of a sparkling white wine. The waiter asked in fluent but accented English if we had questions.

The meal was excellent. Sean pleased everyone with the wine selections. At the end, even though we were all full, we couldn't resist dessert. I never saw the bill, it went to Sean and he paid with a company credit card.

Smiling and satisfied we left the restaurant. The temperature was comfortable and the night was clear.

Abbey said, "Let's walk for a while."

Sean looked at his watch and said, "The water taxi is waiting and I need to report in."

Chad said, "I'll babysit. You go back and we'll catch a cab in a little while."

We walked back to the river, Sean went to the dock, and we continue along the river's edge. It was a beautiful night and I felt like I didn't have a care in the world. There would be plenty of time tomorrow to worry. We walked in silence, each lost in our own thoughts.

An explosion ripped through the night. We turned to see our water taxi engulfed in flames. Chad looked around quickly and then grabbed each of us by an arm. He turned us away from the river and down a side street. He told us to walk slowly and steadily and act as if we heard nothing. Two blocks in, he led us into a crowded bar. He moved us deep inside and up to the bar.

"Stay here, have a drink. I need to make a call," Chad said.

I looked at Abbey, she looked a little white. My stomach was in a knot. He was back in less than a minute. He ordered two beers and a wine for Abbey.

"What now?" I said.

He raised his beer, smiled, and said, "We wait. Pretend you are enjoying yourself. People are starting to look at us."

Abbey raised her glass and touched Chad's mug. I realized my mouth was open so I shut it and tried not to scowl or shake.

Outside we could hear sirens heading to the riverfront.

Chad went on with a grin. "Professor, sometimes I

wonder about you. How did you know it was to be our last supper? Drink your beer."

I looked at the untouched beer in my hand and forced a sip.

"Well look at the bright side. It means we are making progress or they wouldn't be trying to kill us."

I thought it means something else too but I kept that thought to myself. I wasn't sure if he was trying to be funny or he was actually enjoying this. Abbey said nothing but she was doing a better job of acting like we were enjoying a relaxing drink than I was.

In less than twenty minutes two young, fit-looking men approached. Chad put some Euros on the bar and we headed out, one of the new men in front of us and the other behind. There were two black SUVs in the street with two more men standing next to them. We were directed into the back of the first SUV.

As soon as we were in the car I said to Chad, "What about Carol and Mia in Geneva? They could be in danger."

"I already called her company security man and our Geneva station. They are sending men to check on them but her security guard said he was with Carol and there was no sign of trouble. He wasn't sure where Mia was."

Out the window I could see police boats on the river and police cars along the riverside all with their lights flashing. I also saw several ambulances but I thought sadly they wouldn't be needed. There was no way Sean or the boatmen could have survived that blast.

As we approached the Falone Advanced Technologies facility I saw the front gate was all lit up. There were several uniformed police with the company security detail. The gate opened as we approached and the SUVs didn't even slow down.

Chad said, "The police will question us as soon as we arrive. We are here to investigate the theft and black market sale of rare ancient manuscripts. We have a meeting with Europol tomorrow and local museum officials later this week. You two are experts on ancient manuscripts and I'm with company security. The story will check out."

I said, "Will they wonder why eight CIA agents brought us back?"

"I called the US embassy and they sent these people. I'll handle it. And it is OK to look scared and confused now," he said.

That wasn't going to be a problem. There were several police cars in front of our building but no flashing lights and sirens here. Several police and company security men were in front.

They opened the car door and Chad led us in. There was a small crowd of official-looking people inside. A man in a gray suit approached us. He introduced himself as an attorney with the US embassy and said he would assist us during the police questioning. That was fine by me.

I reached out and squeezed Abbey's arm. "Are you alright?"

She gave me a big smile. "No. Looks like we'll earn our pay tonight."

We were taken to a conference room. Someone from the company had already given the police the story of why we were here.

They questioned us together which I took as a good sign, and it became clear that they had already checked with Europol and verified our planned meeting with them and researched our backgrounds. We told and retold our story.

The police captain, after about the third time we told why we were here and the events of the night, said, "For two university archaeology professors you seem to find quite a bit of trouble."

I wasn't sure if he was referring to Mongolia or our earlier time in Peru. I also wondered how he knew so much so quickly.

Finally the questioning came to an end. There would be police stationed out front and we were to stay in the building and clear it with them when we wanted to leave.

Our embassy attorney told them we would voluntarily agree to this but unless the police were going to charge us with something we were free to go.

It was agreed that Europol would meet with us here in the company facility. Everyone seemed satisfied with the arrangement. It was after 2:00AM when we were finally allowed to go upstairs and go to bed.

My sleep was fitful but I managed to stay in bed until after 9:00AM. I did a quick twenty-minute run on the treadmill, showered, and headed to breakfast. The work-out didn't seem to help my mood.

Chad was there neatly dressed and looking well rested.

"Sit down. I won't ask you how you slept. The coffee is good. The breakfast won't stand up to last night's dinner but the eggs Benedict weren't half bad. The meeting with

Europol is set for 1:00PM. I've arranged an 11:00AM videoconference with Mitch and Ned. I sent a text to Carol and Mia to see if they want to join by phone."

I was glad to see Chad had taken charge. I was shaken and I hadn't begun to think about what we should do next. I still had one thought from last night on my mind. I needed to get a grip.

"Thanks, Chad, for your quick thinking last night, handling the police, and keeping the ball rolling today. The bomb, Sean and the boatmen dead, if Abbey hadn't wanted to take a walk we'd be dead too."

"It's not your line of work. You did great. Payback is busting whoever is behind this and stopping whatever they have planned. How's the coffee?" he said.

My eggs came and I ate them as he sent Abbey a text telling her of our meeting time. After last night's dinner I was surprised at how hungry I was. He told me which floor the videoconference room was on and I said I'd meet him there at 11:00. As I left he picked up the *London Times* and read as if he hadn't a care in the world.

Abbey was last to get to the conference room. Her hair was wet and she was back to jeans and a sweater. Carol and Mia had just conferenced in by phone.

"I took a long run," Abbey said as she came in.

"I'm surprised they let you out of the building," I answered.

"They sent two men to run with me and we stayed in the port facility. It's a busy place out there."

The video system was on and it came to life with Ned's face looking at us about twice normal size. He moved back from the camera and bounced into a chair next to Mitch. He said, "You're having all the fun over there. Someone caught the explosion on a cellphone and all the European news channels are playing it at the top of each hour. Holy shit, that water taxi was blown to smithereens."

Mitch was staring at him. He went on more somberly. "No terrorist group has claimed responsibility. Oh we are glad you weren't hurt, but we heard that from Major Campbell before we knew anything else."

As if on cue Major Ian Campbell walked into our room. I looked at him as if he was a ghost then stood and welcomed him. It was reassuring to see him. His six foot five inch chiseled figure exuded command and confidence.

I said, "Did you fly all night?"

"Sean was one of my best men. Walter wanted me here and I wouldn't have it any other way. I'd like to hear whatever is the latest we have and then I'm meeting with the Rotterdam Police and Interpol." He shook hands with everyone and we sat down.

Ned had calmed down a bit but was dying to say something. I realized I was supposed to be in charge. I thought, get a grip, Rob.

I said, "We're glad you're here, Major. Ned, you look as if you are ready to report."

He started. "We have made some progress, well mostly Mitch has made progress. Our software isn't showing any new related incidents like we've seen with the prisons or poacher deaths, just more fallout from the existing ones. I'm making no progress getting into those restricted areas of the do-gooder website. Without Mia to help me I'm not credible as a bioengineering whiz." He looked at Mitch. "You tell them what you found."

"I was able to trace some of the encrypted website messages that had routing instructions that were characteristic of wire transfers. They originated in Europe and went to a business in Taiwan with known ties to the Bamboo Union. I was able to then match major European bank ID codes to what I had using an encryption cracking program.

"I got a match with Société Générale Bank. It is the third largest bank in France by assets and has worldwide operations. That's about it."

She paused and then asked, "Chad, has your Agency made any progress on decrypting the message we flagged for them?"

Chad said, "What they've told me is that they are working on it. But they've made headway in Taiwan. Taiwanese intelligence confirmed that it was the Bamboo Union that blew up the warehouse in Haiphong. But we knew that. What else they said was that the Bamboo Union hasn't been paid for the job. Just the down payment and they are getting pissed off about it.

"I'll have them check on the Société Générale money transfer. Mitch, when was it?"

Mitch tapped some keys on her keyboard. "It looks like a week before the Haiphong warehouse blew up."

Ned interrupted. "One thing that reminded me of, there has been a big fundraising push on the website. Maybe they are running out of money. I don't think I'd shortchange a Chinese gang like the Bamboo Union."

I'd have to think about that.

"Carol or Mia, what are you hearing from the CDC and WHO?"

Mia started. "This is bioengineering like no one has ever seen. The genetic modifying of a rhinovirus to make a new strain is not that hard to do. The fact that the modified virus dies off after a period of time seems to be designed into the RNA to stop replicating after a specified number of generations.

"Rhinoviruses have single-stranded positive sense RNA genomes of between 7,200 and 8,500 nt in length. At the 5' end of the genome is a virus-encoded protein, and like mammalian mRNA, there is a 3' poly-A tail. Structural proteins are encoded in the 5' region of the genome and non-structural at the 3' end. This is the same for other virus. The viral particles themselves are not enveloped and are icosahedral in structure."

I interrupted. "I know icosahedral is a convex polyhedron with 20 faces, 30 edges, and 12 vertices. But you lost me with the rest."

"I see. Well the interesting part is that this virus is over 10,000 nt long and most of the modifications are in the poly-A tail. Without getting into the technicalities of what the poly-A tail does, this is where they have bioengineered the control of how long the virus will live. Both the rhinovirus from the sample from Bolivia and the norovirus samples from ADX Florence prison use this same RNA modification. We are seeing a similar modification in the two different bioengineered bacteria in the UK and South African prisons.

"The part we still are totally unable to figure out is

how the virus and bacteria are confined to a specific area. It is as if they are able to engineer in three-dimensional coordinates."

Abbey said, "Mia, have they looked to see if it resembles any known magnetotactic bacteria?"

"Yes. They're looking at it, but all known magnetotactic bacteria contain fixed magnet crystals that force the bacteria into alignment, even dead cells align, just like a compass needle. What we are seeing is more like migratory birds that allow the virus and bacteria to detect a magnetic field to perceive altitude and location. Nobody has done anything even close to this before."

I asked, "What about vaccine or treatment method?"

"Vaccines are typically designed for a specific virus or group of virus as is done annually for flu shots. A vaccine can probably be developed for the two we have samples of but it seems they can modify a whole host of virus and bacteria. By the time we identify the new one it is too late to create a vaccine."

I said, "Again it sounds like the perfect bioterror weapon. How about the delivery method?"

Carol spoke up. "CDC is quite sure the birth control substance was delivered in the water supply system of the schools. They consider that the most likely delivery method for the virus and bacteria outbreaks but are still working on it."

"Mitch, you and Ned keep working on the money angle. It's clear the prison outbreaks were some kind of test or demonstration. If they need money they are probably looking for buyers. We know they are desperate for money because they are trying to sell the stolen ancient manuscripts. Buyer and seller have to transact somehow, maybe we can get a lead that way.

"Chad, your Agency or the FBI or some one of our government agencies must be setting up a sting operation on this."

Chad was shaking his head. I said, "Right, they're not going to share any info on that with us." He smiled. "Let's hope they figure it out so we can be done with this mess."

Next I said, "Mia, there can't be that many scientists that can do this type of work. These people must have been educated and trained somewhere. They have to be working somewhere with the required equipment. Some list of companies must have made and sold the required equipment. Work with Ned and Mitch to help them check every possibility. Start in the Netherlands and then countries around the Netherlands.

"OK, anything else, anybody? We'll touch base tomorrow."

I wanted to talk to Major Campbell alone. Chad and Major Campbell were talking. Abbey came up and began asking about our Europol meeting. I pretended to be busy checking messages on my phone.

I looked up as if I'd just read something new. "Ian, when you're done can I have a word with you?"

Abbey looked back and forth between us. She knew me too well or I was just a poor actor. I reached out and squeezed her arm low down hidden from the others' view.

Chad finished and left. I didn't want to overly worry Abbey but I could not see how to get her out of the room without an awkward scene.

I closed the door. "Ian, someone had to tip the bombers off. We flew by private jet and were taken straight to the company facility by private car. We hadn't been here a day. We hadn't been out of the facility. Abbey made the dinner plans only hours before we left. How did they know what water taxi we would take or even that we would go by water? It takes time to organize a bombing like that. It takes professionals."

Major Campbell stopped me. "I know. Abbey, how did you book the reservation for the diner and water taxi?"

"I called the people who man the reception desk. They told us to ask for whatever help we needed. I did go online and check to see if Zeezout's had open tables."

I said, "Major, you knew there was a security breach. The quick spotting of Abbey in South Africa at the elephant conference, all the stepped-up security at the ranch, and having Abbey carry a gun. What the hell is going on?"

He said, "Walter was suspicious something was wrong from the resistance our company was getting from some parts of the government on the validity of the connections our software was revealing. It seemed like more than just interagency rivalry.

"When we started to find the bioterror aspects he got more pushback. Once you began to zero in on the Netherlands as the top place to investigate, certain government agencies that had been opposed to buying the company software were now urging NSA to buy it."

Abbey broke in. "How could Walter possibly know that?"

"Since Walter told me to fully brief you two... Falone Advanced Technologies' cyber-security division currently has a contract to test internal government communication systems. Walter had Elizabeth set up a program to examine any communication that NSA had that related to this work."

It didn't sound legal to me but I kept my mouth shut.

He went on. "Some agency or some part of some agency is involved with this. Until now Walter thought it was probably a sting operation to catch whoever it is red-handed and they didn't want us to mess it up. But no legitimate operation would blow up a water taxi killing five people."

I said, "Could it be they warned the bad guys like they had in South Africa but instead of just disappearing they decided to kill us?"

"Let's hope that's it."

I didn't like his answer. I hated to think it but I had to ask. "What about Chad? He is the only one who knew our exact plans in advance. Do we even know his real name? If Abbey hadn't decided to take a walk he could have easily made an excuse not to go back with us and if it is the CIA they would have him out of the country in no time with a brand-new identity."

"We don't think it's Chad."

I said, "Why? And 'we don't think so' isn't that reassuring."

"The communications we have analyzed within the NSA don't indicate the CIA."

I said, "Do we even know Chad is with the CIA or is he with another government agency? Plus how else could they know what our plans were on such short notice?"

"We are working on that. Rob, I understand this is all very disturbing. I'll know more in a day or two. Meet with Europol, see what you can find out. You won't be able to pretend to be agents for a prospective buyer of the stolen manuscripts but maybe you'll learn something from them. Let's talk tonight, now I need to go meet the police."

He left and I sat down. After a minute Abbey sat as well. Finally I said, "This isn't like the trouble we had the other times we worked for Walter. It might be our own government trying to kill us. Before we had real archaeological work to do. That work had real value of its own. We have none of that here. I feel like we are the tethered goats just being used to draw the lion in close enough to shoot it. No one cares much what happens to the goats."

Our meeting with Europol wasn't very productive. We were given the general background on the black market sales of ancient and rare manuscripts in Europe. One of the volumes that we had on our list had been recovered and returned. They said the sale was done through several middlemen. Very friendly and professional but not much help.

After our meeting we took the elevator back up to our rooms. Major Campbell met us as we got off.

He said, "Follow me, please."

I looked at Abbey, shrugged my shoulders, and we followed him around a corner to the service elevator. We got in and he pushed the button for the basement. He didn't say anything and so we didn't say anything.

We followed him out of the elevator and to an underground garage. There was a Range Rover waiting. Abbey and I got in the back and Major Campbell took the front passenger seat.

Finally he said, "Sorry for the mysterious departure but we have rather a problem in our facility. The building was bugged and it looks like Abbey is being tracked."

She held up her arm. He went on, "That's right, the Radio Frequency Identification tag we installed before you went to South Africa. We need to take care of that."

I had visions of him pulling out a knife and cutting it out of her arm. But he took an electronic device and held it over her arm where the RFID was implanted.

"That will deactivate it. We can remove it later. Now let's have your cellphones."

Funny how threatening it is to give up your cellphone. Before they were invented I was perfectly comfortable going all over the world with no phone.

I said, "It hasn't been out of my possession."

Abbey asked, "StingRay?"

I said, "What?"

And Major Campbell said, "We think so. Rob, Sting-Ray is an IMSI-catcher, a controversial cellular phone surveillance device. It was originally developed for counterterrorism purposes by the military; it works by broadcasting powerful signals that cause nearby cellphones to transmit their IMSI number, which is a phone's unique ID number. It pretends to be a normal cellphone tower. Once the phone is connected to the device, there is no way for the user to know that they are being tracked.

"These devices are in widespread use by local and state law enforcement agencies across Canada, the United

States, and the United Kingdom. It isn't that hard to get your hands on the equipment. We will check the phones out and get them back to you with some better software. It isn't foolproof but it should help."

He removed the SIM cards from our phones.

I noticed we had gotten onto route A13 and the sign said 25km to The Hague.

He continued. "It should only be about half an hour. Relax and enjoy the scenery. Once we arrive we will have lots of time for questions."

I looked at Abbey. "What do you think of Texas now?" It was an old joke from the first time we went to work for Walter. She gave me her big warm smile and then we did what we were told and enjoyed the scenery.

We came into the center of the city and then slowed to turn right down an alley. I looked at the building, the address was Lange Voorhout 10, the sign said British Embassy. We drove to a gate, it opened, and we drove to an underground parking area. OK, I was surprised.

Major Campbell got out and opened our door. Only then did I notice that the back door couldn't be opened from the inside. Maybe just the childproof button was on. I tried not to let my imagination run away with me.

A woman with short black hair, dressed in a dark suit, asked us to follow her. We went to an elevator and went up. While we were going up, Major Campbell handed her our phones. Next we entered a very British-looking conference room. On the far wall was a large portrait of the Queen. On the other walls hung paintings of eighteenth-century English country scenes. Walter was sitting with a gentleman with silver hair. They both stood.

Walter said, "Abbey, Rob, how nice to see you. Let me introduce you to Brigadier Sir Sinclair Cumming. I thought perhaps he could help us with our current situation."

"Please call me Sinclair" was his response.

After we all shook hands, I asked, "What exactly is our current situation?"

He spoke up again. "That does seem to be the crucial question. Please sit down."

Major Campbell put a metal device on the table. It was the diameter of a half-dollar and about a quarter-inch thick.

He said, "This is how we believe your exact plans for last night were discovered. It is a bug we found attached to the underside of the phone system at the reception area of our facility. Whoever was monitoring the device would know the arrangements made from that phone. We are working on how it got there."

Sinclair picked it up and turned it over in his hand. "It's made in China and you can get them online. It has a range of about a kilometer but you could set up a repeater station within that distance or a recorder and the operator wouldn't need to be anywhere close to it. The battery might last a month. I doubt you will be able to trace it."

I said, "So Chad isn't our problem."

"We don't see anything that indicates he is involved," Walter said. "But as Major Campbell discussed with you, it appears that some part of the US government is involved. We don't know if they were directly involved in trying to have you killed or not. Someone tipped off the contact that Abbey was to meet in South Africa.

"The CIA head of station in Johannesburg turned his group inside out and concluded it couldn't be any of his people. I tend to believe him. Perhaps whoever it is just tipped them off again and they arranged the bombing. It would support your theory the Netherlands is their base of operation."

I said, "Whoever it was only had a few hours to organize, make a bomb, and get it on the water taxi. The timing had to be just right. I don't know but it would seem like fast work even for a well-organized criminal group. Unless they knew of our plans before we left or were tracking Abbey in Peru and planned to kill us the first chance they got. I can't imagine it is easy to get explosives in Europe. Do we know what the explosive was?"

Sinclair said, "We don't know the exact type but watching the video of the explosion, our analysts believe it was a military-grade explosive. There are a lot of weapons floating around the Mideast now. Getting explosives wouldn't be hard and it would be only a little harder to smuggle them in with the right connections.

"But you're correct. It appears very well organized and quickly executed. That indicates very professional criminals or government help."

The more I heard the worse I felt. I said, "So what happens now?"

Walter said, "That is up to you two. I can arrange for you to go back to Ithaca or even Mongolia if you want and be done with this whole thing. I'll also arrange security but I suspect once you stop pushing, you will be left alone."

Abbey interrupted. "What happens to our investigation?"

"They murdered one of my employees. We will continue. Law enforcement here will be fully investigating the explosion with two people dead. The outbreak of bioengineered diseases at the prisons has lots of governments involvement. The software predicts more to come."

Abbey interrupted Walter again. "So Ned, Mitch, Mia, and Dr. Lord continue to work on this?"

"I will let Mia decide what she wants to do. It is up to the CDC what Dr. Lord does and where she works. I believe we can protect Ned and Mitch at the ranch in Peru. Their work is in cyberspace."

Abbey said, "We'll stay or at least I will. They tried to kill us. I'm not running away and worrying that they might come after me later."

I said, "If she stays I stay. Are we to be the tethered goat to attract the lions or do you have a plan for us?"

Major Campbell looked at his phone and frowned. "Ned is signaling an emergency message."

He looked Sinclair and said, "Ned is a bit excitable."

I smiled as he spoke into his phone. "Ned, I'm putting you on speakerphone. I'm here with Walter, Abbey, Rob, and a friend of mine. He has the proper security clearance.

"We are a little pressed for time, what is it?"

"Hi, everyone, wow where to start. The software predicted a big event in the Middle East. Chad told Mitch that the Taiwanese intelligence service traced large amounts of money being transferred into various companies controlled by the Bamboo Union. Totaling tens of millions of dollars. He gave her bank codes and she's working on tracing them."

Major Campbell asked. "Anything else?"

"I'm tracking rumors of disease outbreaks in Iran. Mitch and I are trying to refine the software search. Mitch is trying to get Elizabeth to help. She invented the software and is way better at this shit than I am."

"Hold on, Ned," Major Campbell said. "I just got a text from Elizabeth in Houston. I'm going to conference her in."

Elizabeth's cheery voice came out of the speaker. "Hi everyone, I miss you." Then she turned to business. "I reset the search focusing on Iran, just bits of info but it looks like more disease outbreaks. The outbreaks appear to be in the Iranian provinces of Kermanshah and Kurdistan. That's about all I know now."

Walter said, "Thank you, Elizabeth. Ned, focus on this and ask Mitch to stay on the money trail. Call Elizabeth when you need to but she already has a lot on her plate."

Major Campbell switched off his phone.

I said, "Those two provinces, Kermanshah and Kurdistan, isn't that where the Iranians fired the missiles against ISIS sites in Syria? Deir ez-Zor area, if I remember correctly." Why I remember certain things is a mystery to me.

Sinclair said, "The provinces of Kermanshah and Kurdistan contain Revolutionary Guard major missile bases as well as missile research and development complexes. The missiles reportedly were Zolfaghar type upgraded Fateh-110 with a longer range and optional cluster munitions warhead with a range of about 470 miles."

Abbey spoke up. "The ones we are trying to find appeared short on money, the Bamboo Union is reportedly very upset about not being paid for blowing up the warehouse full of ivory in Haiphong. At the same time the software indicates a disease outbreak in Iran, the Bamboo Union gets all the money it is due and more.

"Israel, Saudi Arabia, UAE, and maybe even the US wouldn't be sorry to see trouble for the Iranian missile program."

We were all thinking the same thing. I said it first. "My money would be on the Saudis, their young powerful prince seemed a bit reckless."

The others agreed. "So now what do we do?" I said.

Walter said, "You and Abbey stay here a few days. Sinclair will provide accommodations for you. He will arrange it so your phones can connect with us. Major Campbell will have your laptops checked and then sent to you along with your phones. We will decide when you can safely be moved."

Walter was smiling when he said this but I didn't feel any better. I said, "What about Mia and Dr. Lord? Are they safe?"

"Major Campbell has already arranged for more security for them. Things are moving fast now. You two have done great work. Keep digging, work with Mitch and Ned."

I asked, "Where do Chad and the CIA fit in now?"

Major Campbell spoke up. "I'll work the bombing and local leads with him. I'll get better cooperation with the local authorities having the CIA with me."

Walter stood up, shook everyone's hand, and asked Sinclair to take good care of us. With that he left followed by Major Campbell.

"Let me show you to your quarters. It is a restricted area. I'll be one of the very few people you see while you're here," Sinclair said.

He led us down a corridor. No one was around. We rode the elevator to the basement level. Again we saw no one. He unlocked a door and we entered a small hallway with another locked door at the end. The door behind us locked before he unlocked the door in front of us. He opened that door and we stepped into a small room with no windows. It had a table, desk, couch, a few chairs, TV, and small kitchen area. There was a short corridor with doors off each side.

Sinclair said, "These are your bedrooms. It is a bit stark but the bar is well stocked. Everything will be delivered to the short hallway we came in. Once the outer door is locked you can retrieve what was left. At night lock your bedroom doors. The main room will be cleaned each night and the kitchen restocked. Don't leave any identifying items out at night. Safety first, I'm afraid."

Abbey said, "What about clothes?"

"I believe Major Campbell will attend to that," he said. "I'll pop in from time to time to check on you. You can get lots done. No interruptions." Then he left.

Abbey looked around the room and I went to the bar. What time was it anyway? I looked at my watch, almost 6:00PM. Good, definitely time for a drink. Sinclair was true to his word about the bar being well stocked. Lots of those little hotel bottles of booze plus a good assortment of wine. I opened the fridge to find cold beer but no chilled white wine. I stuck two bottles of white in the fridge and opened a third.

"Abbey, do want your wine warm or on ice?"

"Lots of ice, please. This is a creepy place and it is even creepier thinking we need to be here because someone in our government wants us dead. Is this where they keep the secret agents? Does every embassy have one of these facilities?"

I handed her a tall glass of ice and wine then got a beer for myself. "I don't know. Cheers."

I took a big sip of beer. "Since we decided to stay I guess for now we wait."

That black mood was coming over me again but I tried not to show it. I looked in the cupboard. There was quite an assortment of snacks including chocolate-and-pistachio biscotti and "McVitie's Digestives Thins. Delicately thin and crispy biscuits, smothered in a layer of luxuriously smooth chocolate," the package said. Neither of those seemed to go with beer so I took out some mixed nuts and a bag of chips.

"So, Prof, what do we do now?"

"We enjoy our drinks and wait for our computers and phones to arrive," I said setting the snacks on the table and sitting down.

Abbey was walking around the room, she finally pulled out a chair and sat putting her feet up on another chair. She reached behind her back and set the Beretta Nano automatic on the table. I didn't like Abbey carrying a gun even though her quick thinking and proficiency with guns had saved my life more than once.

I pushed the bowl of nuts towards her. I wanted to talk about something besides what was going on here. "I miss Beast." It was lame but it was all I could think to say.

She smiled her warm smile and said, "We'll get this sorted out and life can go back to normal." She raised her glass to me, took a drink, and said, "As if I even know what normal is."

Somehow I felt better. There was a TV so I turned it on and got another beer.

They delivered us dinner and we went to bed early. The next morning there was not only breakfasts but our laptops, phones, and clothes.

I looked at my watch, not quite 8:00AM so about midnight in Peru.

Abbey must have read my mind and said, "They're night owls. I'll call them."

She powered up her computer and used the company's secure videoconferencing link. Ned looked wide awake and was almost bouncing in his chair.

He said, "Major Campbell stashed you away. He won't tell anybody where you are. When Mitch pressed him he said if something happened to him Walter would handle things. Scary shit. I've never heard him talk that way. It even shut Mitch up.

"Speaking of shit the bodies are piling up at those Revolutionary Guard major missile bases in Iran. The government has been trying to cover it up but the chatter on the web is thousands dead on the bases. But it doesn't seem to be spreading beyond the bases. And get this, the rumor is no one who has gone into the bases has come out. The outside is now guarded by soldiers in full biohazard suits."

I said, "Can we patch Chad into this call? The Agency must know something."

Before Abbey could say anything Ned was on it saying, "He'll be with us in a minute."

The screen split and Chad's face appeared next to Ned's.

Ned was still having trouble containing himself. He jumped in again. "I'm hearing thousands dead, what have they told you?"

"Probably not as much as they know but they're reading me in with updates almost every hour and all our intelligence services are all over this 24/7. The missile bases as well as missile research and development complexes in Kermanshah and Kurdistan provinces are all experiencing a deadly disease outbreak. The Revolutionary Guard and regular military are on alert.

"The area is sealed off. It appears that anyone going in now is wearing biohazard suits. Based on communication intercepts it is estimated the outbreak started two days ago. The death toll is unknown but suspected to be in the thousands. The affected complexes together probably have 10,000 workers. Top engineers, scientists, highly skilled workers, and top Revolutionary Guard officials all work there. Plus no one has come out alive and no one outside these complexes is reported as being sickened.

"It sure looks like the ones we have been tracking. Iran isn't saying anything yet. It appears they are worried about setting off a mass panic in the country. There is a rumor spreading that a Revolutionary Guard bioweapons program caused it. For the moment the government seems more worried that rumor could set off mass riots. Iran has been plagued by worker strikes, mass protests over food price increases, unemployment, and the like.

"Our government's fear is it won't be long before they get around to blaming Israel or the US. The US and many other countries have offered assistance but Iran hasn't even officially admitted it has a problem."

I said, "Whoever paid for the attack would love to spread the rumor it was the Revolutionary Guard bioweapons program caused the outbreak. I suppose several other countries would like to see that rumor take hold as well."

The screen split again and Mitch was on the screen with Chad and Ned.

She said, "Lots of money around. The money flowing to companies controlled by the Bamboo Union came from banks in Dubai and Abu Dhabi in the UAE and Beirut in Lebanon. I assume they are all shell companies. I'll send Chad the list, maybe the Agency knows something about them.

"There is also money flowing into the Netherlands from the same banks but it is bounced around through several offshore companies. There were no Saudi banks I've found so my bet is the Saudis are behind this. The more problems Iran has at home the better for Saudi Arabia.

"New money is also flowing into radical animal rights groups."

Ned interrupted. "Professor Wang is calling in. I'll patch her in. It is audio only."

Ned quickly told her who was on the call.

She said, "I guess you all know as much or more than I do about what is going on in Iran. Various agencies of the US and several other countries have briefed the World

Health Organization. WHO has offered to send a team but Iran has refused saying there is no need.

"I've been coordinating with Dr. Lord and the CDC based on what we have seen from the other outbreaks, and the engineered virus and bacteria samples have shown one significant common element. All these engineered viruses and bacteria die out after several generations of reproducing. If this is true the contagion at the complexes in Kermanshah and Kurdistan should die out in a couple more days."

I said, "As we have said, the perfect bioweapon. It can be engineered to a specific place for a limited time period and made in either a lethal or non-lethal form.

"Mitch, how many companies or research facilities are there in the Netherlands that have the sophistication to do anything close to this? Make a list and then Chad, maybe you can get law enforcement agencies to put enough manpower on it to check them all out in detail."

Mitch said, "I can make a list but the Netherlands may just be the banking center used as a cover. Plus pharmaceutical companies are all secretive about their research. Or it could be hidden in among other research and only a very few experts could spot it."

My mood was getting blacker. Why did Walter get us into this? What good was I doing?

"Make the list, Mitch, and we'll see." A plan started to form in my mind, half-baked and perhaps foolish.

I joked about it when we arrived but it may be the best we have for getting a lead. I realized I had abruptly stopped talking.

Abbey said, "Whatever it is, Prof, I don't like it."

"Reading my mind again. Maybe the best way forward is the tethered goat."

Ned jumped in. "Cool, like in *Jurassic Park* when they tied the goat up for the raptor to get. I can still hear the girl screaming."

Mitch said, "Shut up, Ned."

Abbey said, "Major Campbell will never allow it."

I said, "They could set up protective surveillance."

"No top people are going to come after us. Just some thugs from the Bamboo Union or some other hired guns. They probably don't even know who they are working for."

Abbey was right as usual. I said, "All right, contact us if something comes up and we'll see what ideas Major Campbell has."

I looked at Abbey. She shook her head but didn't say anything and started reading something on her computer. Not knowing what else to do I went to take a shower.

Later Sinclair Cumming came in but had little news for us. Abbey asked about a place to work out or take a run. Sinclair said there was a fitness center in the embassy and he would have it cleared for us from two thirty until four.

The next two days went boringly by with not much new happening. The next morning at about 10AM Major Campbell came in with two of his security men and Sinclair.

He said, "Get your things, we are leaving. It looks like we finally got a break."

"What is it?" I said.

"Pack your stuff, we can talk on the way."

We didn't have much so it didn't take long. Sinclair led

us down the empty hall back to the basement garage. It struck me that in the entire British embassy Sinclair might be the only one who knew we were here and most employees didn't know anyone was here.

When we reached the car Sinclair said, "I trust our next meeting will be more enjoyable for you. Godspeed with your work."

With that and a shake of our hands we were put in the back of the car.

As the car drove out of the basement I said, "Major, what's up?"

"It appears we may have located the laboratory that produced or at least help develop the engineered bacteria and virus."

I interrupted Major Campbell and said, "Where?"

He went on and didn't seem disturbed by my interruption. "In an industrial area outside Amsterdam a specialty biotech firm was acquired by a major pharmaceutical company about a month ago. They seem to have found an additional laboratory in a subbasement that was never disclosed during the purchase evaluation. They remembered the inquiry by Interpol and contacted the National Police. The police have secured the lab and a team from the WHO including Professor Wang is heading there now. We will meet them."

A car with the markings of the National Police pulled in front of us with its lights flashing and its siren wailing. We closed in behind and accelerated to keep up.

Abbey said, "What is the name of the biotech firm?"

"Fryrtex Pharmaceuticals," Major Campbell answered.

Abbey sent a text and then started searching the web on her phone.

She started reading. "Fryrtex was founded in 2003 by Bram Visser. Professor Visser was one of the pioneer researchers using an explicit strategy of rational drug design rather than combinatorial chemistry. He then went on to become known as one of the leading experts in bioinformatics and whole transcriptome shotgun sequencing and various applications of multiplexed in-situ hybridization."

She kept scrolling down the screen on her phone.

"Here are a few other areas the company and Professor Visser claim to be expert in. Gene-editing technology, magnetotactic bacteria that orient themselves along the magnetic field lines of Earth's magnetic field, molecular mechanosynthesis, viral phage therapy, and a few other related areas. It looks like his company worked in all the areas needed to bioengineer just what we've been seeing."

I looked out the window, we must have been going close to 90 miles an hour. We'd be there soon if we didn't crash.

We were waved through the main gate of the Fryrtex Pharmaceuticals facility and drove to a building with multiple official-looking cars parked in front. An Interpol officer spoke to Major Campbell and then took us to a conference room.

I saw Mia with a group I assumed were WHO scientists. Some had hazmat kits. There were numerous metal boxes that I assumed contained instruments. It looked like company officials and Interpol officers were arguing about something.

Mia came over. "The company that bought Fryrtex says that the lab they found in the subbasement was never revealed during the purchase negotiations. Most Fryrtex employees didn't even know it existed and the few that did claim they've never been in it and it was Visser's personal lab. The company officials say they see nothing sinister about it, just the type of lab equipment you'd expect in a biotech firm and not much different than the equipment in other Fryrtex labs."

It was finally agreed that hazmat suits weren't needed and we were led to an elevator that below the floor buttons had a key slot. One of the company officials put a key in and the elevator went down. He explained it was a subbasement.

When the door opened there was a short hall with a metal door at the end of it. The door was open and we walked in.

I said to Major Campbell, "No crime scene protocol?"

"When it was found no one thought it was a big deal. Just Visser's private lab. Nobody spotted anything out of the ordinary. People started taking pieces of equipment they wanted for other labs. I don't think they will find anything."

I asked, "Where is Professor Visser?"

Major Campbell said, "Now that is the $64,000 question. No one seems to know. He hasn't been seen since shortly after he closed on the sale of his company."

Abbey was talking to one of the Fryrtex employees. I drifted in that direction.

"What's up, Abbey?"

"Most of the lab equipment is in excellent condition but none of the computers work."

She went over to a laptop and tried to turn it on. Nothing. She turned it over and ran her hand over the seams. Then she found a small screwdriver and began taking the back off.

A police officer came over. "What are you doing?"

"They said all the equipment was working except the computers. Let's see if we can figure out a way," Abbey said.

Another officer came over with Major Campbell. He nodded his head yes.

Abbey took the back off. The memory chips were black and looked melted.

I said, "I've heard of microchips that dissolve in water but this doesn't look like that."

Abbey said, "Actually at Cornell they developed a chip that self-destructs when a certain current is run through it. I suspect this is something like that. I don't think we will find anything here."

Chad strolled in. I said, "Joining the party?"

"This was the spot but they won't find much. The officials will comb through everything in great detail over the next few weeks. If there is anything I'll hear about it."

He turned to Major Campbell and said, "My boss has got a message from your boss. We are all going to Texas. Don't ask me why."

Major Campbell looked at his phone, no signal, and said, "Let's get out of here. I need to call Walter."

I said, "What about Mia?"

He looked around. "Best let her stay with WHO for

now. She still can be helpful to them."

Abbey came over from examining the laptop. "What's up?"

"It looks like we are going to Texas."

"Do you know why?"

"I have a guess and it's that Walter sold his super software package to the government and now they want us out of the picture," I said.

When we reached the ground floor Major Campbell sent a text and went with Chad to talk to the lead Interpol detective.

He came back and said, "Let's go. Walter wants us at his ranch in Houston."

I started to say something and Major Campbell put up his hand and said, "Ask Walter when we get there, I don't know."

He seemed miffed.

We got in the back of the car and Major Campbell got in front with the driver. He was busy texting. Chad was apparently going to make his own way to Texas.

I looked at Abbey. She smiled and took out her phone and began to type. So I watched the scenery out the window. Well maybe I could go home soon.

A jet was waiting for us at the airport. I got on and fell asleep shortly after takeoff.

Chapter 15

We had landed at Ellington Airport and taxied to the Falone Advanced Technologies hangar. A van was waiting to take us to Walter's ranch about fifty minutes away.

As we turned up a dirt road to the ranch I remembered the first time Abbey and I came here. So much has happened since that day we interviewed with Walter.

The dirt road became a paved driveway about a quarter mile in. There was a security detail that waved us through. That wasn't there the other times I'd been here. The ranch was a complex of buildings. No big gate or security fences. There was a main house with a carriage house on one side and a guest cottage on the other. Well, if you could call a place that had to be over 6,000 square feet a cottage. Behind these buildings were several buildings that were the working part of the ranch.

We drove straight to the guesthouse. It was an interesting arrangement, work-professional and homey at the same time. The rooms were more like suites or apartments.

Abbey and I had suites on opposite sides of the center area. The great room had a full kitchen and dining area towards the back and a conference table with several workstations towards the front. This opened out onto a patio and swimming pool area. Off to one side of the great room was another room with a bar, pool table, darts, and several large flat-screen TVs. A different architectural style than the Peru guesthouse but functionally almost the same.

Abbey and I got out, our bags were brought in, and Major Campbell said he would be in touch shortly and went to the security building. He had living quarters in another area of the ranch.

I said, "I'm changing and going for a walk. Do you want to come?"

"No, I'm going to go for a run. I need to burn off some frustration."

So Abbey was feeling it as well. I put on blue jeans, a golf shirt, and sneakers and began walking down the trail that started next to the pool house. A few minutes later Abbey ran by me saying, "See you later, slowpoke." I just kept walking. The trails had a park-like feel down to signposts with photos of the wildlife and detailed descriptions. There was extensive signage at the intersection of the trails from the house and the guesthouse. I stopped to read it just as I had the first time I was here. Actually I'd only been to Walter's Texas ranch a few times, while I'd spent months at the ranch in Peru.

The ranch consists of 3,200 acres and several habitats, including wetland aquatic and hardwood forest. I walked along a trail and then cut over to the working part of the ranch. There were cattle, of course. No self-respecting Texas billionaire can have a ranch without a few thousand head of cattle. There were also large herds of sheep and goats grazing. I came to the riding complex. If we were here for a few days I'd see if we could do some riding. After the months we spent on horseback in Mongolia both Abbey and I were horse lovers and strong riders. Beyond the stable was another set of barns and fenced areas. There were llamas, alpacas, and guinea pigs, now those are not the Texas rancher's usual livestock but much the same as when I first came here.

Walter had told me that the livestock was work related. They were developing remote sensing of animals, primarily wildlife. The company had a team working on large-scale detailed noninvasive tracking of wildlife in Africa and Asia that could be invaluable to saving species while allowing the people in these areas to continue economic development. It wasn't just tracking and counting herds from aerial or satellite photos. They were developing thermal bio-patterns of species; remote vegetation and water consumption assessments in real time as herds migrate; and patterns of interaction of a particular herd and predators, in real time. Adapting what the company had developed for the mining and petroleum exploration industry to wildlife management could be transformative. If I remember correctly, they were mostly obtaining thermal body signatures for the animals here in a controlled environment. Which is hard to do in the wild. It probably made the whole ranch a tax write-off.

I checked my watch and decided to head back to shower.

When I came out Abbey was on her computer. She said, "Prof, you have to see this."

I said, "It seems like a lot more security people here than the last time we were here."

She just shrugged her shoulders so I sat next to her at the table. She turned her laptop my way. There was a picture was of an old Jeep rattled with bullets and three bloody bodies inside. The caption read "Elephant poachers and soon their families will join them in hell."

She clicked to the next picture. It showed a man hanging by his feet. He was naked, his throat had been cut, and his genitals cut off and stuffed in his mouth. The caption read "An ivory smuggler soon all four of his sons will be dead."

Next was a longer-range view of an airport front entrance. There was a bloody body with police all around. The caption read "Chinese ivory buyer. Many more to die."

I said, "Where is this?"

"It is Jomo Kenyatta International Airport in Nairobi, Kenya. Ned said he is getting dozens of reports of killings at all points of the illegal ivory trade: poachers, middlemen, buyers, shippers, and even ivory carvers in Asia who carve illegal ivory.

"The software predicts lots more incidents to come. Mitch is seeing all sorts of money movement and not just to the Bamboo Union."

I said, "So the money Professor Visser, if he is our bad guy, got for the bio-attack on the missile research and development complexes in Kermanshah and Kurdistan provinces is being used to kill off poachers. Plus what he got for the sale of the company, he could have hundreds of millions. You can cause a lot of mischief with that much money.

"Let's have Mitch see if she can trace the money Professor Visser got from the sale of Fryrtex Pharmaceuticals."

Abbey said, "No time like the present."

She sent a text then went over and powered up the videoconference screen in the work area.

A minute later Mitch's image popped up on the screen. She said, "In Texas and out of hiding. What gives?"

Abbey said, "Are you up to speed on Fryrtex Pharmaceuticals and Professor Visser?"

"Ya. Major Campbell filled Ned and me in. My bet, he's our guy."

I broke in. "Can you get a line on where the money went from the buyout?"

"I can tell you where it didn't go," Mitch said. "Our Professor Visser didn't get a dime of it. The company was practically insolvent, all the purchase funds went to assuming debts and paying off creditors.

"It does look like Visser made a bundle from the attack on the Iranian missile research and development complexes. Plus he could be selling his technology. Major Campbell said nothing resembling the technology of the attacks we've been following was part of what was acquired from Fryrtex Pharmaceuticals. Yet lots of the things the company did were in the areas of research that would be needed to bioengineer the bugs we're seeing.

"Lots of money going to radical animal rights groups and from what I can tell the Bamboo Union got way more than they earned just blowing up the warehouse full of ivory."

I said, "Was the Bamboo Union behind the poacher killings Abbey has been showing me? Also where is Ned?"

"To answer your second question, I sent him a text a minute ago and told him to get his ass over here. As for your first question, I don't know, Ned was keeping track of who's getting killed and who's doing it. He's the self-proclaimed cyber warrior," Mitch replied.

Just then Ned jumped into the chair next to Mitch. He said, "What did you do to piss off Major Campbell? He had a million questions and chewed my ass for not having answers."

"He doesn't like when his people get murdered and he didn't seem to like whatever Walter told him when we were all ordered to Texas.

"I've got some questions for you but I'll try leaving the ass chewing to Major Campbell. What's the status of the bio-attack on the Iranian missile research and development complexes? Mia said that all the engineered viruses and bacteria we previously encountered seemed to die out in about a week."

Ned started bouncing in his chair. "Lots of stuff on the web. Dozens of conspiracy theories out there. The most interest thing is the campaign to say it was Iranian bio-weapon research run amok. It's all over the web. Someone is publishing the names of all the people who are in the complex. Satellite images show everyone moving inside the complexes in biohazard suits. I only can access commercial satellite pictures. I'm sure our government has far better. All the bodies were moved inside buildings.

"They have the area for miles around the complexes sealed off by the military. No journalists, no photographers. Crowds are forming demanding to know what is happening to their relatives who are in the complex. The government isn't saying anything. That is causing people to believe the wildest of rumors.

"Plus there is an organized campaign to spread fear and that it was Iran's fault. Not just online and social media but on the ground. Someone is paying to spread the rumors on the ground. Kermanshah and Kurdistan provinces both border Iraq. Most people in Kurdistan province are Kurds, and the majority of them are Shafi'i Sunni Muslims. They have no love for the Persians Shiite majority that controls the military and the government. Kurdish traders from Iraq that travel across the border are saying that Iran's government is covering up the death of tens of thousands caused by the Revolutionary Guard biological weapons program that has contaminated the scientists working on the project, and they spread it to the rest of the government complexes. That is why the military has sealed off the area. There are printed pamphlets written in the local Sorani-Kurdish dialect with pictures of the military checkpoints and satellite photos.

"The same tactic is being used with the Azerbaijani Turks minorities in Kurdistan province and the Yarsanists minority in Kermanshah province. Now the Sunni Arab states such as Bahrain, Egypt, Saudi Arabia, and the United Arab Emirates are having their official news agencies broadcast the story saying the suspected cause is Iran's bioweapon program. The demonstrations are bigger every day. The ayatollahs must be shitting their robes."

I stopped him. "Nothing has spread outside the compounds, right?"

"It doesn't seem like it."

"What about the animal rights groups?"

Ned thought a minute. "Lots and lots of money going to both radical and traditional animal rights groups that Mitch identifies. The groups getting the money all focus on endangered species. Those photos I sent Abbey were almost certainly the work of the Bamboo Union and only because they were paid a bundle. Now there are copycat killings and lots of nervous people all along the illegal ivory trade."

"Ned, do you think you can figure out where Professor Visser is?"

He looked disappointed. Perhaps this was below the dignity of a cyber warrior but he said he'd try.

Mitch elbowed him in the ribs and he said, "OK, any idea where to start?"

I said, "There must be photos of him online someplace, family, friends, favorite vacation spots. Does Fryrtex Pharmaceuticals have facilities in other countries? You're the cyber warrior, you figure it out."

He said, "I'll get on it along with the thousand things Major Campbell gave me to do."

Then he got up and walked away. Mitch just shook her head. "I'll help him. There isn't much more I can do on the money trail." Then she signed off.

I said, "Maybe we'll get lucky and they'll find something."

"That is if Walter still wants up to find something," Abbey said.

"There is that. I wonder where Walter is. Major Campbell didn't seem to know. I'll text Mrs. Lopez."

The reply was immediate. "Come over in half an hour and I'll have dinner for you."

I showed it to Abbey. "Time for a drink, wine?"

She nodded and went to the fridge and poured two glasses.

She held up her glass. "Let's go home."

I drank to that but it didn't turn out to be that simple.

Mrs. Lopez met us at the door to the main house. She had a warm smile and a disarming charm. I knew from experience that she was very sharp, extremely efficient, and could be steely hard if the occasion required it.

"Professor, Abbey, so nice to have you two safely back with us. Oh excuse me, Abbey, you are also a professor now. Walter isn't here yet. Come in and have a drink."

After discussing how her niece and family were doing caring for my place in Ithaca, we exchanged a few more words of greeting and she led us to a sitting room.

When our drinks came Mrs. Lopez said, "Walter thought you might enjoy wandering through his archaeological collection. He has added quite a bit to it since you were last here."

Walter's collection would have been a respectable archaeological gallery in almost any museum. It was filled with expert replicas of pre-Columbian objects acquired at auction by an anonymous bidder and then donated to the Natural History Museum, that anonymous bidder being

Walter. The only original pieces are ones where almost every major museum has fine examples and these would add little or nothing to their collections. Walter felt deeply that these ancient objects should be for many to enjoy and study and not to be hidden away by the rich.

We spent almost an hour examining the collection before Mrs. Lopez returned. She led us to a dining room that was set for two.

"Walter has been further detained and won't be arriving until late tonight," Mrs. Lopez informed us.

Abbey looked at me. I said, "I'm sure we'll enjoy the dinner. Thank you, Mrs. Lopez."

The dinner was excellent but without seeming fancy or in any way over the top. The wine was excellent, perhaps eighty dollars a bottle. It was above my normal price range but not outrageous, especially for a billionaire. Walter seemed to spare no expense for required technology and equipment but no needless frills. The two of us ate without saying much. We were wondering what was next.

We finished, thanked Mrs. Lopez, and left.

I said goodnight to Abbey and went to my room and read.

In the morning I swam and Abbey took a run. I was having coffee when Major Campbell arrived with Chad. With a curt hello he went to the videoconference unit and powered it up. Neither of them looked happy. Once the unit was on, Mitch and Ned were staring at us from the screen.

I sat and said nothing.

Abbey came out of her room, her hair still damp, and said, "That bad?"

As she got herself coffee, Major Campbell said, "Chad,

fill them in on what you have."

"In Holland we have four people killed in a car crash and one person with a broken neck in a canal. Three were outstanding scientists that worked for Fryrtex Pharmaceuticals. The two others are yet to be identified."

I immediately thought of the missing Cornell grad student Justin Barry.

Chad went on. "The CIA believes the three Fryrtex Pharmaceuticals employees worked closely with Professor Visser before he sold the company. Dutch authorities are trying to identify the two bodies in the car that don't appear to have worked for Fryrtex."

I said, "Do we know who was working in Professor Visser's secret lab with him?"

"The Dutch police are questioning company employees now to see what they can find out. Most, if they know anything, say it was Professor Visser's private lab and they don't know anything else."

I broke in again. "Does the Agency have any idea where Professor Visser is?"

Chad gave me his shit-eating grin that I find so annoying. "Not a clue but Ned might."

I looked at Ned on the video screen.

"You asked me to see if I could find Professor Visser so I've been trying. I've hacked into the camera systems in countries where Fryrtex has or had facilities and then fed the camera streams into facial recognition software. Every method has its advantages and disadvantages. Technology companies have amalgamated the traditional 3-D recognition and Skin Textual Analysis. What I've done is combined what our cybersecurity division has with some from the Israeli security company Check Point. Plus I was able to borrow a few things from the Chinese.

"Then I just started hacking as many camera feeds as I could at airports, train stations, ports, etc. It gets easier all the time because all the newer systems use the web, not just a few cameras hooked to a video recorder on site. Automated border control systems or eGates are making it real easy because people have to look right into the camera. It's not like having to pick out someone walking in a crowd in an airport terminal."

Abbey was first to interrupt Ned. "Fascinating, but did you find Professor Visser?"

Ned started bouncing again. "Better, much better, I found Justin Barry."

I thought, interesting, our lost Cornell grad student that was a major reason we got dragged into this mess.

He continued. "According to my calculation I have a 92 percent certainty of a match. He is traveling on a Dutch passport under the name Jan Bakker. In 2007 it was the seventh most common name in the Netherlands. There were then 55,273 people named Bakker in the Netherlands. I didn't check to see how many Bakkers there were worldwide."

Mitch glared over at him. Ned visibly flinched under her stare.

"Anyway I showed it all to Mia and she said she is sure it is Justin. He flew into Perth, Australia, yesterday, or maybe it is today over there, from Hong Kong."

He put up a picture of Justin Barry or Jan Bakker and said, "See, the same initials. I read in a spy novel people often use the same initials with fake names."

I couldn't tell if it was Justin but I'd only seen his Cornell ID photo.

I said, "Why is he on the run? He could just reappear as Justin Barry and who would know what he's been doing?"

Ned jumped in. "He might be running from the same people who killed the other five. Professor Visser is probably killing anyone that knows about his secret work. I saw a movie like this."

Mitch poked him in the ribs.

Chad said, "He is probably right that Justin is on the run. The Agency is trying to track down a missing Georgian researcher from the Tbilisi Institute. They just received a report he has been missing for months."

Mitch cut him off. "I've been following that, the researcher is Alexander Pshavians. He is a professor specializing in bacteriophage, microbiology, and virology at Tbilisi Institute. He was scheduled to deliver a paper in London on viral phage therapy to treat pathogenic bacterial infections. Phages are much more specific than antibiotics. They are typically harmless not only to the host organism, but also to other beneficial bacteria, such as the gut flora, reducing the chances of opportunistic infections.

"Anyway he took an Air France flight to Paris and never made it to London and hasn't been seen since."

I said, "Chad, either Mitch knows more than the CIA or they aren't reading you in on everything."

"Probably both. The only reason the Agency took any notice is the Ministry of Internal Affairs of Georgia put out an official missing person notice to Interpol. The GIS or Georgian Intelligence Service forwarded the notice to the CIA," he replied. "But what else do you know, Mitch?"

"Ned started running the photos we had through his facial recognition software but that is a long shot."

I said, "Have the police ask employees at Fryrtex Pharmaceuticals if they recognize him from the photos we have."

Mitch said, "I bet he's one of your unidentified bodies in the Netherlands."

"Let's find out. Send me the photos," Chad said.

I started thinking out loud. "So is Justin traveling and still working with Professor Visser or is he on the run so he doesn't get killed? Is Visser closing everything down and having anyone who worked on the project with him killed or just eliminating some who think he has gone too far and they were planning to turn him in?"

Major Campbell said, "Alexander Pshavians won't be one of those two unidentified bodies."

He looked as disturbed as I'd ever seen him.

"The CIA knows who they are even if Chad doesn't and the Dutch police are never likely to find out. This whole thing is blowing up and I doubt Walter is going to be able to patch it up.

"It was some intelligence group in the US Defense Department that tried to kill you and succeeded in killing one of my men. They were negotiating with Visser for his bioweapon knowhow. He told them he needed more time. We were getting too close and since we had been authorized to do this from another part of the government someone in the chain of command decided it was easiest just to kill us.

"Then Visser double-crossed them and killed the two agents who were stationed with Visser and negotiating the deal. As the news of what happened in Iran leaked out every major government in the world knew they had a new problem to deal with. The way the rest of the world felt when the US set off the first nuclear bomb.

"The Defense Department all of a sudden told Walter they'd pay his price for the software. They probably realized that it was their best shot at getting Visser and his technology. They threatened to seize it but Walter's company is technically Canadian and he has Canadian citizenship. Plus Walter was careful to make sure the development work was done outside of the US and he has lots of high-level connections."

I said, "Anybody who worked closely with Visser has got to be someone numerous governments would want to get their hands on and I imagine some governments wouldn't be above just grabbing them."

I'd barely finished my sentence when Major Campbell looked at his phone, jumped up, and went to the other side of the room.

He came back. "Get your things, we have to go. They just tried to grab Elizabeth and Walter thinks we may be next.

"Chad, do you want to stay or go with us?"

"I'll stay and see if I can slow them down."

"Don't kill anybody here. I don't want to deal with the paperwork."

Chad answered, "They are supposed to be on the same side as me. I'll try charm."

I looked at Abbey and we each headed to our rooms. It wasn't hard to pack, I'd been living out of one small case for over a week now.

I returned to the center room, unplugged my laptop and slid it into my case. I heard a car door slam. Major Campbell came in and said, "Let's go now. They're at the front gate."

"Who's at the front gate?" Abbey grabbed my arm and pulled me with her to the door.

"Get in the back."

Abbey slid into the back of the Jeep and I followed. Major Campbell got into the driver's seat and headed off towards the complex of barn buildings.

I said, "Where the hell is Walter and where are we going?"

Major Campbell said, "Abbey, under the seat is a SIG Sauer P226R. I don't think we will need it but keep it close."

Abbey felt around and came up with the pistol in a holster. It was the kind Major Campbell usually carried. She methodically checked it, chambered a round, double-checked the safety, set it on the seat next to her, and gave me a big smile.

Abbey's USMC skills had saved my life several times. It felt strange whenever I saw Abbey with a gun. Reassuring and yet sad.

Behind the barn complex we came to a barn converted into a hangar and there was a grass runway. Two men were standing next to a single-engine plane with floats.

Abbey said, "A Cessna 206 with amphibious floats."

Major Campbell said, "Let's go. Get in the back. Abbey, you should bring the pistol."

One of the men took our bags and put them in the back of the plane. He then opened the rear double doors on the right side of the plane. We climbed into the middle seat and then he got into the copilot's seat.

Major Campbell did a quick walk around the plane, got in the pilot's seat, yelled "Clear!" and started the engine.

Abbey looked at her phone and said, "Chad says they are headed our way."

Major Campbell taxied to the end of the grass strip and headed down the runway but he wasn't picking up speed. Abbey saw the look on my face and pointed to the windsock. Right, take off into the wind. He reached the end of the runway, spun the plane around, ran the engine up, checked a few gages and we took off. The runway was surprisingly smooth.

I saw two black SUVs stopped next to the hangar and two men in dark suits were talking to Major Campbell's man. He was shaking his head and holding his hand in a way it was obvious he was saying he didn't know. I thought, why do government agents always wear dark suits?

The plane lifted off and we headed away from the ranch. No hail of bullets followed from the men on the ground.

After a few minutes I shouted, "What now and what just happened?"

The copilot shouted back for us to put on our headsets. I heard Major Campbell say. "Ellington approach control, this is Cessna 9712 X-Ray VFR in route to Pearland Regional Airport." I looked out the window and listened as the flight controller assigned him an altitude, told him about traffic in the area, gave him the winds aloft, and wished him a good day.

After a minute Major Campbell said, "To answer your questions. What now? We get to someplace safe. What just happened? Well we will try to figure that out when we get to someplace safe."

In another few minutes he was talking to the Pearland Regional Airport controller and preparing to land. Abbey had been quietly looking out the window the whole time. The pistol was in the large backpack-style purse she usually carried.

We taxied to the fixed base operator's modest blue one-story terminal building and killed the motor. The copilot got out and headed to the terminal. Before he reached the door Elizabeth came out with a Falone Advanced Technologies security guard on each side of her. All she had with her was a purse and briefcase.

The copilot took the briefcase and opened the plane's back door.

Elizabeth said in her usual cheery voice as she climbed into the third row seat, "Hi Abbey, hello Professor Johnson. It is wonderful to see you two."

There wasn't any hint in her voice or manner that there was anything out of the ordinary.

Before she could say any more the copilot told her to fasten her seatbelt and put on the headphones. As he climbed back into the copilot's seat Major Campbell started the engine. We headed back to take off, the process taking less than five minutes.

As we flew I saw the massive Port of Houston, it extended miles and miles. Then I could see Galveston Bay. The plane began to descend. I realized we were going to land on the water. OK, that's what amphibious floats are for.

The bay was calm but the landing was noisy and it felt like we were landing on a washboard. As we slowed a powerboat was heading towards us. The copilot opened his door and stepped on the pontoon as the boat slide alongside.

He opened our door and told us to get on board. Abbey climbed out followed by Elizabeth and me. Our bags were loaded, the copilot jumped on board, and the boat went to the other side. Major Campbell got in the boat and the copilot got in the plane's pilot's seat. We motored anyway. I looked back over the boat's twin 300-horsepower Mercury outboards to see the plane taxiing for takeoff.

Elizabeth and Abbey were having an animated conversation so I sat back and enjoyed the ride. Major Campbell wasn't going to tell me much and it wouldn't matter at this point anyway.

Finally Elizabeth said, "Major, where are we going?"

Major Campbell pointed his arm to the front and left. In the distance was a ship. It was some type of work vessel.

"It is one our company ships, the FAT 7. It is a Stalwart-class auxiliary general ocean surveillance ship. The US Navy built eighteen of them. Their original purpose was to collect underwater acoustical information using the surveillance towed array sensor system. The ship served as an anti-submarine surveillance ship during the Cold War, then as an anti-drug smuggling vessel as part of the US War on Drugs.

"There are only two still in service with the US military. The rest were sold off. Several went to the National

Oceanic and Atmospheric Administration or NOAA, a few went to marine research institutes associated with major universities, the EPA got one, and the rest went to private companies. Walter bought this one third-hand and had it re-equipped for petroleum exploration and research."

It didn't look particularly graceful. I knew that FAT stood for Falone Advanced Technologies but fat seemed to fit the way it looked. Definitely a workboat. Two squat smokestacks, cranes, winches, and a submersible were now visible as we got closer.

Major Campbell seemed happy to talk about the ship. Perhaps he was trying to take our minds off the danger we were in.

"It is 244 feet long and 43 feet wide. Its draft is 15 feet and it is powered by two 1600-horsepower diesel-electric engines with twin screws. It is a bit of a clunker, its top speed is 11 knots or 13 mph. A fast swimmer can keep up with it. It is designed for a complement of crew and researchers of thirty-six. Some Stalwart-class ship had crews of sixty-four. I'm not sure how many are onboard now."

Elizabeth broke in. "Where are we going in it?"

"Walter will have to tell us that."

I said, "Let's hope we don't have to outrun anybody in that thing." No one seemed to appreciate my comment.

We pulled alongside and were helped on board. The ship's captain welcomed us and I noticed the speedboat was being secured to the aft of the ship. We were shown to our quarters, and told to settle in and meet in the dining hall in twenty minutes.

Chapter 16

I could smell cooking in the galley as I entered what was the dining hall and main meeting room. Walter was in conversation with the captain.

He finished what he was saying and headed over to me. "Rob, how good to see you. It seems we've stirred up quite a hornets' nest."

He looked more drawn and tired than I'd ever seen him. In the past he always seemed vibrant and upbeat. His look, his words, our rushed escape from Houston, and being on this ship all gave me a sinking but somehow energized feeling.

I said, "It would be nice to know what is going on and where we are going."

"Well I'm afraid none of us know exactly what is going on and where you and Abbey are going is up to you two. Once she, Elizabeth, and Major Campbell join us we can go over what we do know. Ned and Mitch have uncovered quite a bit recently."

A man came out of the galley with a platter of sandwiches, then coffee, iced tea, and fruit. I looked at my watch, almost one in the afternoon.

Another crewman powered on the videoconference machine as the others arrived.

Walter said as a way of introduction, "You all had an interesting morning. I'm happy to have you here and looking so well."

There really wasn't time for us to worry or even think much about what just happened.

We all sat on the same side of the table and waited for the connection to Ned and Mitch. After a few seconds they both appeared on the screen. Ned again seemed to bounce in his seat.

He jumped right in. "Elizabeth, I hear the G-men tried to grab you right out of your office. If they got you they probably…"

Walter cut him off. "Mitch, please tell us what you and Ned found out in the last few hours."

"Ned ran the photos of Alexander Pshavians through the video feed where he found Justin Barry and he was on the same flight from Hong Kong to Perth as Justin. Major Campbell put me in touch with a detective agency in Perth and they've tracked them to the Cottesloe Beach Hotel in Cottesloe that is a suburb of Perth on the Indian Ocean. Looks like a cool place from the hotel website. They are booked into separate rooms but too much of a coincidence that they are there together. The question is why?"

Major Campbell asked, "Anything on Professor Visser?"

"Nothing but I'm still hacking into as many camera

systems as I can. Somebody must have noticed me by now but so far they haven't tried to stop me."

Walter said, "NSA has but they want you to find something and don't want to hack into those systems of friends and allies that you are trampling all over. It is easier just to track you. I suspect the Chinese, Russians, Brits, and several others are also watching your handiwork."

Ned looked deflated but said, "They're probably just jealous."

Walter said, "There were two additional deaths of researchers who worked with Visser. Both were in France. It looked like professional hits. Visser or someone is killing any of the researchers who had close knowledge of what he was doing."

I said, "Back to my questions. What happened back in Houston and where are we going?"

"As Major Campbell told you, a group within US military intelligence was trying to acquire Visser's biotechnology. Someone who is part of it at some level went too far and tried to have you killed. For the greater good of the country, you know how their excuses go. Visser double-crossed them and killed the two agents sent to negotiate with him. We got this from MI6 who seemed to be more forthcoming and concerned about your lives than our government."

I thought back to hiding in the British Embassy so my own government didn't kill me.

Walter went on. "The group is being shut down and low-level heads have rolled but no one yet knows how high up it goes. I'm working with the State Department,

Homeland Security, and the CIA. DOD has agreed to pay for the company software and the various agencies are now negotiating over who will run it and oversee its use.

"I wasn't sure if the government visitors in Houston were completely with us or part of the rogue group. Best we stay away until the government figures all that out.

"To your second question, you and/or Abbey may join Major Campbell and Professor Wang and go to Perth or I'd be happy to deliver you to any number of places where we can assure your safety until this matter is resolved. I'll be going to Washington because I want to make sure the top person who is responsible for killing one of my employees is caught and sent to prison."

I turned to Major Campbell. "I assume you have a plan."

"We will meet with Justin and Alexander Pshavians to determine if they are on the run or still working for Visser. Assuming they are running, as we believe, we will see if they know where Visser is and we will offer them lucrative research positions at Walter Reed National Military Medical Center. They will also be offered immunity for any crimes they may have committed while working for Visser. Alexander Pshavians will be given asylum if he wants it. They will be required to sign on for a five-year contract to help understand and control Visser's technology. Professor Wang has agreed to join the team if Justin agrees to the plan. Needless to say their work will receive the funding and support it requires. Walter has arranged this with the State Department and DOD."

"I'll go," Abbey said.

I said, "What about Elizabeth. Is she in danger?"

"Elizabeth will go with me to Washington. She will lead the team that customizes and sets up software for the government. There will be very good security," Walter said.

I looked at Abbey. She said, "They tried to kill me. They will probably try to kill Justin. I believe I can help convince Justin that what Walter has set up is best for him and for mankind. Plus I don't know where else I would go right now. Prof, let's finish this."

Abbey was close to Justin's age, confident, and respected in her field, she may be able to relate to Justin in a way the rest of us can't. Plus I told her parents a few years back I'd look out for her. More often she was the one that saved me.

"I'll go but I'm not sure how much help I'll be. I assume we aren't taking this ship to Perth," I said.

Walter smiled. "Very astute observation. We are headed to Port Fourchon, Louisiana. It is the southernmost port in the state. Port Fourchon currently services over 90 percent of the Gulf of Mexico's deepwater oil production. There are over 600 oil platforms within a 40-mile radius of Port Fourchon.

"From there you will fly to London meet Professor Wang and go on to Perth. It will take about twenty-four hours to get to Port Fourchon. So rest and relax I suspect you will have a busy time ahead.

"Elizabeth, let's go, we also have a plane to catch."

After a few goodbyes they left in the speedboat we arrived in.

We agreed to touch base with Ned and Mitch in the morning. I found the captain and asked if someone could give me a tour of the ship. He said he'd be glad to. After my tour was done I stood at the front rail looking into the Gulf and wondering when all this was going to end and how. What little this had to do with archaeology when we arrived had long passed. At least Australia has one of the oldest known pieces of rock art on Earth with a confirmed date of 28,000 years ago or perhaps I should just go home.

Chapter
17

On our eighteen-hour, 9,000-mile Qantas Air flight from London to Perth, I had an opportunity to think about what Mitch and Ned added when we spoke before the ship reached Port Fourchon.

More riots and discontent in Iran. The unofficial tally of the people who worked in the missile research centers is up over nine thousand. The country was on full military alert.

The list was full of top scientists, plus high-ranking officers of the Basij or Islamic Revolutionary Guard, and Air Force. It was reported that the basements of several large building were being excavated to bury all the dead since cremation is forbidden for Muslims. It appears they didn't want satellite picture of mass graves. The plague had run its course and people were in the compounds without bio-suits according to satellite photos.

The killing of endangered animal poachers was continuing in Africa and Asia. The software predicted more of the same.

Justin Barry and Alexander Pshavians were schedule to check out of the hotel today for parts unknown.

I ate and slept. I woke to a warm washcloth and another meal. I looked out as the plane descended into the Perth airport. I could see the slender white concrete control tower and off in the distance about a dozen high-rise buildings of the downtown Perth skyline.

We cleared customs and Major Campbell was approached by a man who looked like he was sent from central casting of a Crocodile Dundee movie. He wore an Australian bush hat and his shirt had cut-off sleeves. He wore it untucked over faded jeans. I didn't see a big knife sticking out of his boot. They greeted each other warmly and obviously knew each other.

I was standing with Abbey and Mia. Major Campbell came over and introduced his friend Ron Shadie.

He stared at the two women with the eyes of a hungry wolf. Mia began to flush under his grinning stare. Abbey didn't seem a bit fazed.

She said, "SAS?" pointing to the tattoo on his arm.

It was stylized bird wings with a dagger through the center and the motto WHO DARES WINS. I'd seen it before on the company's security employees who had served in the British Special Air Service.

She continued. "So you're a Brit?"

"Missy, I am not."

He seemed deeply offended.

"Not all Brits are assholes. Take Major Campbell here, he's a good bloke. My family has been in Australia since the Brits sent my ancestors by prison ship to Port Jackson in the 1700s for something they didn't do, I might add."

Staring straight at him and pointing to his arm she said, "So why do you have the British SAS insignia tattooed on your arm?"

Sensing things were going from bad to worse, Major Campbell stepped in. "It is the insignia of the Australian Special Air Service Regiment and it was modeled after the British SAS insignia. Flight Lieutenant Shadie and I served in a joint operation in southern Afghanistan conducting long-range vehicle patrols around Kandahar and into the Helmand Valley.

"Ron, this is Dr. Abbey Summers."

He was leering at her.

Abbey continued to stare right back at him and said, "You can call me Dr. Summers."

The rest of the introductions went more smoothly.

As we waited for what little luggage we had, Ron said, "Your two boys checked out of their hotel and flew to Darwin this morning. I had a friend in Darwin meet the flight and follow them. They took separate cabs so my man followed the Barry kid but they both ended up at the Argus Hotel at 13 Shepherd Street downtown. No more flights today but I can book a flight for the morning."

"Is your man watching them?" Major Campbell said.

"They're booked for two days so we should have time to get there. He'll check on them from time to time. You're booked into the Cottesloe Beach Hotel. The same place they were staying. It's right on the ocean, go enjoy the afternoon. I'll pick you up tomorrow at 8:00 to go to the airport."

He hailed us a cab, gave the cabby the hotel address, and then walked away.

"Not your type, Abbey?" I said. She frowned and didn't bother to answer.

We checked in and agreed to meet at the Beach Club bar in an hour. I took a shower, changed, and was the first one at the bar. I looked across the white sands to the blue of the Indian Ocean. There were boys playing beach cricket.

Abbey and Mia joined me and we ordered drinks. There wasn't much conversation. We drank and enjoyed the sunshine. I ordered a second beer. Eventually Major Campbell joined us.

Abbey said, "We're being watched."

"I know," replied Major Campbell. "Ron's men are watching the men who are watching us. He'll let us know who they are."

I foolishly looked around and then stopped, a little embarrassed.

"So what is the plan?" I said.

"We fly to Darwin in the morning and talk to Justin and Dr. Pshavians. I'm having a jet sent to Darwin and hopefully we all fly back to the States together," Major Campbell said as he finished his beer.

The rest of the evening was peaceful, we walked around the town, I tried not to keep looking to see if someone was following us, we ate dinner and went to bed.

The next morning Major Campbell told us to stay in the hotel, have breakfast, and be ready to leave together at 8:00AM. Mia was a nervous wreck. I tried to act calm. Abbey had a heightened sense of alertness like an athlete in the zone before the big moment. I'd seen it before and that more than anything scared me.

"OK, let's walk out together and get in the middle car," Major Campbell instructed.

Abbey took Mia's hand. We walked out into the sunshine. There were three Range Rovers. Abbey, Mia, and I got in the back seat and Major Campbell got in the front. We drove smoothly away. No hail of bullets. No gunning of engines and squealing of tires. The ride to the airport was totally uneventful.

We arrived at the airport without incident, checked in, and went to the gate. Ron Shadie was traveling with us.

I asked Major Campbell, "So who was watching us?"

Ron answered, "Bamboo Union. We don't see much of them in Perth. They mostly operate out of Sydney. There is a big Chinese population there. They probably came up here especially for you folks. Kind of makes you special."

He was playing with me but that wasn't what bothered me. They were probably there because of Justin Barry and Alexander Pshavians and then spotted us.

We boarded the plane for the four-hour flight to Darwin. I drank coffee, read about Darwin, and tried to think why this location?

Darwin International Airport is Darwin's only airport, it shares its runways with the Royal Australian Air Force's Base Darwin. As we approached I could see the city's downtown section and the Timor Sea in the background. Darwin was the biggest city in the Northern Territory of Australia but not big by world standards with a population of only about one hundred and fifty thousand.

We grabbed our bags and went out front. Mia said, "What is that thing?"

Ron again seemed offended. "It is an OKA 4WD, an Australian made all-terrain vehicle and one of the best in the world."

It looked part bus, part truck, part SUV and rather ugly.

Ron went on, "I use it as a mobile command center. I had it driven up from Perth and I'm billing it to your boss, Ian. Get in."

It was set up for eight people and equipped like a military command vehicle. Two of Ron's men were in the front. We piled in the back.

The driver said, "Your boys are meeting with Uncle Duong this afternoon."

Ron asked, "What do they want with that crooked old snake?"

"From what we heard from bugging Barry's room they want equipment, transport, and a guide to take them to Kakadu National Park. It seems they are willing to pay for a no questions asked arrangement."

Ian asked, "Just who is Uncle Duong?"

Ron replied, "He is a Vietnamese smuggler and cheat who fronts as a supplier to the bush safari trade. We've had a few dealings over the years. When is this meeting?"

The driver answered, "It should be about now."

"OK, take us to Uncle Duong's and let's see what's up." He looked at Ian and he nodded yes.

So after all the countries we were in and all the miles we traveled we were finally going to see Justin Barry.

We drove about thirty minutes to a run-down industrial

park. Uncle Duong's was a warehouse with an office storefront.

Ron said to his men in front, "Wait here."

We all piled out. I don't think Ron wanted us all with him but since Ian didn't object he said nothing.

We walked in without knocking. Justin and Alexander were talking to a slight older man I assumed was Uncle Duong. The only other person was an elderly lady working at a desk on a stack of paper. Seeing us she got up and slipped out.

Ron said, "Uncle Duong, long time no see."

Uncle Duong didn't seem happy to see him.

Mia rushed in and said, "Justin, we have been so worried about you."

The shock on Justin's face was almost comical. His mouth fell open and at first the words wouldn't come out. Finally he said, "Professor Wang, what are you doing here?"

Alexander Pshavians was edging towards the door and Abbey stepped in front of him sticking out her hand. "Professor Pshavians, I'm Professor Abbey Summers. It's a pleasure to meet you. Your work with phages is most interesting."

This seemed to stop him in his tracks. He looked at Justin and then at each of us.

Mia said, "Justin, you've got to come home with us. We've arranged amnesty for you, actually both of you, with the Justice Department. We need your help with our work."

They now seemed even more confused. Justin said, "We can't, we've got to stop him. He's gone completely mad."

Then it all happened so fast. The back door banged open and Oriental men with pistols stepped in. Uncle

Duong ducked behind the counter. Ron drew his pistol and was shot before he could raise it. I pulled Mia to the floor and Abbey dove for Ron. Tap-tap, tap-tap, tap-tap.

I can still see it all in my mind like it was a slow-motion movie. When Ron is shot, I pull Mia down to the floor and Major Campbell hurls a chair at the men, hitting the first one who stumbles into the others.

Abbey dives on top of Ron. I can hear him grunt when she lands on him. As she rolls off, I see Ron's blood on her blouse. She rolls to her stomach and then braces up on her elbows. Somehow she had grabbed Ron's automatic in her diving roll. Then two shots, the first man is down, two more and the second man is down, and two more shots and the third man goes to the floor. The fourth man runs out the back door.

Ron sits up as his two men come in the front door, pistols drawn. He takes a quick look around and says, "The fourth man?"

One of his men shakes his head. "He drove off as we were coming in."

Abbey pulls the bandanna off Ron's hat that had fallen to the floor and makes a tourniquet around his wounded arm. He looks down at it as if he'd forgotten all about it.

He says, "Ian told me you were special, now I see what he meant. Thank you, that was quite good."

Abbey pulls the tourniquet tighter and Ron grunts.

I can still see it so clearly.

After that, Ron turned to Major Campbell and said, "Ian, I suggest you folks take Justin and his buddy out of here and I'll clean this up just like you were never here.

Plus I'd rather let the police think I did this than admit they got the drop on me and Abbey saved my ass. Take the driver and go. Uncle Duong and I need to get our story straight."

Major Campbell took Justin's arm and the driver guided Professor Pshavians out to the OKA. The six of us got in the back and the drive asked where to? Ian told him to get away from here and find a quiet place to park so we could talk.

Justin looked at me. "You're that Cornell archaeology professor who made those discoveries in Peru." He looked at Abbey. "You were his grad student. What are you two doing here?"

It was obvious he was keyed up and confused. I said, "The short answer is to bring you home and stop Bram Visser."

He interrupted me. "He's gone mad, completely mad. When I started, Dr. Visser was all about cutting-edge science and saving endangered species. We were all excited and working hard for the good of the planet. A few bad people would die, poachers who killed not only animals but also park rangers if they got in their way. Now he doesn't care who he kills. Thousands were killed in Iran just for money."

I told him we knew about killing poachers, the Zulu curse, Bolivia, the prisons, the Philadelphia schools, the stolen manuscripts, and the graves of ancient plague victims being dug up. He seemed surprised.

I said, "Did you know he had several of his own scientists murdered just a few days ago?"

He nodded yes and said, "Al and I ran but when we understood what he was going to do next, we decided we needed to stop him. That's why we're here, to stop him."

I said, "We will have lots of time to go over the other things later. Where is Visser?"

"We don't know but he's planning to use the next generation of the engineered virus that was used in Iran on the Ranger Uranium Mine."

The driver cut in. "The Ranger Uranium Mine is one of the biggest and most productive uranium mines in the world. It is right in the middle of Kakadu National Park, which is a national treasure, and on the UNESCO World Heritage List. So the mine is controversial. The park is about a hundred miles from here."

Justin went on. "The park has the most amazing animals: dingoes, antilopine kangaroos, black wallaroos, agile wallabies, and short-eared rock wallabies. Plus smaller mammals such as northern quolls, brush-tailed phascogales, brown bandicoots, black-footed tree-rats, and black flying foxes.

"There are 180 species of birds, over a hundred species of reptile, plus frogs and insects. The flora is among the richest in northern Australia with almost 2,000 plant species recorded which is a result of the park's geological, landform, and habitat diversity."

Then Alexander Pshavians broke in. "Visser has gone crazy. He plans to use a virus on the area of the uranium mine but unlike the ones released at the military facilities in Iran this strain is not programmed to die off after a few weeks. He wants it to contaminate the area of the uranium mine forever so no one can mine it."

Mia asked, "What about the other mammals? The mine area must be large if it is one of the world's biggest. Animals roam all over."

Alexander went on. "The virus is designed to target humans. But we don't really know about other animals. This is the newest engineered virus and one of the most deadly. But that's not the real problem. You can't remove the time limit of the virus reproducing without losing the dimensional restriction. I kept telling Dr. Visser this but he wouldn't listen. As time passes it will continue to spread geographically."

I could hear Abbey on her secure phone. She was talking to Mitch and telling her to have Ned focus his search for Visser on Australia. She told Mitch to ask Chad and find out what the CIA and Taiwanese intelligence had on the Bamboo Union activity in Australia and with Visser. She said she'd check back once we were in our hotel at the park.

Justin said, "Dr. Visser doesn't have to be here. He didn't personally go to those other places where he ran tests of the engineered virus and bacteria. He always hired someone to do it."

"What about another laboratory? Where did he manufacture the stuff for the other attacks? Did it all come from his lab in Amsterdam?" I asked.

Alexander answered, "Now that you ask, I don't think it all came from our lab in Amsterdam, especially for Iran. I would have noticed the quantity being produced. The lab we worked in was relatively small. We did some parts of our work in other areas of the Fryrtex Pharmaceuticals facilities but only for routine things that could be used in various pharmaceutical research activities. So he must have another production facility."

"Abbey, ask Ned to research all the other Fryrtex Pharmaceuticals facilities. The authorities must have asked about other places where Visser might have had a secret lab.

"Major Campbell, I say we head to Kakadu National Park," I said.

"I agree. How long a drive?" he asked the driver.

"Two and a half hours down Stuart Highway then the Arnhem Highway. We can be there by six."

"Ok. May I have the key to the gun locker?" Ian asked.

The driver didn't ask any questions. He just took the key out of his pocket, handed it to Ian, and pointed to one of the lockers.

It was an impressive array of weapons. High-powered rifles, shotguns, and pistols. Major Campbell selected the smallest automatic and handed it to Abbey. I didn't like it because I knew he would only do this if he expected trouble. But we had just killed three Bamboo Union gunmen and unlike the police they knew who actually shot them. I'm sure the Bamboo Union wouldn't be happy about that.

Abbey took it and ejected the magazine, it was loaded. Next she completely checked the workings of the pistol and reinserted the magazine. Major Campbell handed her two more magazines. Abbey put them in her backpack-style purse.

Ian selected another automatic, checked it, holstered it at his back, and relocked the cabinet.

As we drove, the driver booked us into the Mercure Kakadu Crocodile Hotel. He said it in the middle of the park near the mine in the town of Jabiru.

The roads were in fairly good condition, although we had to brake several times for wandering cattle, buffalo, and kangaroos. I wonder if the local Chamber of Commerce put them out by the road to please the tourists.

The Mercure Kakadu Crocodile Hotel was in the shape of a giant green crocodile. That's different, I thought, but once we checked in it was much like any other small resort hotel.

After checking in and taking a shower I went to the bar. There at the bar chatting up one of the waitresses was Chad Dillon, my favorite CIA agent.

He looked up, held up his drink, and said, "Welcome to Jabiru."

I ordered a beer and joined him. "Who were our visitors at Walter's ranch?"

"They weren't real specific on which branch of our government they worked for. If I had to guess I'd say military intelligence. They were a bit surprised to be met by me but I didn't slow them down much. I informed the Agency and then made flight arrangements to Sydney with plans to meet you in Perth. But then I heard you are headed here so here I am.

"I also heard you had a little fun earlier today."

It was only a few hours ago. I wondered how he knew about it so quickly. "Not my idea of fun," I said.

"They were Bamboo Union. Two of them were known to authorities in Sydney and the other two probably are in from Taiwan. The Agency is trying to find out what others might be in the area," he said.

"Good luck, two thirds of the tourists here are Asian looking. Do they know anything about where Professor Visser is?"

He just shook his head and ordered another drink. Major Campbell joined us.

I asked him, "So what now?"

"We have lots of company from AFP and ASIO."

He saw the look on my face and said, "That is the Australian Federal Police and the Australian Security Intelligence Organization. Jointly they handle terrorism issues in the country. They work closely with MI6. Brigadier Sir Sinclair Cumming spoke with the top people at ASIO. For now they're leaving the Americans out of the loop, with the exception of our friend Chad."

Interesting the way Ian had phrased that and I thought again about my own government trying to have us killed.

"Any word from Ron Shadie?" I was curious how his story was holding up with the police.

"The AFP should be there by now and once they confirm that the bodies belong to the Bamboo Union and it relates to a terrorist investigation the local police will probably be happy to turn it all over to the AFP," Ian said.

"Will Ron stick with his story or will Abbey be dragged into it?"

"I think Ron will stick with the story, it's simpler all the way around. We left for the park and the Bamboo Union hit men went to Uncle Duong thinking they'd find Justin and Alexander but were too late."

The Zulu Curse

I hoped he was right for Abbey's sake.

"What about security? The Bamboo Union must know we would come here. They can't be pleased that we killed three of their people," I said.

"The hotel is secure. There are over two dozen AFP and ASIO agents here. They've established a command center in the hotel and all of our rooms are being carefully watched."

I felt better but it sounded a bit creepy. This time I resisted looking over my shoulder to see who was watching us.

He continued. "Relax, have dinner, and get a good night's sleep. Just stay on the hotel grounds. Tomorrow is likely to be a busy day."

With that he walked off.

Not knowing what to do, I ordered another beer. Chad had gone back to talking to the waitress.

Chapter 18

Major Campbell found Abbey and me having breakfast. He sat down and ordered coffee.

"In twenty minutes we all meet in the command center. I'm afraid Mia, Justin, and Alexander didn't get much sleep last night. Once AQIS arrived they wanted to start understanding the threat immediately and put them right to work."

Again he saw my puzzled look.

"That is the Australian Quarantine and Inspection Service, like your Centers for Disease Control," he said.

We finished our breakfast and Major Campbell led the way. There were two men guarding the hallway we entered. They smiled and waved us by. We went through a set of double doors into a large meeting or ballroom.

There were rows of folding tables set up with computer and communication equipment on them. There seemed to be four or five groups of people working on different tasks.

Abbey went to an empty table and powered up her

laptop. I saw Mia, Justin, and Alexander in animated conversation with the people from AQIS so I wandered over to listen in.

I didn't follow a lot of the conversation but they were discussing containment methods in case the virus was released. It didn't sound like there were a lot of good options.

Then I went over to check on Abbey. She had Mitch and Ned on videoconference. I watched over her shoulder as they updated her on what they found. It turned out they had no leads on Visser's location.

Then my mind snapped, whirled, and a picture replayed in my head. I shouted. "Stop, don't drink that."

The man at the water cooler had the paper cup halfway to his mouth. He looked at me like I was crazy. All the conversation in the room stopped.

I tried to calm my voice. "That's how they introduced the virus into the prisons and the school building. In the water supply."

Then it came to me. I said, "That's how they are going to contaminate the mine. Every workstation and trailer on the mine must have a water cooler like that one. They are going to hijack the bottle delivery truck and deliver contaminated water throughout the mine."

Justin and one of the AQIS people went over to the man who was now staring at the cup and then back at me. The AQIS person took the cup and held it like it was a live grenade.

I went on. "It didn't hit me at first but just a few minutes ago someone dressed like a hotel employee changed the water bottle. The old bottle was still a third full.

"They may have already poisoned the mine's water cooler."

The captain of the AFP snapped, "Get the head of security for the mine on the phone now."

Major Campbell made a quick call and said, "Rob, Abbey, let's go."

He grabbed Justin by the arm, saying, "Let's move."

The AFP captain started to protest but between Ian's six foot five inch chiseled frame and his commanding presence, instead he said to one of his lieutenants go with us.

We ran out the front door and our ugly OKA 4WD was waiting, engine running. Obviously Major Campbell's call was to the driver. We piled in the back and Major Campbell got in front.

The AFP lieutenant was on his phone. At the same moment both Ian and Abbey drew out the automatics, checked and rechecked them, then put them away. Military training. As the Marines say, "Take care of your equipment and your equipment will take care of you."

We were met at the Ranger Uranium Mine gate by the head of security. He'd just got off his phone with the AFP captain and didn't look happy. Several of his men were milling about.

The AFP lieutenant showed him his credentials. We were all now standing next to the head of security who was saying, "What the hell is going on?"

Major Campbell and the lieutenant were starting to explain. I cut them off. "Shut the mine down now. Don't let anybody drink the water from any of the water cooler."

"Who the hell are you?" was his reply.

I said, "You know what happened at those two Iranian military bases? Well it's about to happen here."

A security man ran over to his boss. "The water bottle delivery truck entered the service gate almost an hour ago. Our man at the service gate said it wasn't the usual two men. He was told our regular men were on vacation."

Now the mine security chief looked truly panicked.

Half a dozen police vehicles came screaming up to the gate. The AFP captain was in the first car and jumped out as it stopped. A van pulled up, and several men jumped out and began putting on biohazard suits.

I said it again, "Shut the mine down. You must have an emergency shutdown procedure. Tell everyone don't drink the water."

He looked at me and then at the AFP captain. He said, "You heard him, shut it down now."

A dozen men in full SWAT gear had now assembled.

The security chief gave the order. Sirens began to wail.

"Have everyone hold in place," I said.

Abbey came over with a man from the gatehouse in tow. "He says he knows the normal route the delivery truck takes."

He went off with two police officers to show them the delivery route on a map of the mine.

The chief of security was trying to get a grip on the situation.

I said, "Justin, go work with the biohazard team on a containment plan."

I saw that Mia and Alexander had arrived with several AQIS folks.

Major Campbell said, "Let's go, get in. You come with me." He pointed to a security guard standing next to an open-top Range Rover.

I jumped in the back and Abbey followed me. Major Campbell barked at the AFP lieutenant to get in and the driver of our OKA handed him a Remington Model 700 rifle.

The security chief started to protest. I thought the AFP captain was going to agree with him and try to stop us. But he told the chief to have all gates secured and radio us as soon as he had a report on the bottle delivery truck's location.

As we drove by I shouted, "And pray no one drinks the water."

As we drove towards the main processing area the contrast between the pristine parkland outside the mine area and scarred wasteland ahead of us couldn't have been starker. The pit we drove by was well over 200 feet deep. The place looked to be thousands of acres in size.

The driver's radio crackled and a voice said the water delivery truck driver shot a guard when he approached him and then ran back to the truck. There appeared to be two men in the truck. It was now heading toward the far side of the property.

"What's over there?" Major Campbell asked the driver.

"There isn't much, just the pond of treated water that discharges to a stream that leads to the East Alligator River."

"Go that way."

The AFP lieutenant relayed that the SWAT unit and the biohazard team were on their way. Water bottles had been to only three places and these buildings were being secured with everyone staying in place.

The Range Rover bounced down the gravel road with a dust trail flying up behind us. We rounded a corner and saw the truck parked several hundred yards ahead. Then a hail of bullets struck the road just in front of us. The driver slammed on the brakes as bullets hit the front of the Rover.

Abbey pulled me down and said, "Stay here."

Major Campbell was out the door and behind the vehicle. Abbey followed him. Only then did I notice that the AFP lieutenant was slumped over and bleeding. I reached over to help him and saw the entire back of his head was blown off.

After throwing up I checked on the driver. He was down on the floor screaming into the radio for help. He seemed unhurt.

I heard Major Campbell say to Abbey, "He's on the roof of the truck, and has some type of light machine gun."

Abbey said, "It sounds like the Belgium FN Minimi light machine gun or the M249 US version."

Both of them had their pistol drawn but there was no way they could do much damage from this range. The firing had stopped so I peeked over the seat.

"There are three of them, one on the roof and the other two are unloading the water bottles. It looks like they're planning to dump then in the pond," I said as I pulled my head back down.

Abbey said, "Get the rifle from the front and hand it out the back door to me."

The driver slid it over the seat and I opened the door and stuck it out butt first. This was enough activity for the gunmen to send us another spray of bullets.

Abbey told Major Campbell, "You're too big to do this so don't argue with me. I'm going to crawl under the car. From down there I don't think I'll have the angle to shoot the gunmen on the roof so I'll go for one of the other two. Once I fire, you spray as many shots as you can at the truck. Hopefully it will distract the gunmen long enough to let me get a second shot off and then duck back."

"I don't like it but we don't know how much destruction it will cause if those water bottles are dumped," Ian said.

I ventured another look. They had over a dozen bottles out of the truck now.

Abbey said, "Three, two, one, now."

The same second Abbey took a shot, Major Campbell started blazing away with his pistol from the side of the Rover.

As I ducked my head I saw one of the men go down. Before the machine gun fired I heard Abbey take the second shot. Major Campbell emptied his clip and ducked back.

Both of them were behind the Rover that was being riddled with bullets. Finally the firing stopped. I assumed he was changing his ammunition clip.

Abbey thought the same thing. She jumped up, steadied the rifle on the back of the Rover, and fired.

I ventured another look. The gunman rolled off the roof. From behind I heard the vehicle of the SWAT unit followed by several police and mine security cars. They rushed past as our driver radioed that the three men in the water delivery truck were down and we had wounded, send an ambulance.

I climbed out of the Rover. Abbey rushed to me with a look of horror on her face. I looked down. My shirt and slacks were covered in blood.

I said, "It's not mine."

Epilogue

The third man was Professor Visser. He was dead, as was one of the other two; the second would live to stand trial. It turned out Visser had terminal cancer and this was his last crazy effort to save wildlife.

No one was infected and the virus-contaminated water bottles were all recovered.

Justin Barry and Alexander Pshavians agreed to the arrangement to work for the US government and help to try to understand and contain what Visser created. It wasn't going to be as easy as officials hoped. Visser kept each piece of his work separate and Justin, Alexander, and the other scientists working with him were limited to specific tasks. Only Visser knew how all the pieces fit together. Various law enforcement agencies were rounding them up.

In Washington some people were jailed and others were fired for trying to kill us and various other excesses in the name of national security. I doubt they ever got the top folks responsible for the whole mess, they seldom do.

Walter's company got its rich contract with the government for his software.

Abbey went back to Mongolia. She left with such short notice that most of her belongings were still there.

I was happy to be back in Ithaca. I missed my dog, my little farm, and the other animals. I missed teaching and I found I even missed the Dean being so fussy over small details.

Walter really didn't need to involve Abbey and me. The archaeological link turned out to be very small and irrelevant to what was really happening.

The funniest thing is you can be so right and so wrong at the same time. I was right that the people at the Ranger Mine were going to be infected via contaminated water bottles and we arrived just in time to prevent a major disaster. But I was also completely wrong about the water bottle in the hotel conference room. It wasn't infected. The hotel employee was getting close to the end of his shift and seeing all the people in the room he decided to put a full bottle on the cooler so we wouldn't run out. No terrorist, just a thoughtful dedicated employee trying to do a good job.

About
the Author

BRADFORD G. WHELER is the former CEO, President and Co-owner of Allan Electric Company. He sold Allan Electric to a New York Stock Exchange listed company. After staying on as President during the transition, Brad retired.

Brad's lifelong love of history, art, books, and the inherent humor in man's nature led to the founding of BookCollaborative.com and the publishing of *MONGOLIA AND THE GOLDEN EAGLE: An Archaeological Mystery Thriller*, as well as *INCA'S DEATH CAVE: An Archaeological Mystery Thriller, LOVE SAYINGS: wit & wisdom of romance, courtship, & marriage, GOLF SAYINGS: wit & wisdom of a good walk spoiled, CAT SAYINGS: wit & wisdom from the whiskered ones, HORSE SAYINGS: wit & wisdom straight from the horse's mouth, DOG SAYINGS: wit & wisdom from man's best friend,* and *SNAPPY SAYINGS: wit & wisdom from the world's greatest minds.*

His community involvements include being a Trustee of Community General Hospital in Hamilton, NY, and chairing their Finance Committee. He is the former Chairman of the Board of Trustees of Cazenovia College, and former Chairman and member of the Board of Directors and Alumni Association and President of the Sigma Phi Society at Cornell University in Ithaca, NY. He is also a former member of the Board of Directors of the Greater Cazenovia Area Chamber of Commerce and several other boards.

Brad played polo on the Cornell University men's polo team for four years and was a member of the Cazenovia Polo Club. In 2012 he was inducted into the Manlius Pebble Hill Athletic Hall of Fame.

He holds a BS and Masters of Engineering in Civil and Environmental Engineering from Cornell University in Ithaca, NY as well as an MBA degree from Fordham University in New York, NY. He is a licensed Professional Engineer.

Brad, his wife, Julie, and their golden retriever Finlay live in Fort Pierce, FL. And summers in Cazenovia, NY.

Acknowledgments

A few clarifications: First, this book is a work of fiction. However the countries, regions, cities, archaeological sites, rivers, and national parks are all real. The major historical figures and experts, plus their works, are real.

To the extent of my ability I have tried to accurately describe the cultures and landscapes. The same is true with the technology. Most of what I describe exists in some form today. The company spyware was made up. But who knows, the NSA may have this type of software.

Any errors are completely my fault.

First and foremost I would like to thank the readers of this book. Thank you for giving it a chance. I hope you enjoyed it.

I would like to thank the following individuals for their direct help with this book.

My wife, Julie, not only encouraged me to write the book, she did the first proofread of the book when it needed a lot of work.

Marcia Abramson for her professional proofreading and editing.

Lorie DeWorken at Mind*the*Margins for her wonderful book design work and producing the ebook files.

My website consultant Brian Hoke of Bentley Hoke Consulting who continually helps with all things web related.

The artist Tanya who did the cover painting artwork. Find her work at tproud on Fiverr.com.

Finally I'd like to thank all those book consultants and experts who help authors and small publishers survive in today's rapidly changing media world.

Buy These Books at a discount on www.BookCollaborative.com

They are also available on Amazon.com and Barnes&Noble.com. You can order them at any bookstore in the US, UK, and Canada for delivery within a few days. All books available in eBook form on Amazon.com.

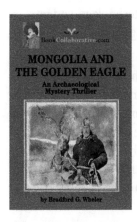

MONGOLIA AND THE GOLDEN EAGLE An Archaeological Mystery Thriller

By Bradford G. Wheler

Nine 5 Star reviews

Adventure, archaeology, high-tech cyber spying, and mystery mix to form a breathtaking, action-packed tale.

MONGOLIA AND THE GOLDEN EAGLE: An Archaeological Mystery Thriller. Why is Cornell archaeology professor Robert Johnson, a pre-Columbian scholar, selected to head up a multimillion-dollar project in Mongolia? Why is this so important to high-tech billionaire Walter Falone? Why is he using consultants from Israel Aerospace Industries for his government contract in Mongolia?

For Johnson and his colleague, brilliant and beautiful assistant professor Abbey Summers, it becomes the adventure of a lifetime. Cyber security threats, high-tech spying, and Chinese agents mix in this ingenious and thrilling plot of full of twists and turns. Somewhere in spectacular snowcapped Altai Mountains of western Mongolia there is a mysterious object that people are willing to kill for.

INCA'S DEATH CAVE
An Archaeological
Mystery Thriller

By Bradford G. Wheler

Twenty-one 5 Star reviews

Adventure, archaeology, technology, and mystery mix to form a breathtaking action-packed tale.

A 500-year-old puzzle catapults an archaeology professor and his brilliant grad student into the adventure of a lifetime in *INCA'S DEATH CAVE*, a new mystery thriller from author Bradford G. Wheler. What happened to a band of Inca rebels who journeyed north in Peru to seek the fabled cave of the true gods – and escape the disease and destruction brought by Spanish conquistadors? They were never heard from again. Did they just melt back into their villages or was something more sinister involved? What trace or treasure did they leave behind?

The ingenious plot of this thriller is full of twists and turns, excitement and adventure, archaeology and technology. Readers will meet fascinating characters they'll never forget: a high-tech billionaire, a quick-witted professor, his beautiful young student, and her still-tough grandfather, a retired Marine gunny sergeant.

Cornell University professor Robert Johnson and his star PhD student are hired by a billionaire entrepreneur to solve a 500-year-old archaeology mystery in northern Peru. But first, they will have to survive corporate skullduggery and drug-lord thuggery. And why, 6,700 miles away in Vatican City, is the old guard so upset? What dark secrets could centuries-old manuscripts hold?

This assiduously researched, fast-paced novel brings the Incas and their ancestors to life against the backdrop of the Peruvian Andes.

LOVE SAYINGS: wit & wisdom of romance, courtship, and marriage

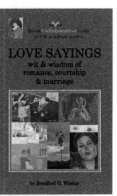

By Bradford G. Wheler

Nineteen 5 Star reviews

Dedicated to love and romance, and featuring art from around the globe, *LOVE SAYINGS: wit & wisdom of romance, courtship, and marriage* is an exciting and vibrant collection of beautiful art and text designed to celebrate the joy, humor, and bittersweet struggles of love. This art-themed quotation book covers topics including Love Through the Ages, Women, Men, Dating, Sex, Children, and more. This collaborative publication has two goals in mind: first, to honor and highlight the power and humor of love through text and art-work, and second, to showcase the talents of new and emerging artists. BookCollaborative.com provides artists with a platform through which they can gain exposure and recognition. Both professional and nonprofessional artists were invited to submit their work to be a part of this art-themed quotation book. The end result showcases 48 artists from countries including the US, UK, Poland, Australia, India, Switzerland, and South Africa. *LOVE SAYINGS* features a variety of art media including paintings, sculpture, and photography. Among the selected artists whose works are featured in *LOVE SAYINGS* is Ninh Le, who lives in the city of Dien Bien Phu, Vietnam. He is a junior high school teacher and finds inspiration in the gentle and romantic struggle of the ethnic people of the Vietnam highlands. Another artist is Kayla Ascencio, who has a wonderfully captivating fantasy art style.

GOLF SAYINGS: wit & wisdom of a good walk spoiled

By Bradford G. Wheler

Seven 5 Star reviews

Lots and lots of wisdom on these pages and a lot of chuckles

By D. Blankenship, Amazon top 50 and Hall of Fame reviewer

I have quite a few books whose subject matter deals exclusively with "golf sayings." I have been collecting these books since I first started playing some 55 odd years ago. Of all the wonderful reading I have on my shelf; all the wisdom, humor and frustration documented in their pages concerning what is probably the greatest game ever invented, this little work is most certainly in the exclusive top five I own.

CAT SAYINGS: wit & wisdom from the whiskered ones

By Bradford G. Wheler

Thirteen 5 Star reviews

Feline Art and Words: For cat lovers and those who attempt to understand them

By Grady Harp, Amazon top 50 and Hall of Fame reviewer

Brad G. Wheler has curated an art and words spectrum devoted to Cats (note the capital C and you'll get the gist of this book!). There is about as much variety of artwork reproduced on every page of this enormously entertaining book as is mirrored in the variety of excerpts of words from the ancients to the moderns. Wheler wisely keeps the reader's interest by dividing his book into chapters: Cats Rule, Wild Cats, Kittens, Humor, Of Cats and Dogs, The Cat Personality, Death of a Friend, Love Of, Cats Vs. People – each topic is generously illustrated with art and comments pertinent to each subsection.

HORSE SAYINGS: wit & wisdom straight from the horse's mouth

By Bradford G. Wheler

Nine 5 Star reviews

Horse Enthusiasts Rejoice!

By Dr. Joseph S. Maresca, Amazon top 1000 and Hall of Fame reviewer

Horse Sayings: Wit and Wisdom Straight from the Horse's Mouth by Bradford G. Wheler depicts the horse in all of its glory together with the continued human interest in the equine. The presentation has pearls of wisdom from horse humor, competition, ancient wisdom, training and many other aspects of horses unbeknownst to the public generally but well known to horse enthusiasts. There are illustrations by 61 artists from 11 countries.

DOG SAYINGS: wit & wisdom from man's best friend

By Bradford G. Wheler

Three 5 Star reviews

A Choice Read, Solidly Recommended

By Midwest Book Review

The simple mutts can be far wiser than they let on. *Dog Sayings: wit & wisdom from man's best friend* looks at a collection of humor and knowledge as well as plenty of art focusing on man's constant canine companion. For centuries, there has been much said about the relationship of man and dog, and much inspiration has been drawn from them. Presented in full color throughout, *Dog Sayings* is a choice read, solidly recommended.

SNAPPY SAYINGS:
wit & wisdom from the
world's greatest minds

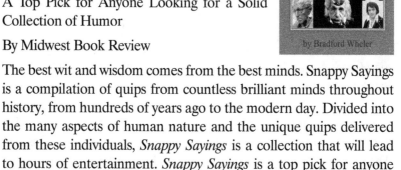

By Bradford G. Wheler

Nine 5 Star reviews

A Top Pick for Anyone Looking for a Solid Collection of Humor

By Midwest Book Review

The best wit and wisdom comes from the best minds. Snappy Sayings is a compilation of quips from countless brilliant minds throughout history, from hundreds of years ago to the modern day. Divided into the many aspects of human nature and the unique quips delivered from these individuals, *Snappy Sayings* is a collection that will lead to hours of entertainment. *Snappy Sayings* is a top pick for anyone looking for a solid collection of humor.

EIGHTEEN 6/10/71:
The Poetry of John G. Hunter III
is a collection of poems written by John G. Hunter III and given to Bradford G. Wheler for his eighteenth birthday on June 10, 1971. Each poem is accompanied by a color photograph. The layout and design was done by the renowned Italian book designer Adira Cucicov. Wheler has said many times, "I'm sure I received many fine gifts on my 18th birthday but this is the only one I remember and still treasure."

CPSIA information can be obtained
at www.ICGtesting.com
Printed in the USA
FFHW020059100719
53528423-59178FF